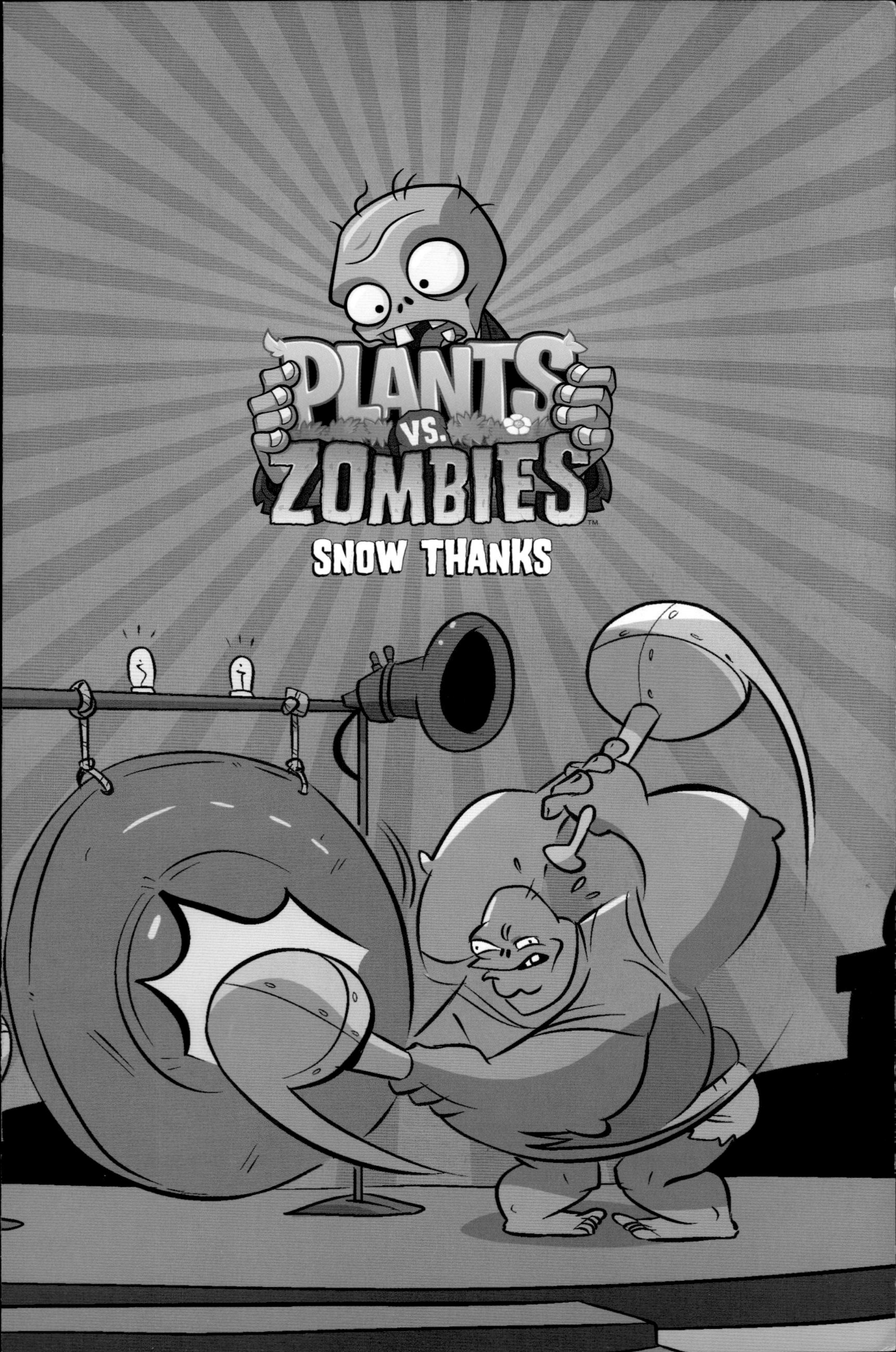
PLANTS vs. ZOMBIES™
SNOW THANKS

Publisher **MIKE RICHARDSON**
Senior Editor **PHILIP R. SIMON**
Associate Editor **MEGAN WALKER**
Designer **BRENNAN THOME**
Digital Art Technician **CHRISTIANNE GILLENARDO-GOUDREAU**

Special thanks to A.J. Rathbun, Kristen Star, and everyone at PopCap Games.

Scholastic edition: August 2019
ISBN 978-1-50671-533-9

10 9 8 7 6 5 4 3 2 1
Printed in Shenzhen, China.

DarkHorse.com
PopCap.com

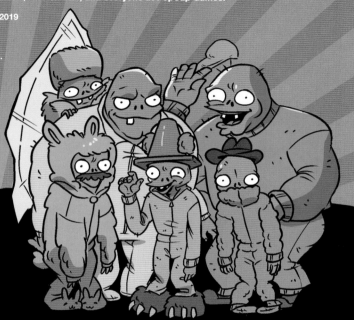

▷ No people or pets of Neighborville were harmed in the making of this graphic novel. However, many plants almost got frostbite and had to warm up inside a cabin by the fireplace with steaming mugs of hot cocoa, which really wasnt all that bad, now that we think of it. Also, when snow melts, it makes for soggy Pop Smarts, which are super gross.

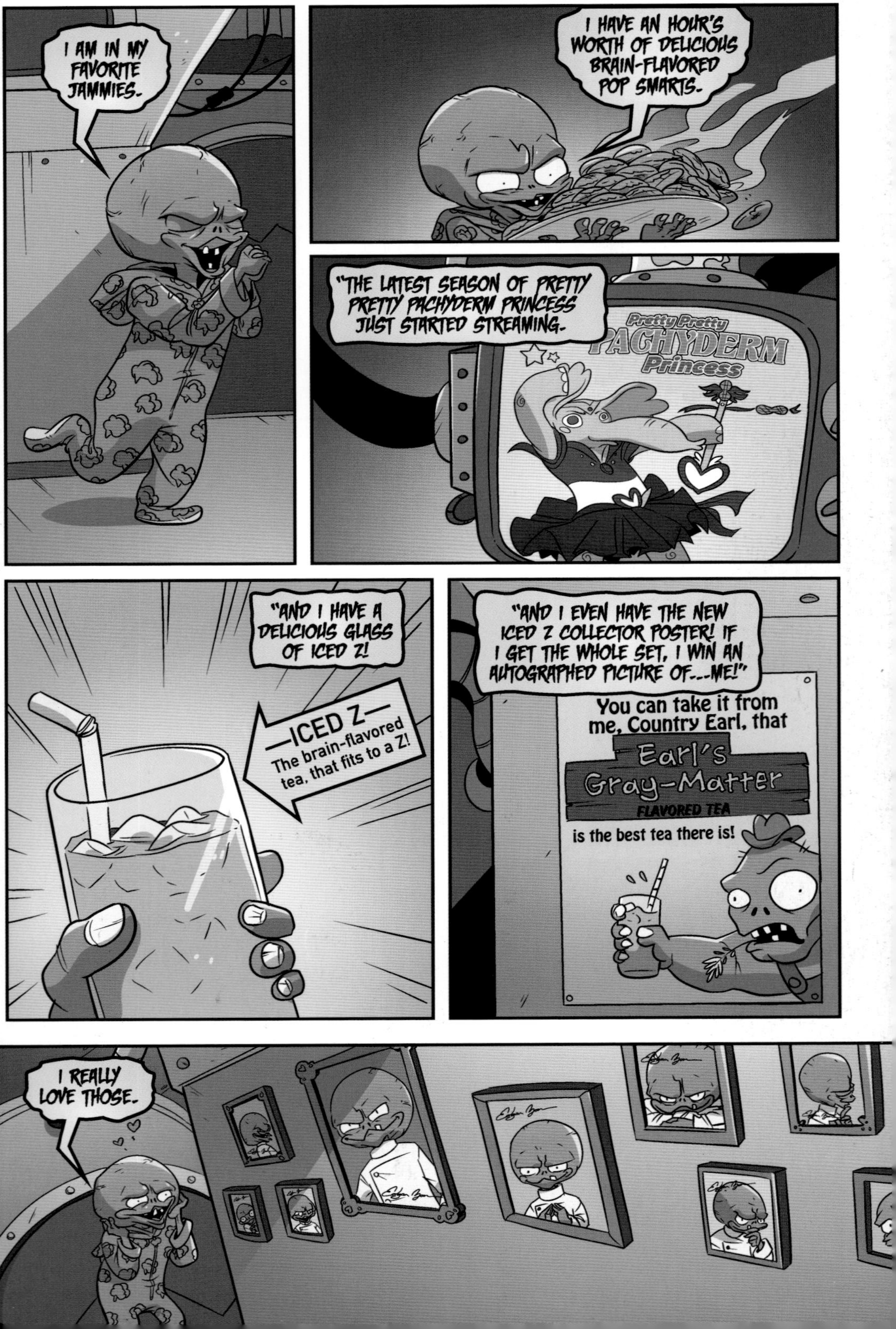
I AM IN MY FAVORITE JAMMIES.
I HAVE AN HOUR'S WORTH OF DELICIOUS BRAIN-FLAVORED POP SMARTS.
"THE LATEST SEASON OF PRETTY PRETTY PACHYDERM PRINCESS JUST STARTED STREAMING.
Pretty Pretty PACHYDERM Princess
"AND I HAVE A DELICIOUS GLASS OF ICED Z!
—ICED Z—
The brain-flavored tea, that fits to a Z!
"AND I EVEN HAVE THE NEW ICED Z COLLECTOR POSTER! IF I GET THE WHOLE SET, I WIN AN AUTOGRAPHED PICTURE OF...ME!"
You can take it from me, Country Earl, that
Earl's Gray-Matter
FLAVORED TEA
is the best tea there is!
I REALLY LOVE THOSE.

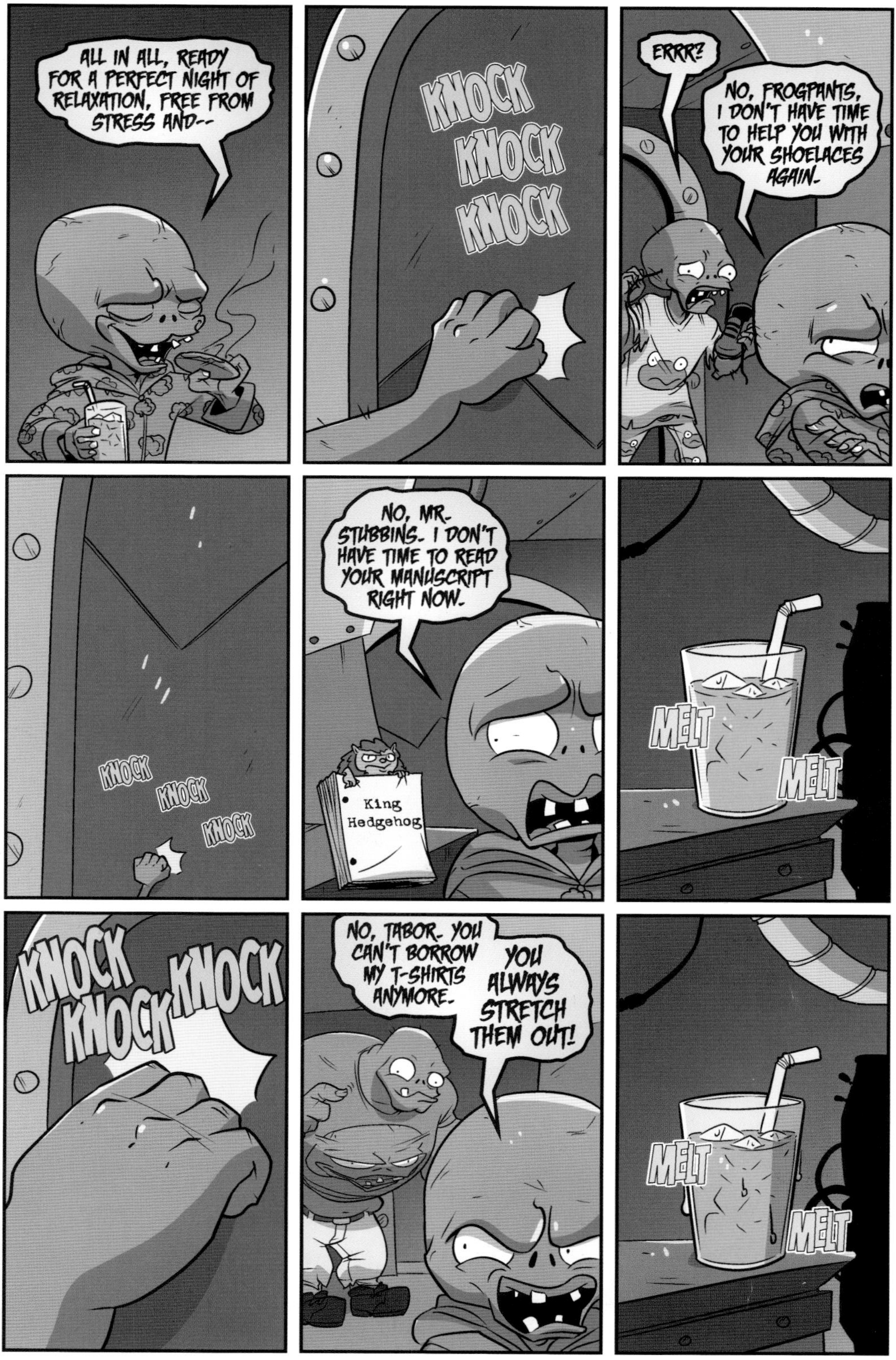

ALL IN ALL, READY FOR A PERFECT NIGHT OF RELAXATION, FREE FROM STRESS AND--
KNOCK KNOCK KNOCK
ERRR?
NO, FROGPANTS, I DON'T HAVE TIME TO HELP YOU WITH YOUR SHOELACES AGAIN.
KNOCK KNOCK KNOCK
NO, MR. STUBBINS. I DON'T HAVE TIME TO READ YOUR MANUSCRIPT RIGHT NOW.
King Hedgehog
MELT
MELT
KNOCK KNOCK KNOCK
NO, TABOR. YOU CAN'T BORROW MY T-SHIRTS ANYMORE.
YOU ALWAYS STRETCH THEM OUT!
MELT
MELT

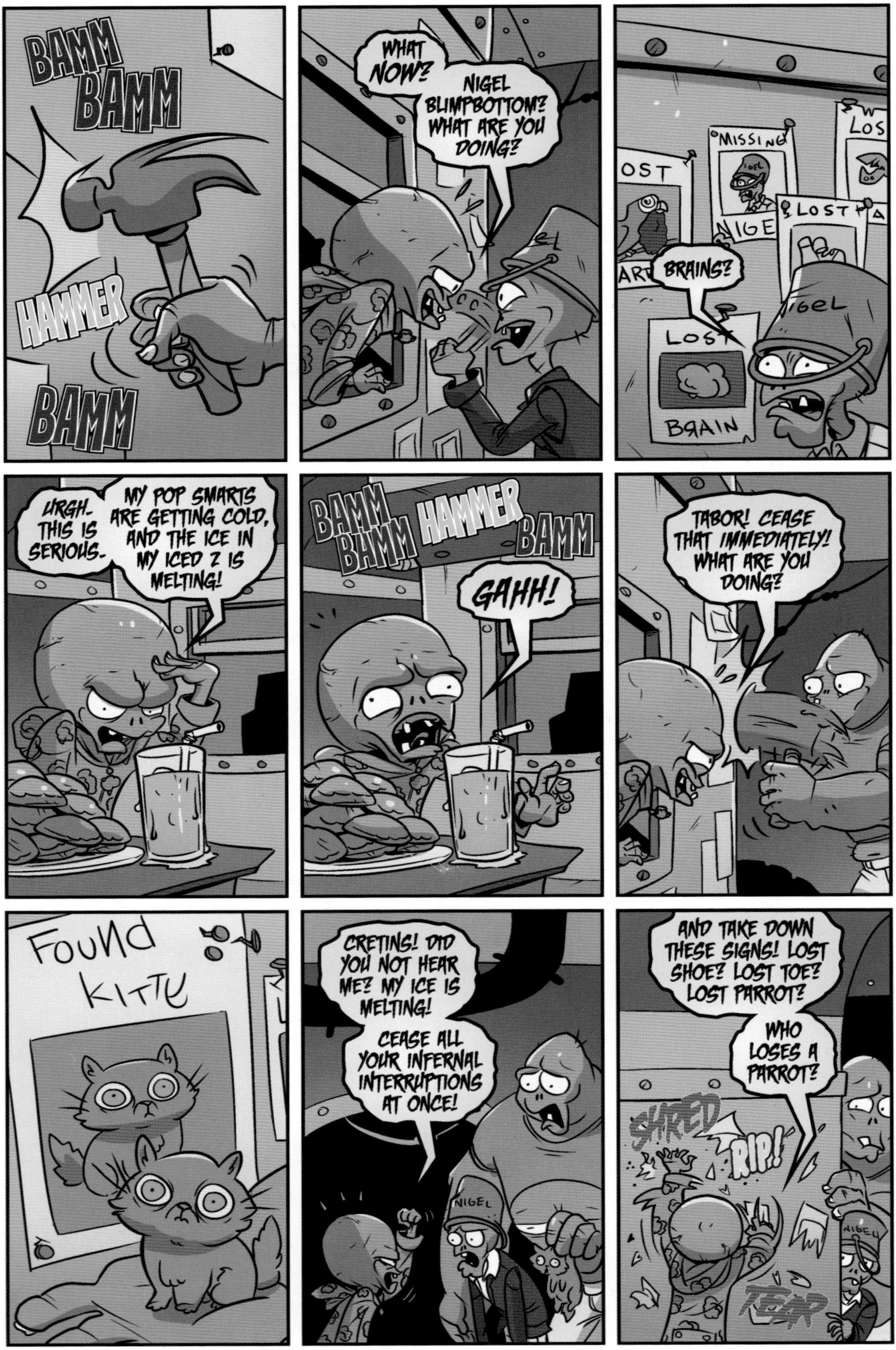
BAMM
BAMM
HAMMER
BAMM
WHAT NOW?
NIGEL BLIMPBOTTOM? WHAT ARE YOU DOING?
MISSING
OST
LOS
LOST
NIGE
BRAINS?
LOST
BRAIN
NIGEL
URGH. THIS IS SERIOUS.
MY POP SMARTS ARE GETTING COLD, AND THE ICE IN MY ICED Z IS MELTING!
BAMM
BAMM
HAMMER
BAMM
GAHH!
TABOR! CEASE THAT IMMEDIATELY! WHAT ARE YOU DOING?
Found kitty
CRETINS! DID YOU NOT HEAR ME? MY ICE IS MELTING!
CEASE ALL YOUR INFERNAL INTERRUPTIONS AT ONCE!
NIGEL
AND TAKE DOWN THESE SIGNS! LOST SHOE? LOST TOE? LOST PARROT?
WHO LOSES A PARROT?
SHRED
RIP!
TEAR

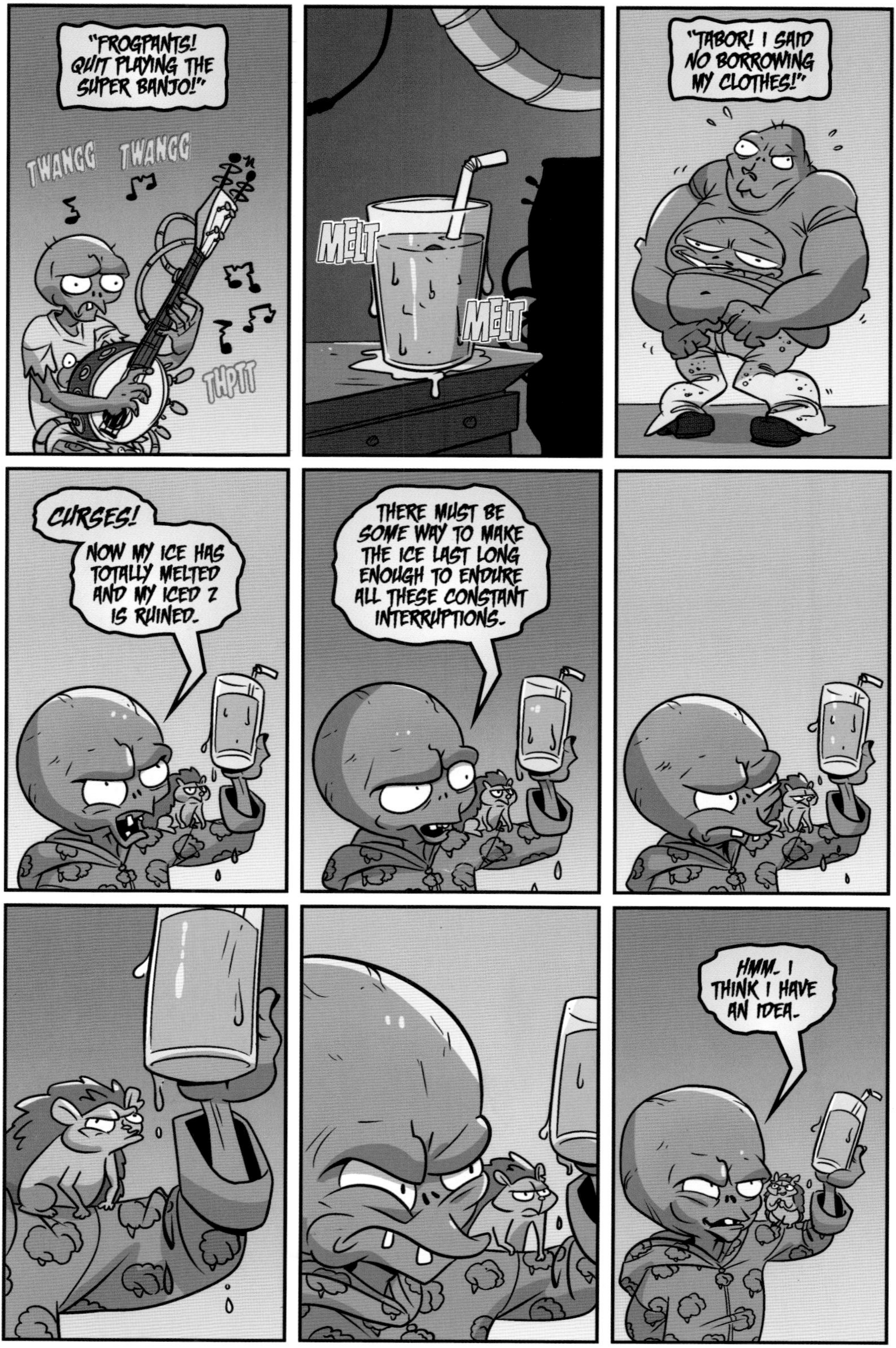
"FROGPANTS! QUIT PLAYING THE SUPER BANJO!"
TWANGG TWANGG
THPTT
MELT
MELT
"TABOR! I SAID NO BORROWING MY CLOTHES!"
CURSES!
NOW MY ICE HAS TOTALLY MELTED AND MY ICED Z IS RUINED.
THERE MUST BE SOME WAY TO MAKE THE ICE LAST LONG ENOUGH TO ENDURE ALL THESE CONSTANT INTERRUPTIONS.
HMM. I THINK I HAVE AN IDEA.

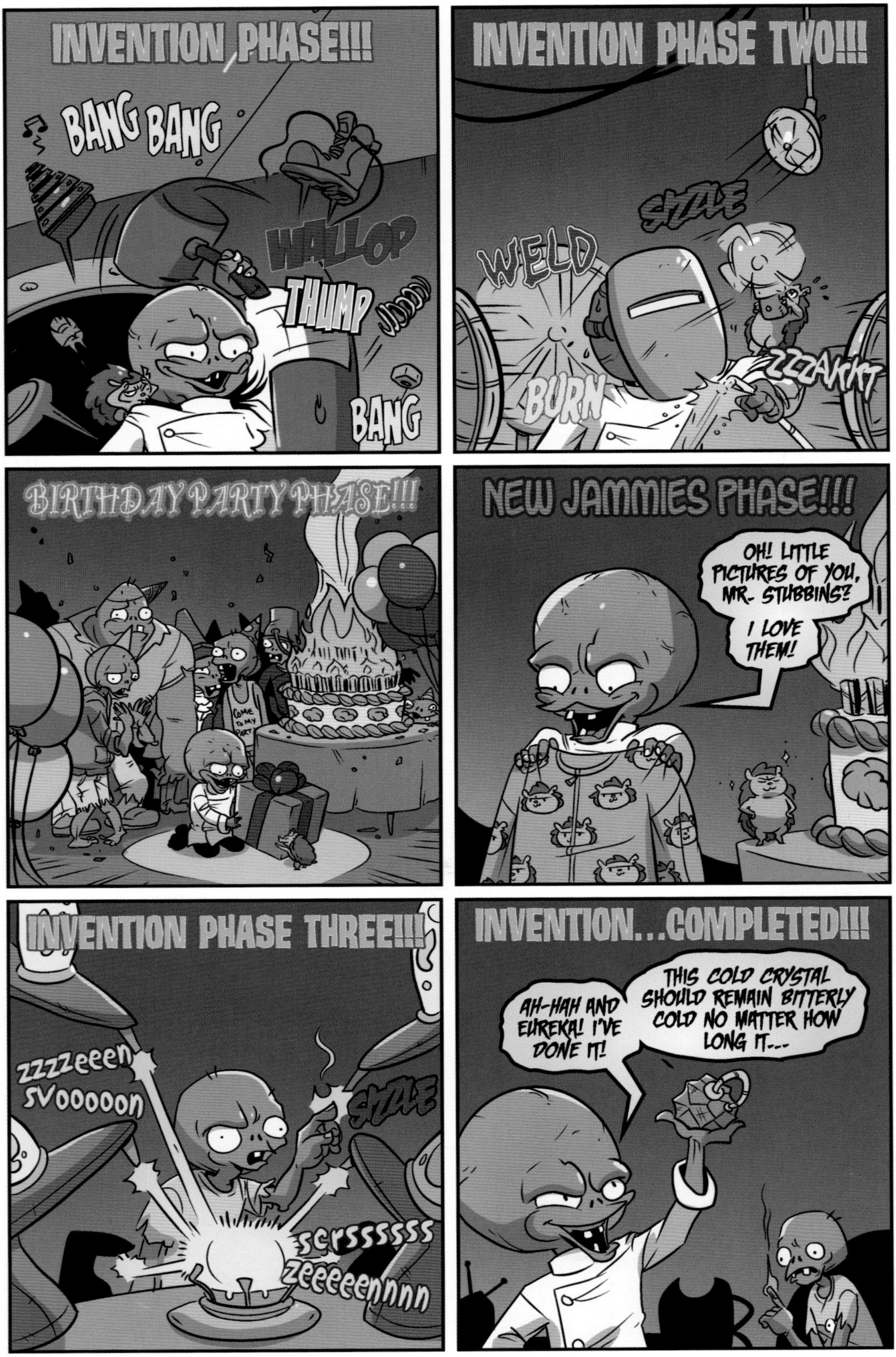
INVENTION PHASE!!!
BANG BANG
WALLOP
THUMP
BANG
INVENTION PHASE TWO!!!
SIZZLE
WELD
BURN
ZZZAKKT
BIRTHDAY PARTY PHASE!!!
COME TO MY PARTY
NEW JAMMIES PHASE!!!
OH! LITTLE PICTURES OF YOU, MR. STUBBINS?
I LOVE THEM!
INVENTION PHASE THREE!!!
zzzzeeen
svoooooon
SIZZLE
scrssssss
zeeeeeennnn
INVENTION...COMPLETED!!!
AH-HAH AND EUREKA! I'VE DONE IT!
THIS COLD CRYSTAL SHOULD REMAIN BITTERLY COLD NO MATTER HOW LONG IT...

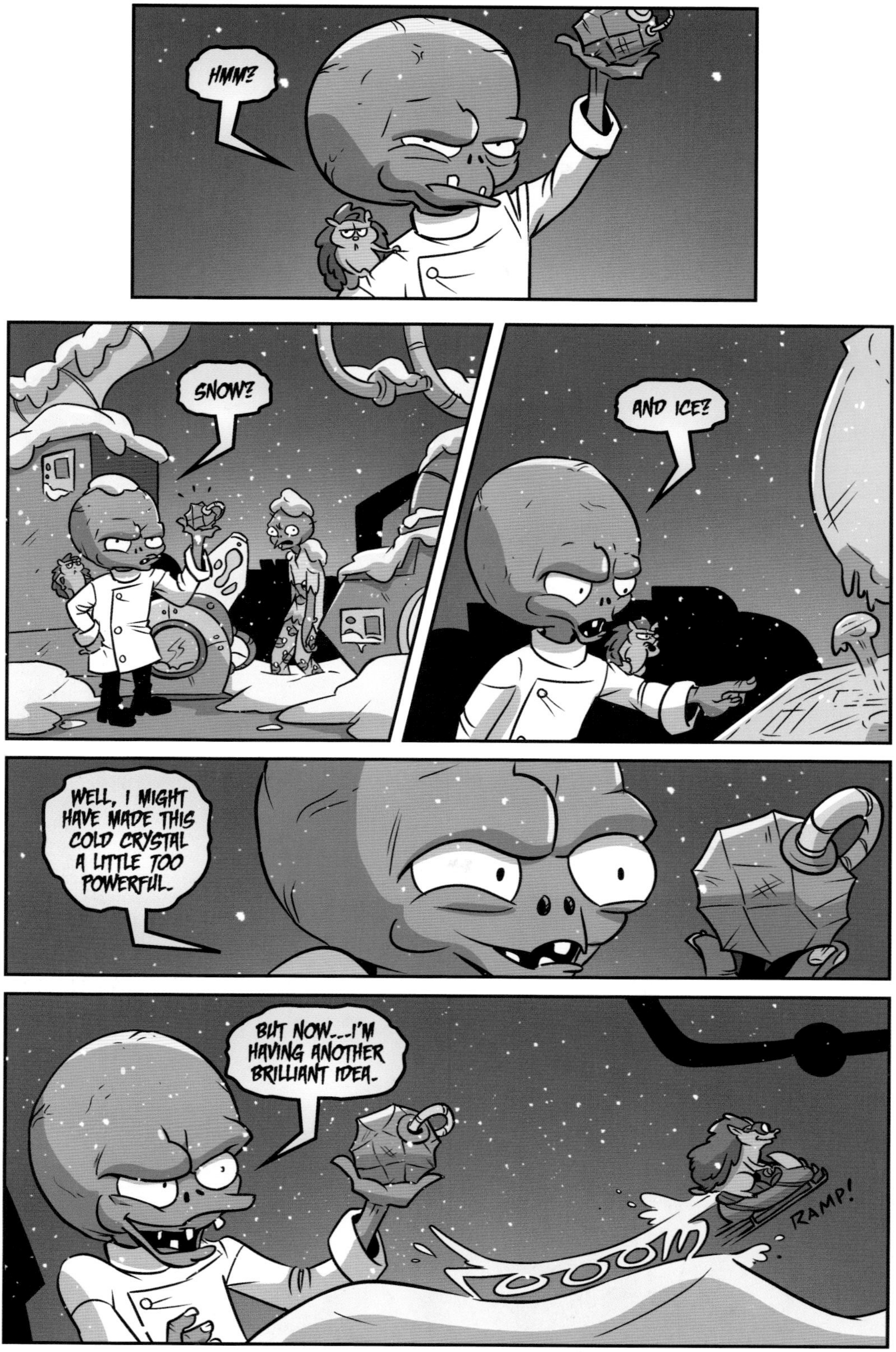
HMM?
SNOW?
AND ICE?
WELL, I MIGHT HAVE MADE THIS COLD CRYSTAL A LITTLE TOO POWERFUL.
BUT NOW...I'M HAVING ANOTHER BRILLIANT IDEA.
ZOOOOM
RAMP!

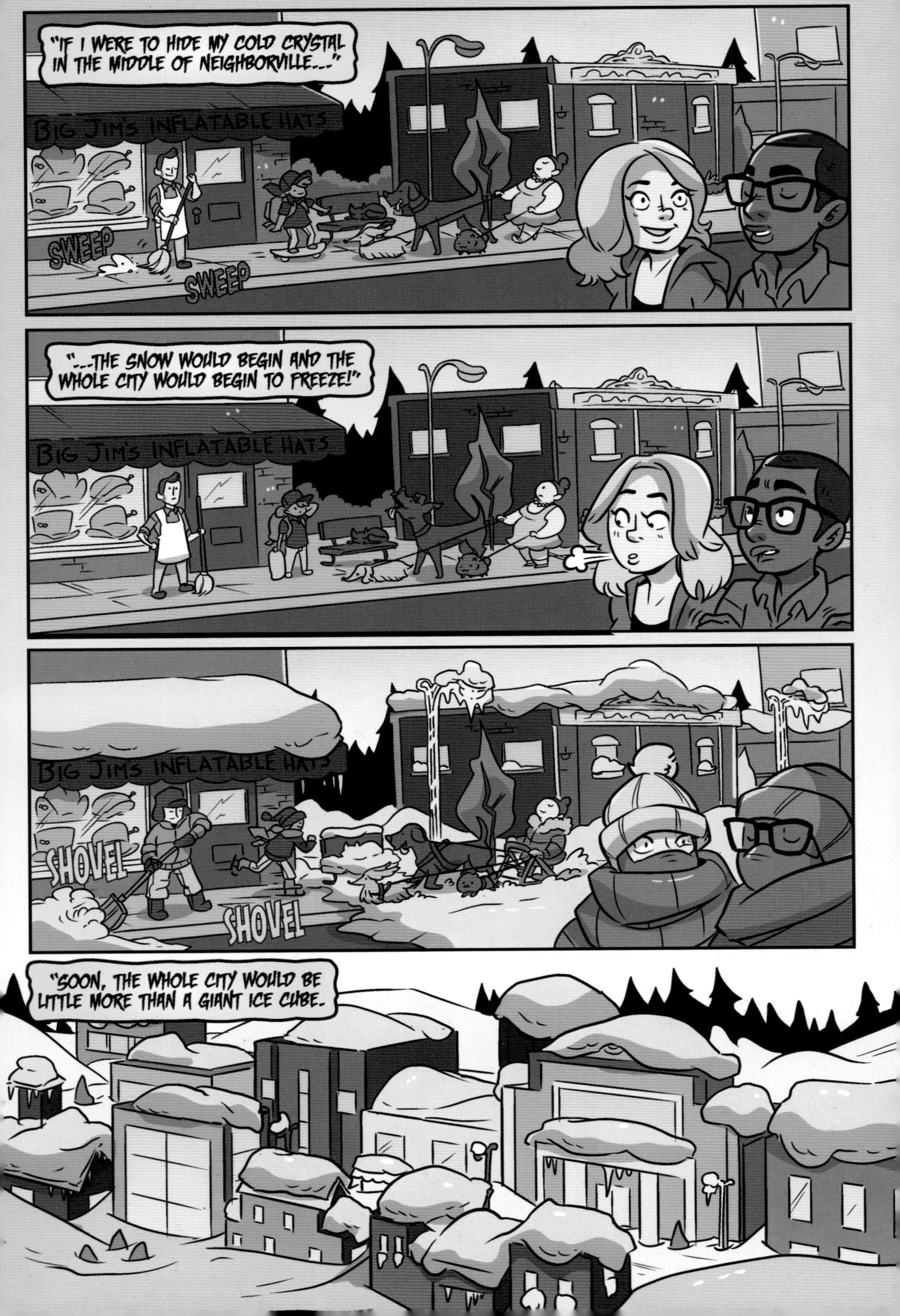
"IF I WERE TO HIDE MY COLD CRYSTAL IN THE MIDDLE OF NEIGHBORVILLE..."
BIG JIM'S INFLATABLE HATS
SWEEP
SWEEP
"...THE SNOW WOULD BEGIN AND THE WHOLE CITY WOULD BEGIN TO FREEZE!"
BIG JIM'S INFLATABLE HATS
BIG JIM'S INFLATABLE HATS
SHOVEL
SHOVEL
"SOON, THE WHOLE CITY WOULD BE LITTLE MORE THAN A GIANT ICE CUBE.

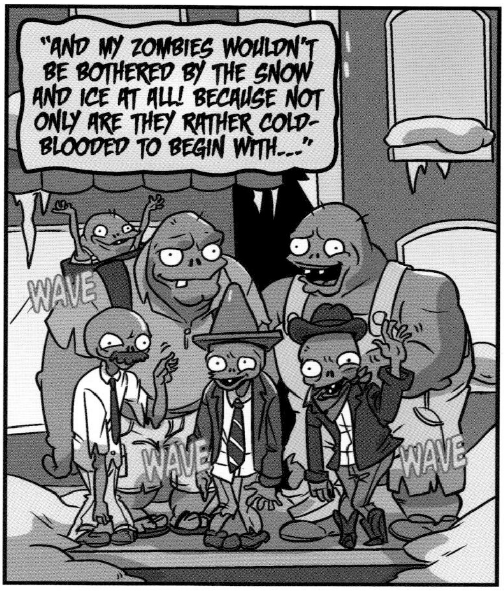
"AND MY ZOMBIES WOULDN'T BE BOTHERED BY THE SNOW AND ICE AT ALL! BECAUSE NOT ONLY ARE THEY RATHER COLD-BLOODED TO BEGIN WITH..."
WAVE
WAVE
WAVE

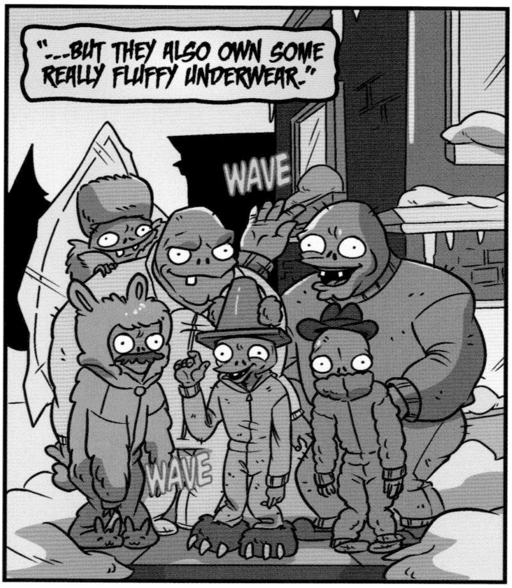
"...BUT THEY ALSO OWN SOME REALLY FLUFFY UNDERWEAR."
WAVE
WAVE

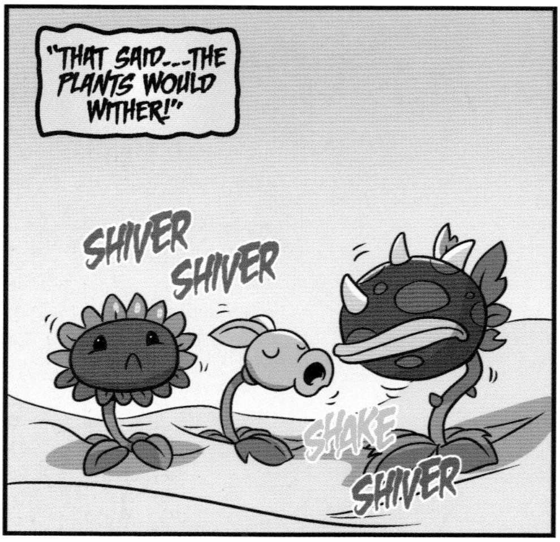
"THAT SAID...THE PLANTS WOULD WITHER!"
SHIVER
SHIVER
SHAKE
SHIVER

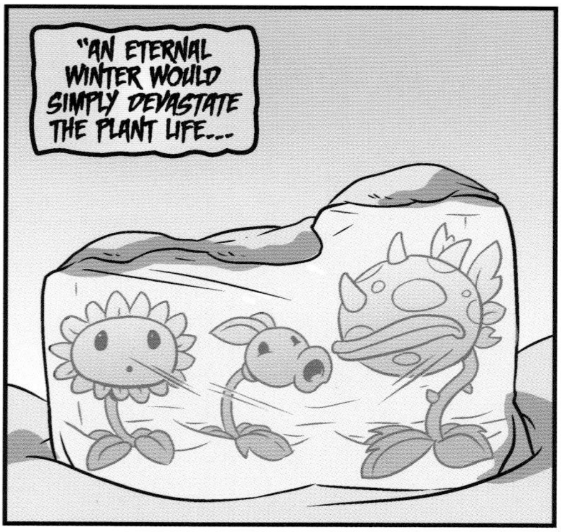
"AN ETERNAL WINTER WOULD SIMPLY DEVASTATE THE PLANT LIFE...

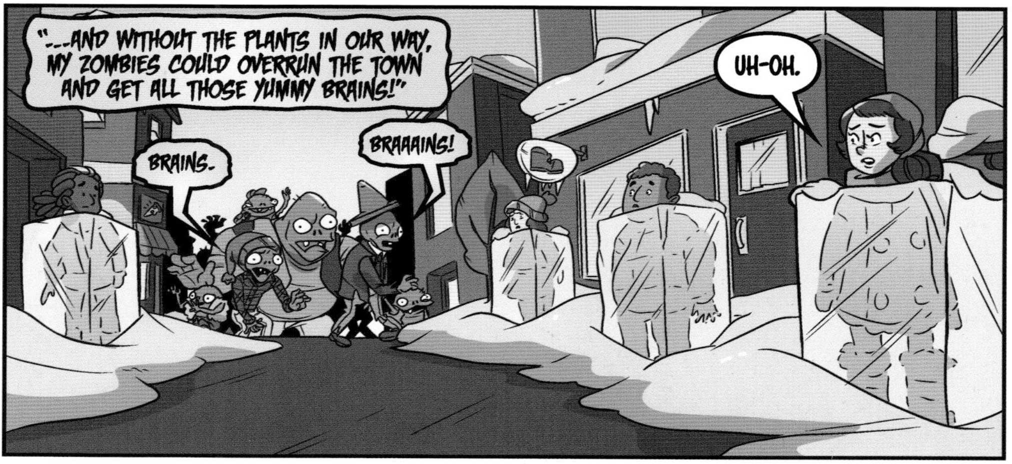
"...AND WITHOUT THE PLANTS IN OUR WAY, MY ZOMBIES COULD OVERRUN THE TOWN AND GET ALL THOSE YUMMY BRAINS!"
BRAINS.
BRAAAINS!
UH-OH.

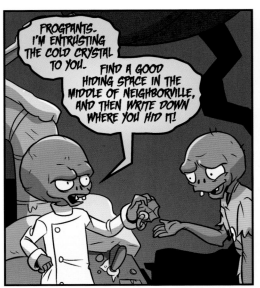

FROGPANTS. I'M ENTRUSTING THE COLD CRYSTAL TO YOU. FIND A GOOD HIDING SPACE IN THE MIDDLE OF NEIGHBORVILLE, AND THEN WRITE DOWN WHERE YOU HID IT!

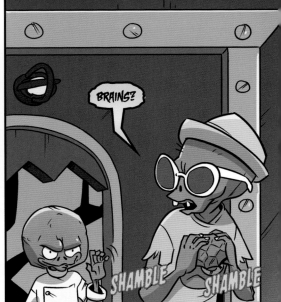

BRAINS?

SHAMBLE SHAMBLE

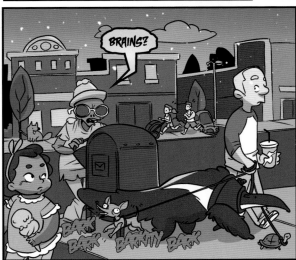

BRAINS?

BARK BARK BARKITY BARK

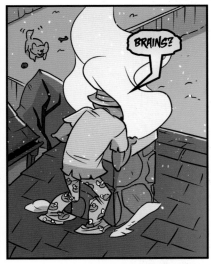

BRAINS?

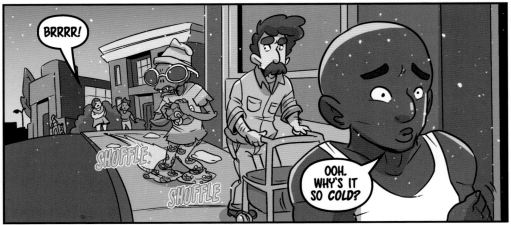

BRRRR!

SHOFFLE

SHOFFLE

OOH. WHY'S IT SO COLD?

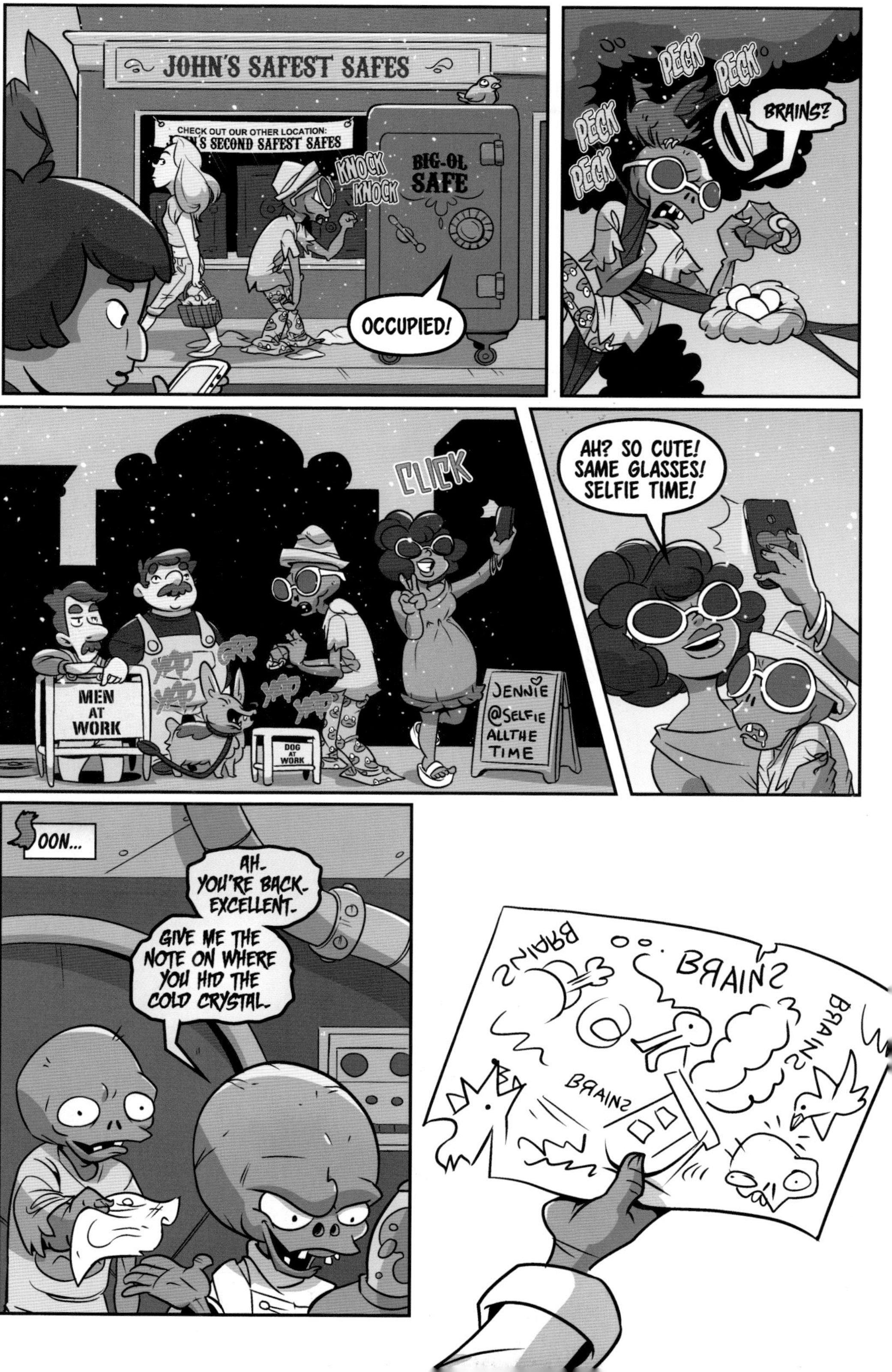
JOHN'S SAFEST SAFES
CHECK OUT OUR OTHER LOCATION:
N'S SECOND SAFEST SAFES
KNOCK KNOCK
BIG-OL SAFE
OCCUPIED!
PECK PECK PECK PECK
BRAINS?
CLICK
MEN AT WORK
YAP YAP
GRR
YAP YAP
DOG AT WORK
JENNIE @SELFIE ALLTHE TIME
AH? SO CUTE! SAME GLASSES! SELFIE TIME!
OON...
AH. YOU'RE BACK. EXCELLENT.
GIVE ME THE NOTE ON WHERE YOU HID THE COLD CRYSTAL.
BRAINS
BRAINS
BRAINS
BRAINS

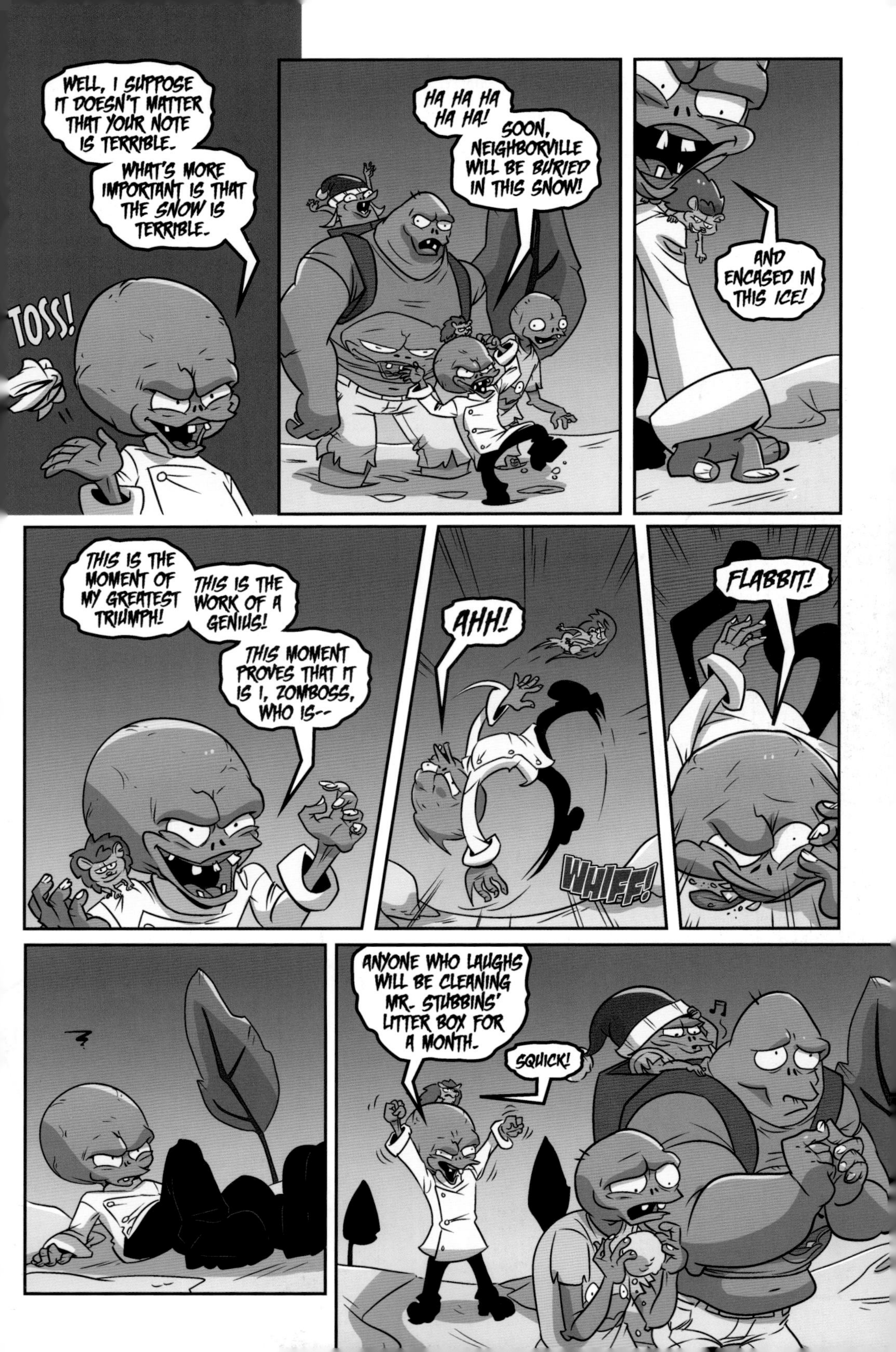
WELL, I SUPPOSE IT DOESN'T MATTER THAT YOUR NOTE IS TERRIBLE.
WHAT'S MORE IMPORTANT IS THAT THE SNOW IS TERRIBLE.
TOSS!
HA HA HA HA HA!
SOON, NEIGHBORVILLE WILL BE BURIED IN THIS SNOW!
AND ENCASED IN THIS ICE!
THIS IS THE MOMENT OF MY GREATEST TRIUMPH!
THIS IS THE WORK OF A GENIUS!
THIS MOMENT PROVES THAT IT IS I, ZOMBOSS, WHO IS--
AHH!
WHIFF!
FLABBIT!
ANYONE WHO LAUGHS WILL BE CLEANING MR. STUBBINS' LITTER BOX FOR A MONTH.
SQUICK!

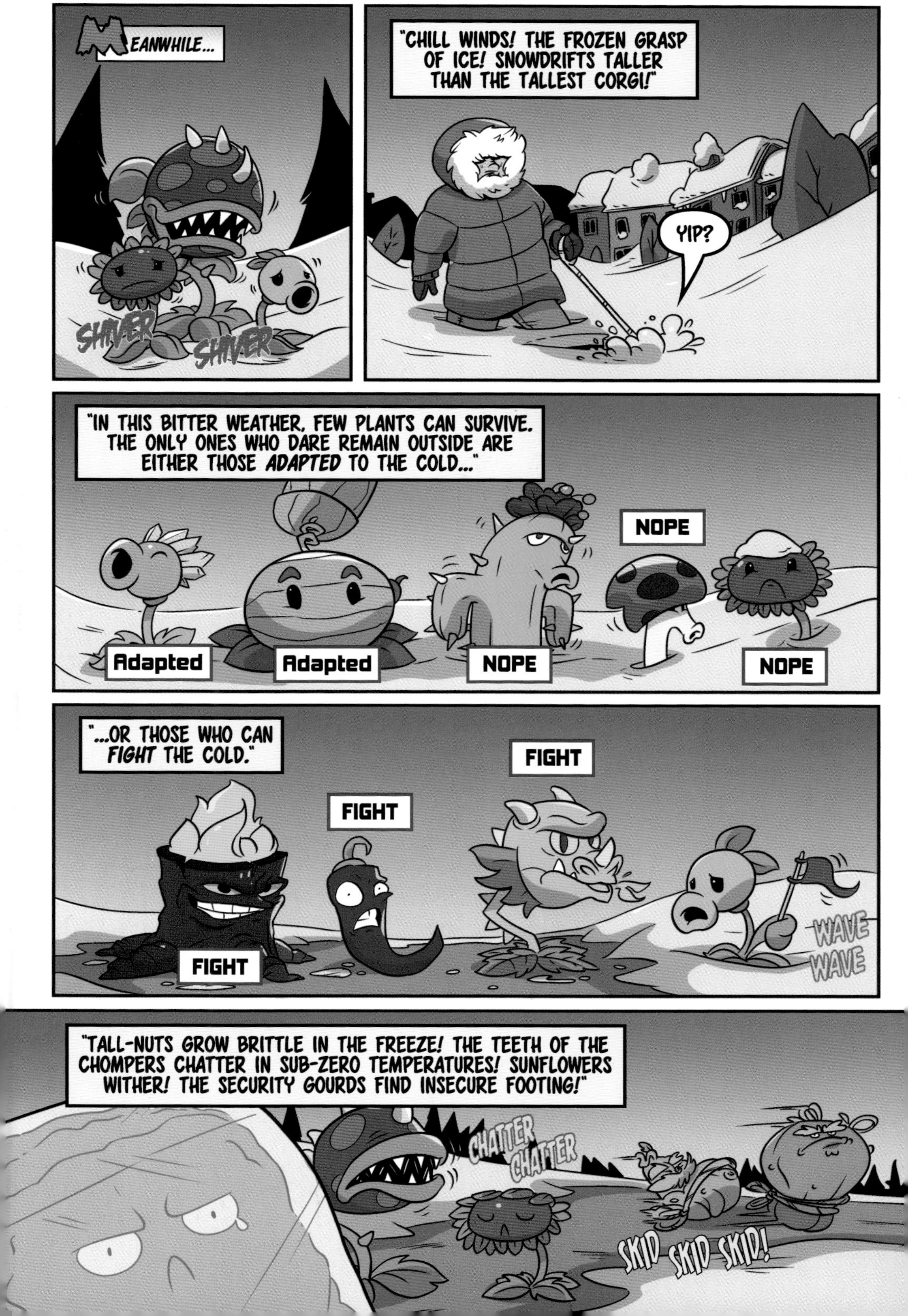
MEANWHILE...
SHIVER
SHIVER
"CHILL WINDS! THE FROZEN GRASP OF ICE! SNOWDRIFTS TALLER THAN THE TALLEST CORGI!"
YIP?
"IN THIS BITTER WEATHER, FEW PLANTS CAN SURVIVE. THE ONLY ONES WHO DARE REMAIN OUTSIDE ARE EITHER THOSE ADAPTED TO THE COLD..."
NOPE
Adapted
Adapted
NOPE
NOPE
"...OR THOSE WHO CAN FIGHT THE COLD."
FIGHT
FIGHT
FIGHT
WAVE
WAVE
"TALL-NUTS GROW BRITTLE IN THE FREEZE! THE TEETH OF THE CHOMPERS CHATTER IN SUB-ZERO TEMPERATURES! SUNFLOWERS WITHER! THE SECURITY GOURDS FIND INSECURE FOOTING!"
CHATTER
CHATTER
SKID SKID SKID!

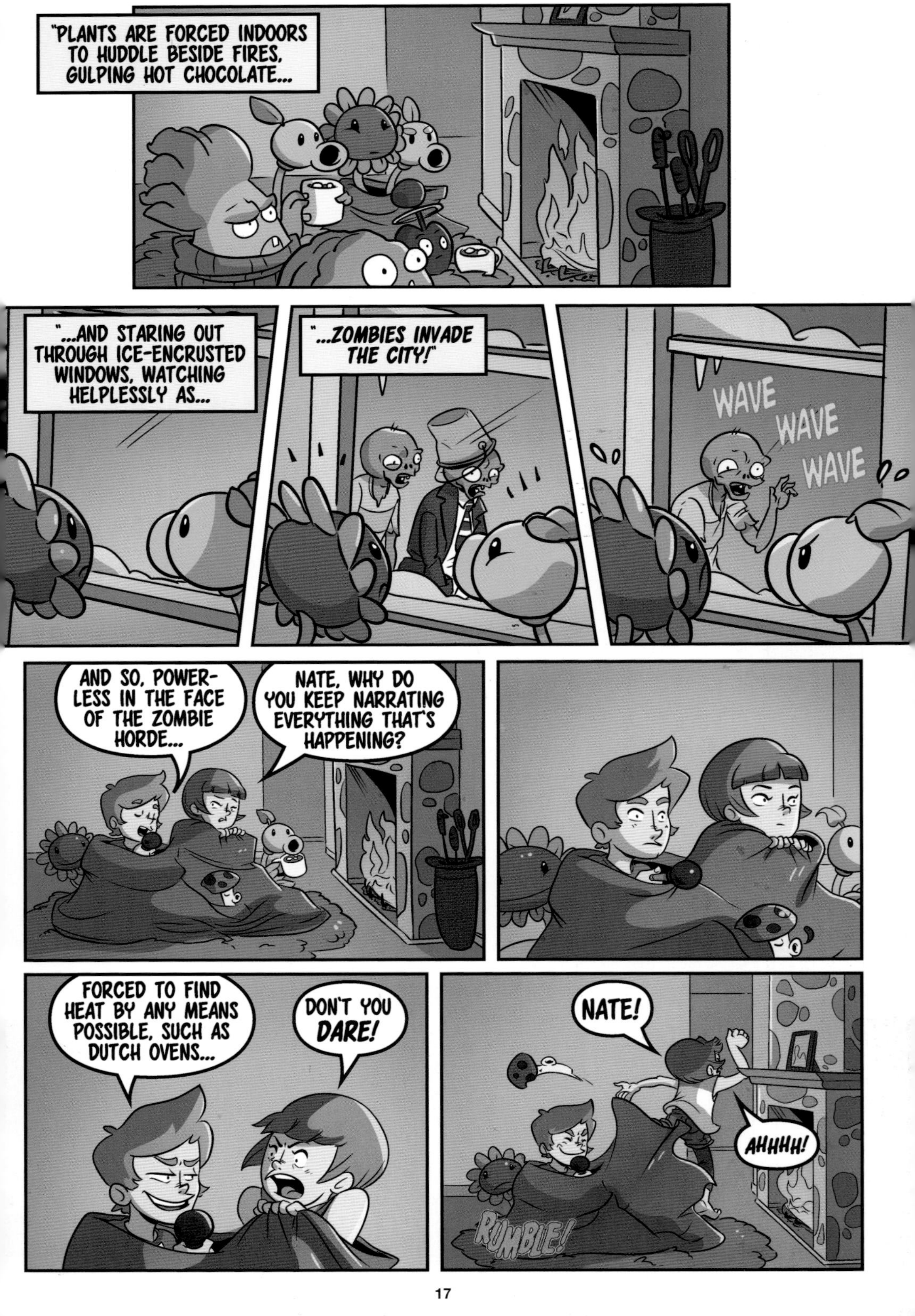
"PLANTS ARE FORCED INDOORS TO HUDDLE BESIDE FIRES, GULPING HOT CHOCOLATE...
"...AND STARING OUT THROUGH ICE-ENCRUSTED WINDOWS, WATCHING HELPLESSLY AS...
"...ZOMBIES INVADE THE CITY!"
WAVE
WAVE
WAVE
AND SO, POWERLESS IN THE FACE OF THE ZOMBIE HORDE...
NATE, WHY DO YOU KEEP NARRATING EVERYTHING THAT'S HAPPENING?
FORCED TO FIND HEAT BY ANY MEANS POSSIBLE, SUCH AS DUTCH OVENS...
DON'T YOU DARE!
NATE!
AHHHH!
RUMBLE!

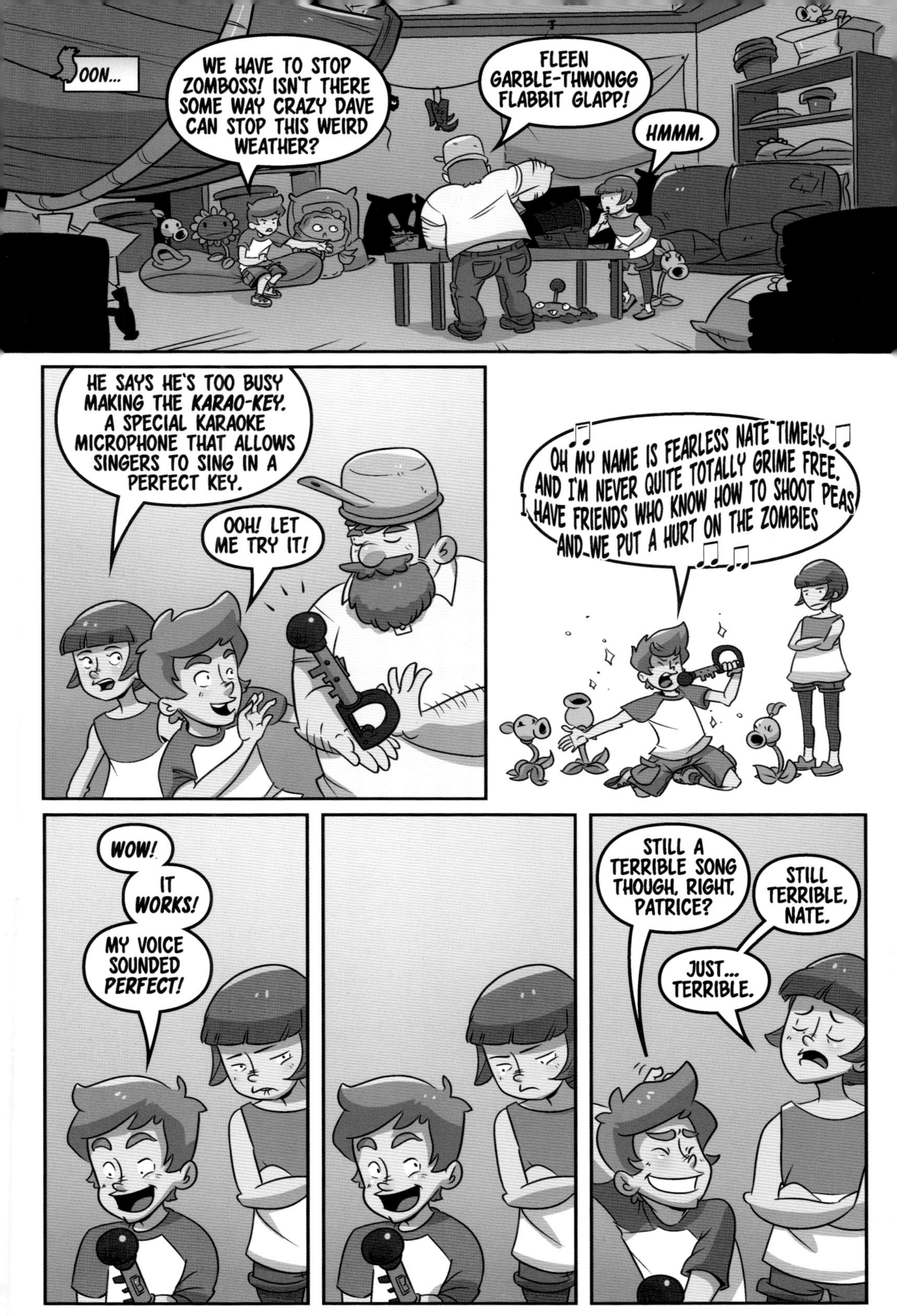
SOON...
WE HAVE TO STOP ZOMBOSS! ISN'T THERE SOME WAY CRAZY DAVE CAN STOP THIS WEIRD WEATHER?
FLEEN GARBLE-THWONGG FLABBIT GLAPP!
HMMM.
HE SAYS HE'S TOO BUSY MAKING THE KARAO-KEY. A SPECIAL KARAOKE MICROPHONE THAT ALLOWS SINGERS TO SING IN A PERFECT KEY.
OOH! LET ME TRY IT!
OH MY NAME IS FEARLESS NATE TIMELY, AND I'M NEVER QUITE TOTALLY GRIME FREE. I HAVE FRIENDS WHO KNOW HOW TO SHOOT PEAS AND WE PUT A HURT ON THE ZOMBIES
WOW!
IT WORKS!
MY VOICE SOUNDED PERFECT!
STILL A TERRIBLE SONG THOUGH, RIGHT, PATRICE?
STILL TERRIBLE, NATE.
JUST... TERRIBLE.

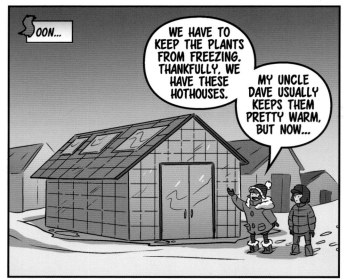

OON...

WE HAVE TO KEEP THE PLANTS FROM FREEZING. THANKFULLY, WE HAVE THESE HOTHOUSES.

MY UNCLE DAVE USUALLY KEEPS THEM PRETTY WARM, BUT NOW...

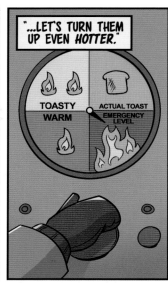

"...LET'S TURN THEM UP EVEN HOTTER."

TOASTY WARM

ACTUAL TOAST

EMERGENCY LEVEL

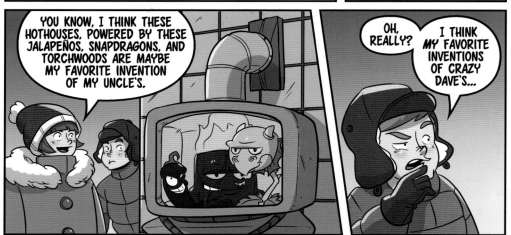

YOU KNOW, I THINK THESE HOTHOUSES, POWERED BY THESE JALAPEÑOS, SNAPDRAGONS, AND TORCHWOODS ARE MAYBE MY FAVORITE INVENTION OF MY UNCLE'S.

OH, REALLY?

I THINK MY FAVORITE INVENTIONS OF CRAZY DAVE'S...

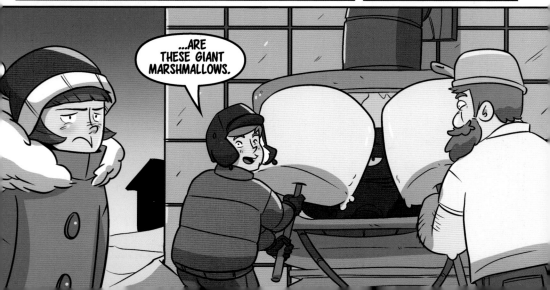

...ARE THESE GIANT MARSHMALLOWS.

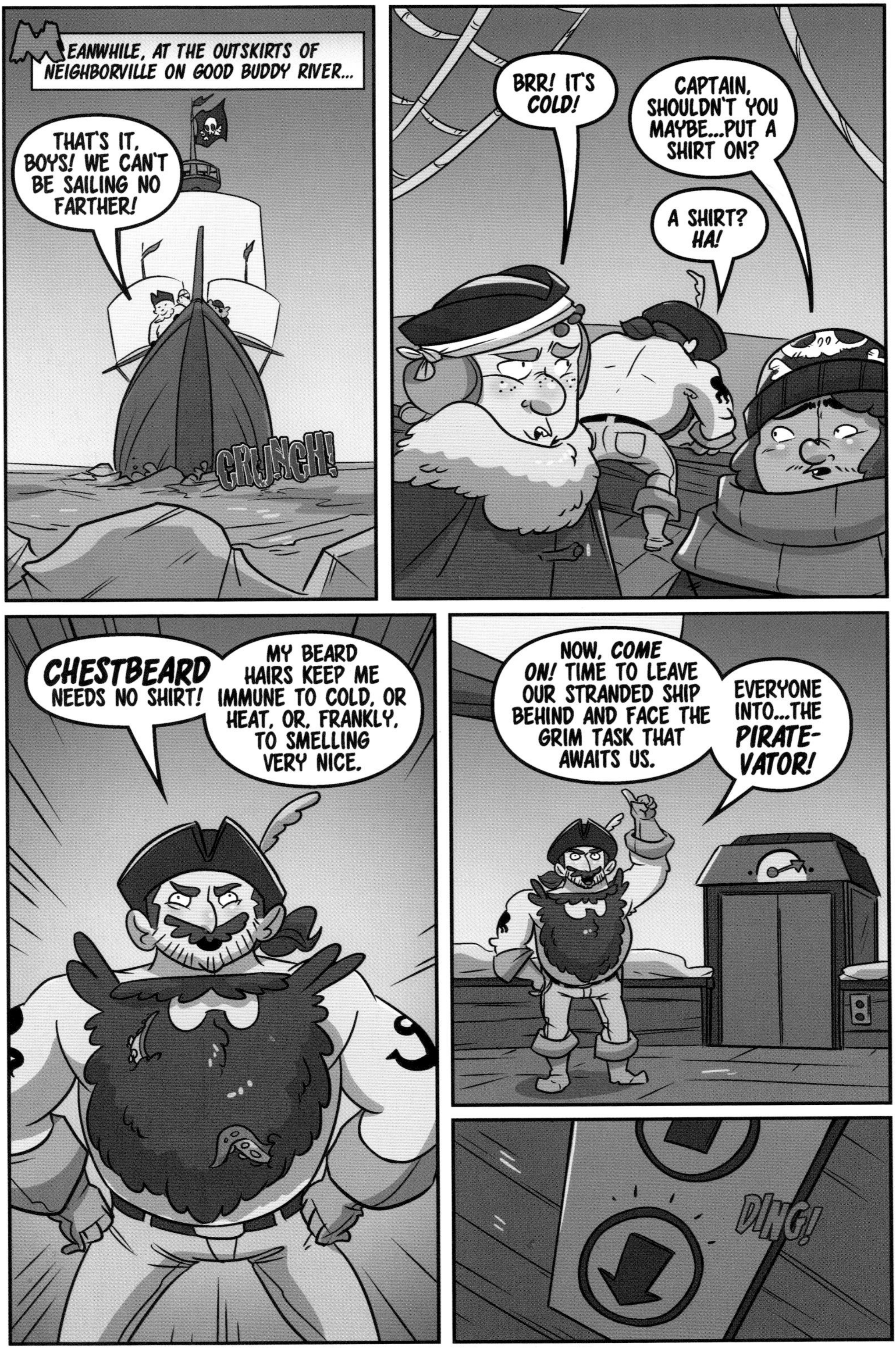
MEANWHILE, AT THE OUTSKIRTS OF NEIGHBORVILLE ON GOOD BUDDY RIVER...
THAT'S IT, BOYS! WE CAN'T BE SAILING NO FARTHER!
CRUNCH!
BRR! IT'S COLD!
CAPTAIN, SHOULDN'T YOU MAYBE...PUT A SHIRT ON?
A SHIRT? HA!
CHESTBEARD NEEDS NO SHIRT!
MY BEARD HAIRS KEEP ME IMMUNE TO COLD, OR HEAT, OR, FRANKLY, TO SMELLING VERY NICE.
NOW, COME ON! TIME TO LEAVE OUR STRANDED SHIP BEHIND AND FACE THE GRIM TASK THAT AWAITS US.
EVERYONE INTO...THE PIRATE-VATOR!
DING!

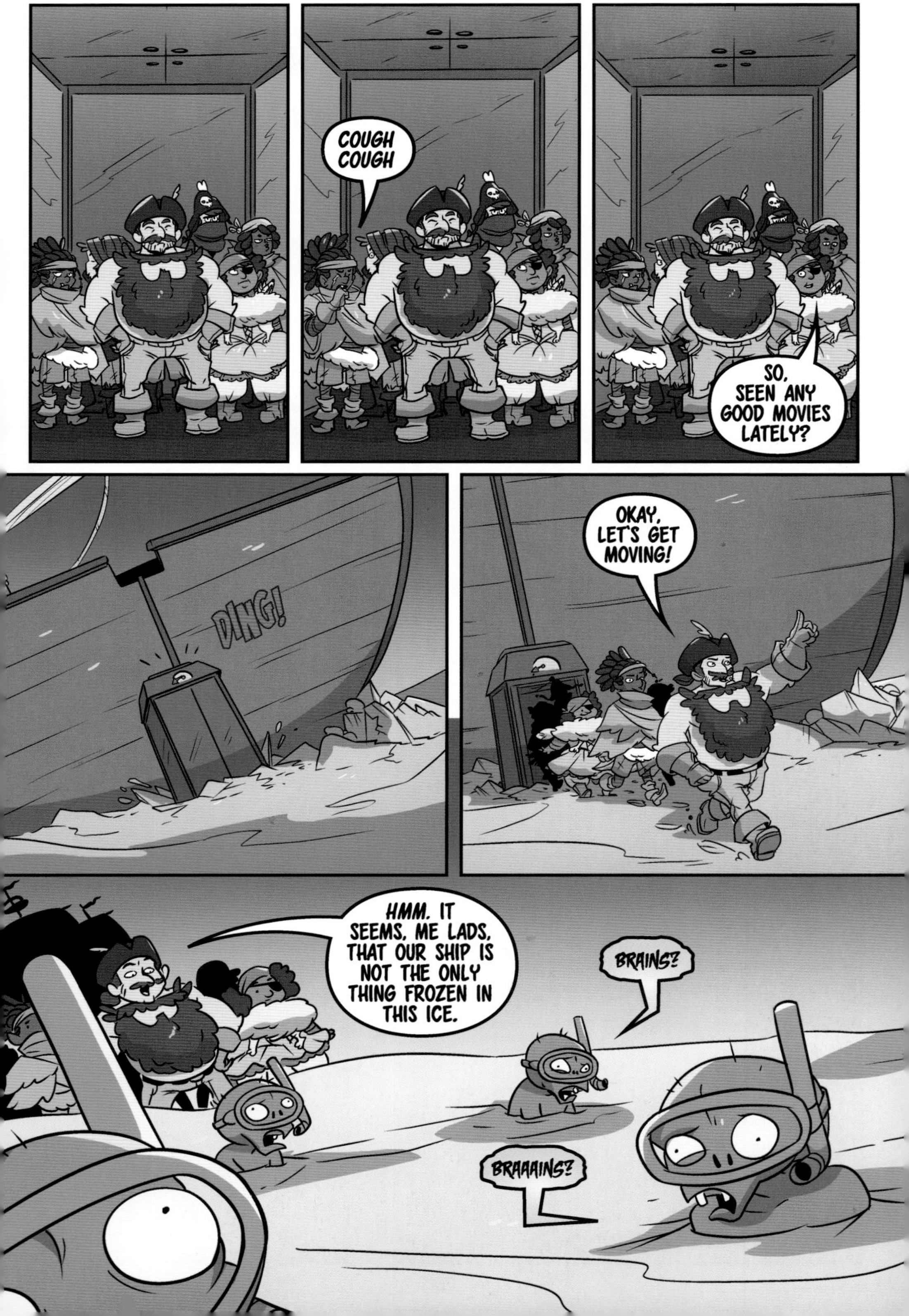
COUGH COUGH
SO, SEEN ANY GOOD MOVIES LATELY?
DING!
OKAY, LET'S GET MOVING!
HMM. IT SEEMS, ME LADS, THAT OUR SHIP IS NOT THE ONLY THING FROZEN IN THIS ICE.
BRAINS?
BRAAAINS?

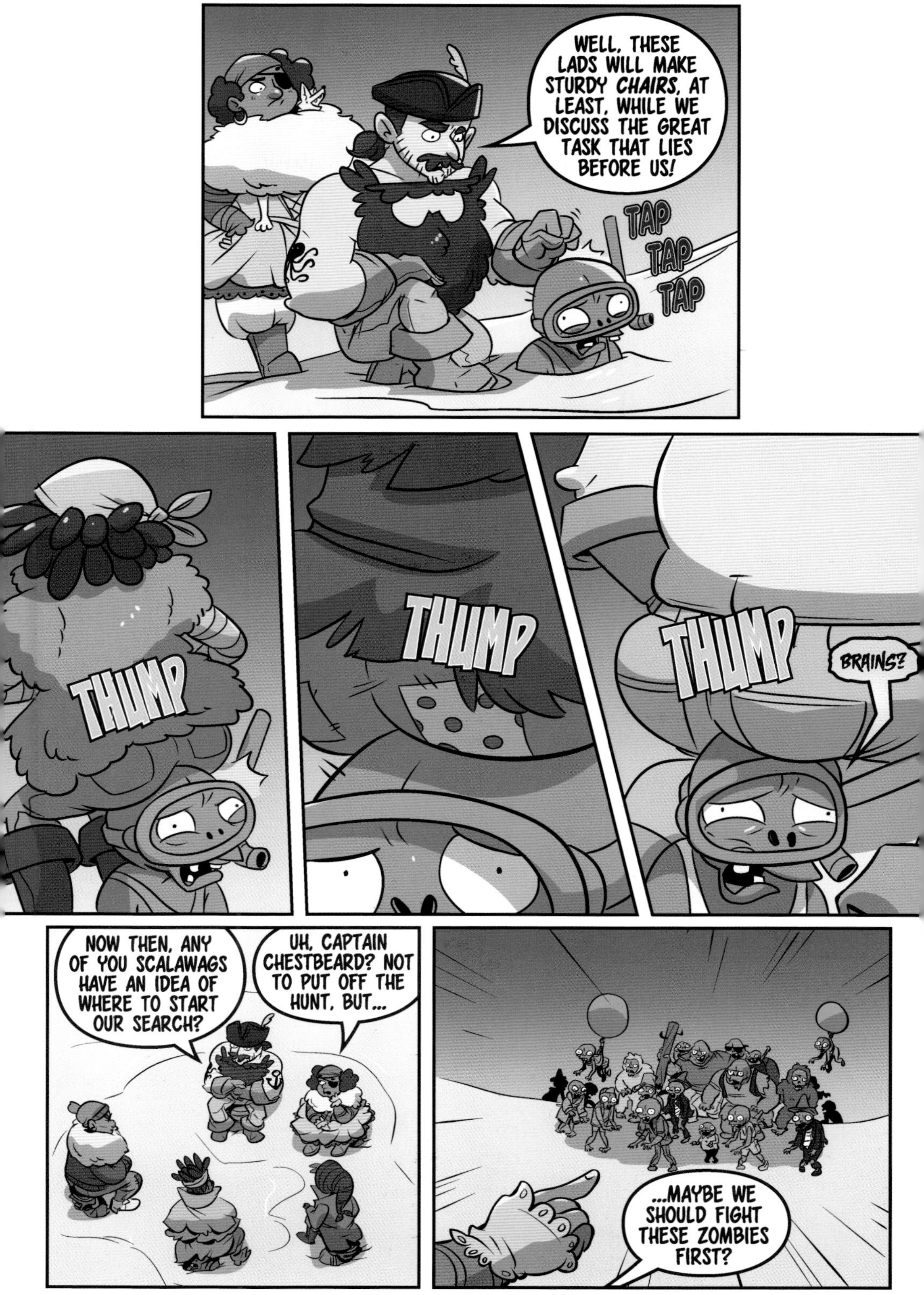

WELL, THESE LADS WILL MAKE STURDY *CHAIRS*, AT LEAST, WHILE WE DISCUSS THE GREAT TASK THAT LIES BEFORE US!
TAP
TAP
TAP
THUMP
THUMP
THUMP
BRAINS?
NOW THEN, ANY OF YOU SCALAWAGS HAVE AN IDEA OF WHERE TO START OUR SEARCH?
UH, CAPTAIN CHESTBEARD? NOT TO PUT OFF THE HUNT, BUT...
...MAYBE WE SHOULD FIGHT THESE ZOMBIES FIRST?

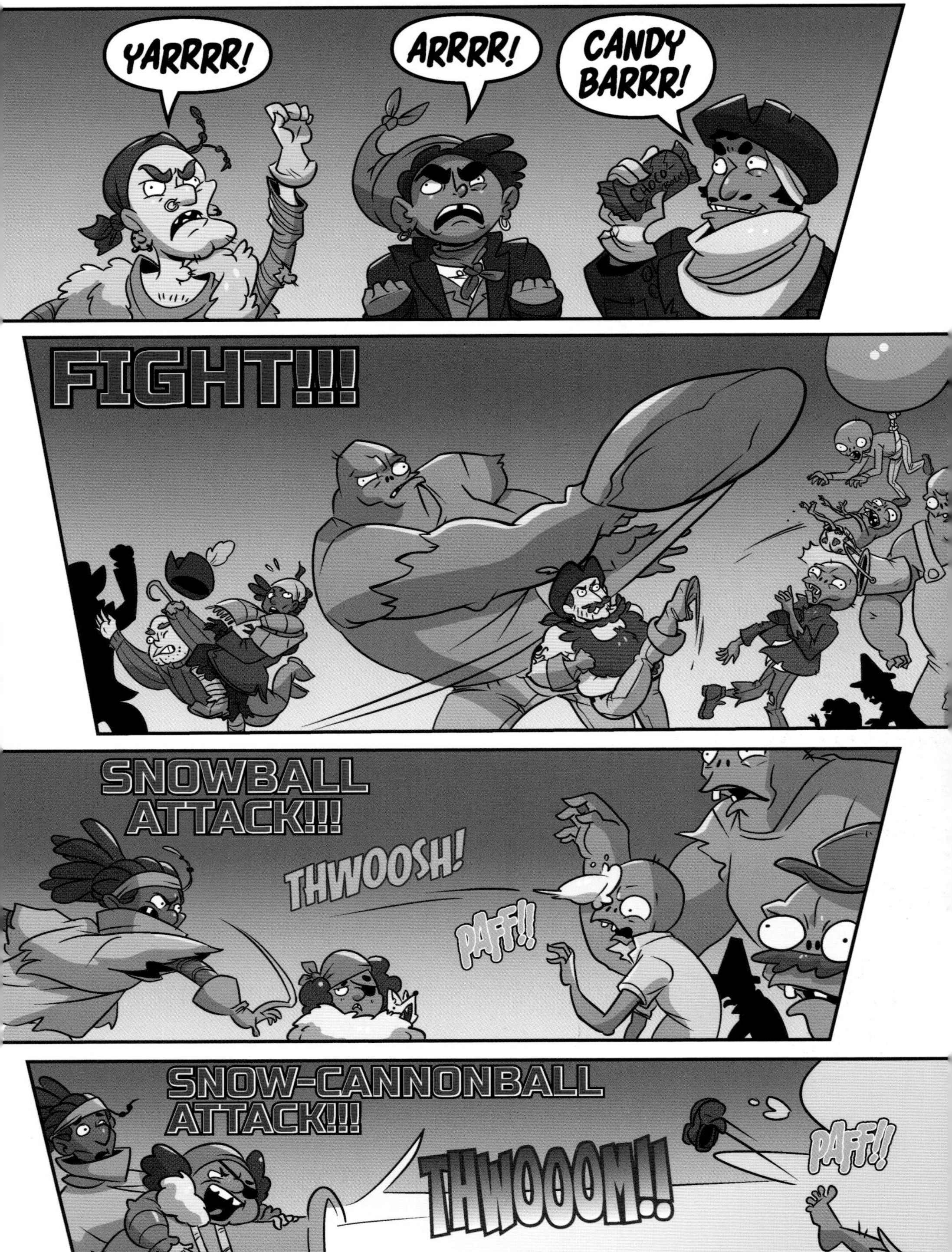
YARRRR!
ARRRR!
CANDY BARRR!
FIGHT!!!
SNOWBALL ATTACK!!!
THWOOSH!
PAFF!!
SNOW-CANNONBALL ATTACK!!!
THWOOOM!!
PAFF!!

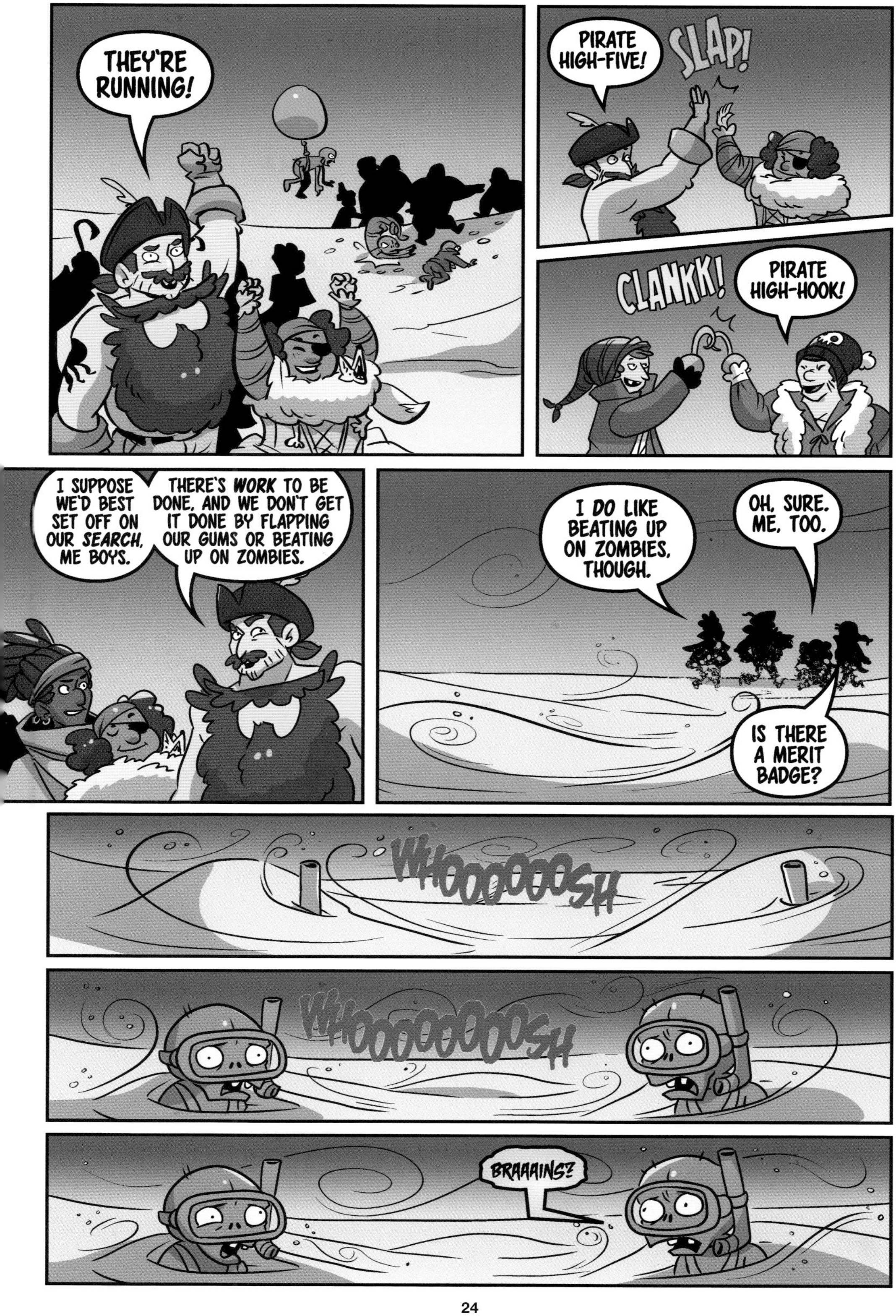
THEY'RE RUNNING!
PIRATE HIGH-FIVE!
SLAP!
CLANKK!
PIRATE HIGH-HOOK!
I SUPPOSE WE'D BEST SET OFF ON OUR SEARCH, ME BOYS.
THERE'S WORK TO BE DONE, AND WE DON'T GET IT DONE BY FLAPPING OUR GUMS OR BEATING UP ON ZOMBIES.
I DO LIKE BEATING UP ON ZOMBIES, THOUGH.
OH, SURE. ME, TOO.
IS THERE A MERIT BADGE?
WHOOOOOOOSH
WHOOOOOOOOOSH
BRAAAINS?

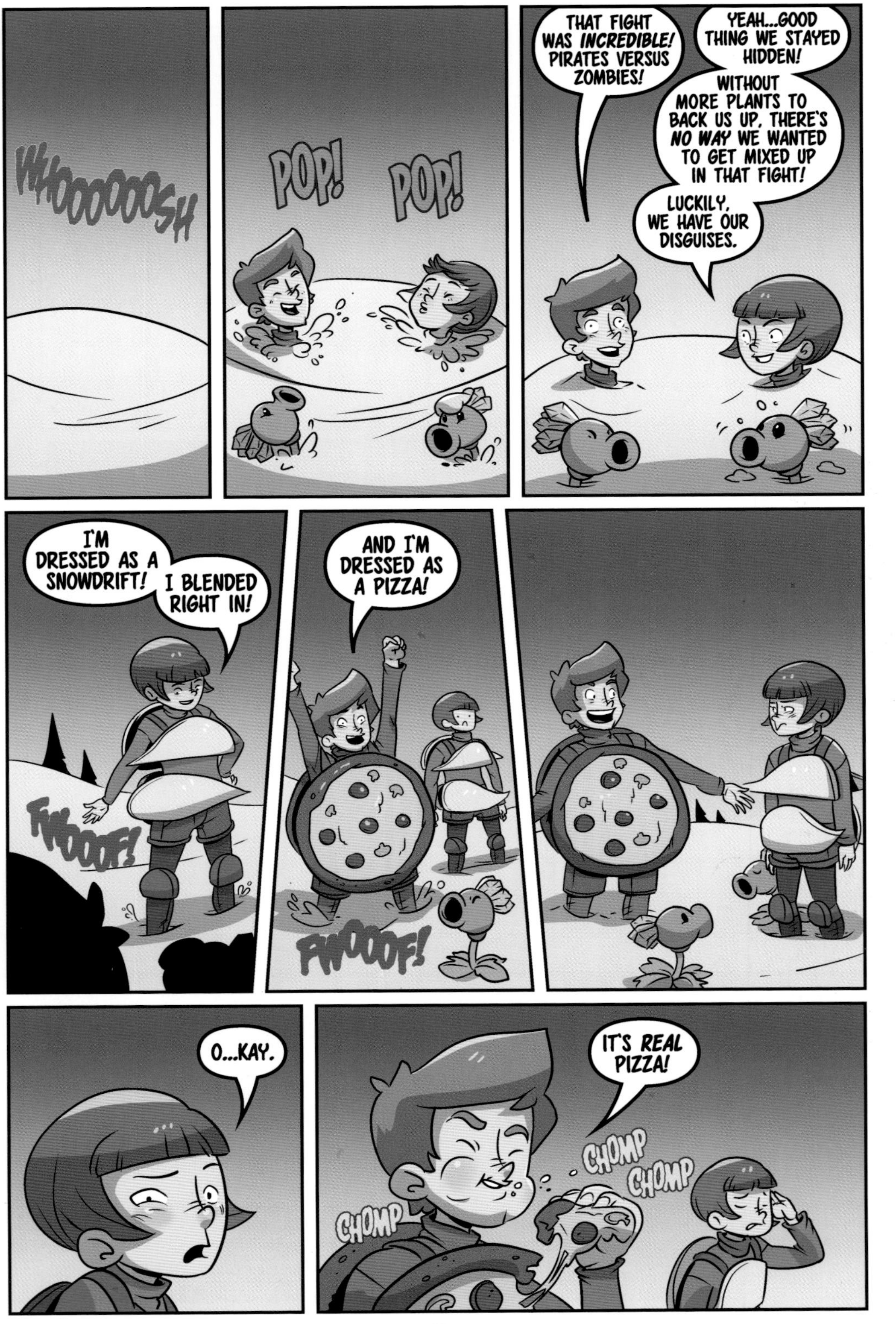
WHOOOOOOSH
POP!
POP!
THAT FIGHT WAS *INCREDIBLE!* PIRATES VERSUS ZOMBIES!
YEAH...GOOD THING WE STAYED HIDDEN!
WITHOUT MORE PLANTS TO BACK US UP, THERE'S *NO WAY* WE WANTED TO GET MIXED UP IN THAT FIGHT!
LUCKILY, WE HAVE OUR DISGUISES.
I'M DRESSED AS A SNOWDRIFT!
I BLENDED RIGHT IN!
FWOOOF!
AND I'M DRESSED AS A PIZZA!
FWOOOF!
O...KAY.
IT'S *REAL* PIZZA!
CHOMP
CHOMP
CHOMP

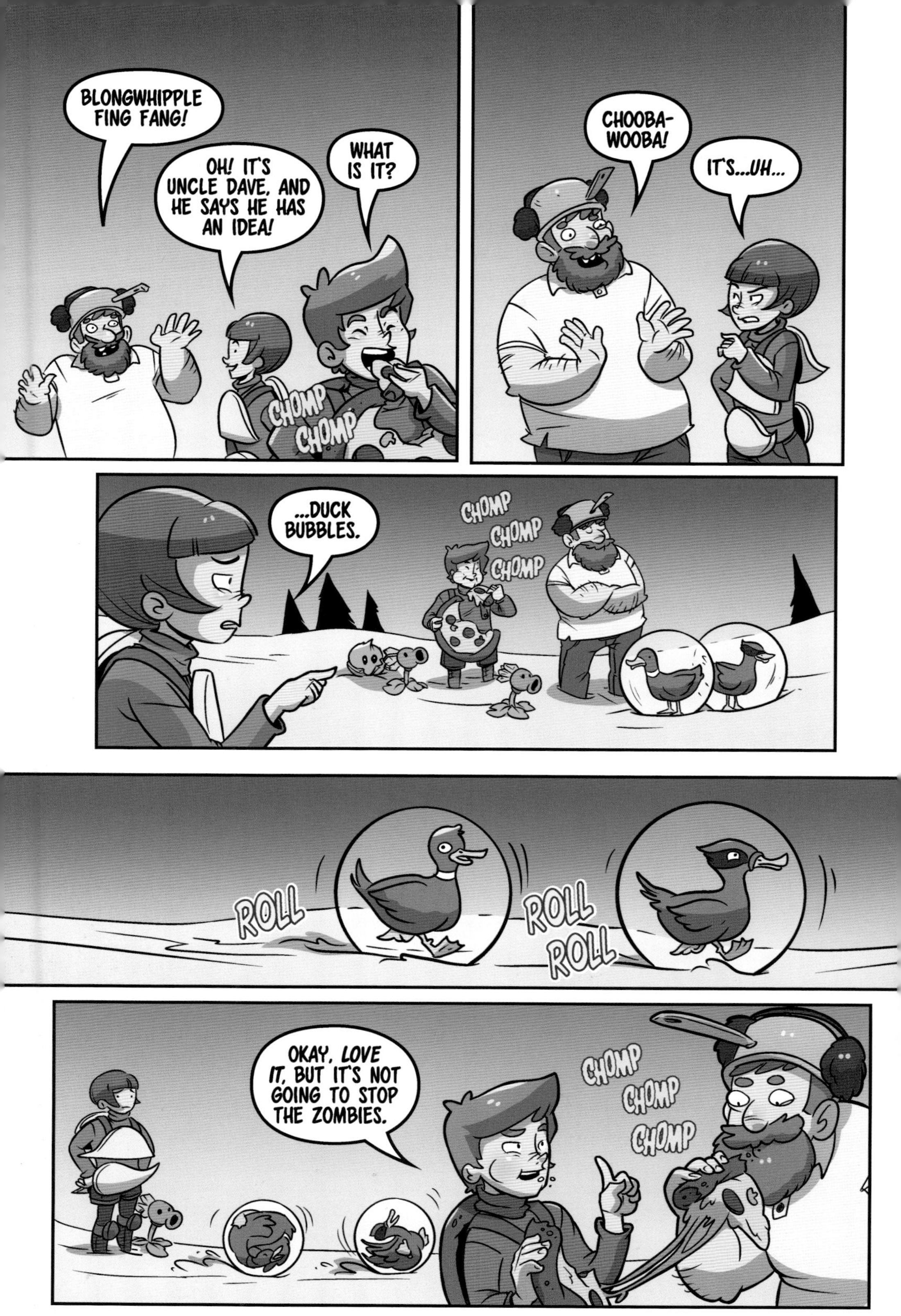
BLONGWHIPPLE FING FANG!
OH! IT'S UNCLE DAVE, AND HE SAYS HE HAS AN IDEA!
WHAT IS IT?
CHOMP
CHOMP
CHOOBA-WOOBA!
IT'S...UH...
...DUCK BUBBLES.
CHOMP
CHOMP
CHOMP
ROLL
ROLL
ROLL
OKAY, *LOVE IT*, BUT IT'S NOT GOING TO STOP THE ZOMBIES.
CHOMP
CHOMP
CHOMP

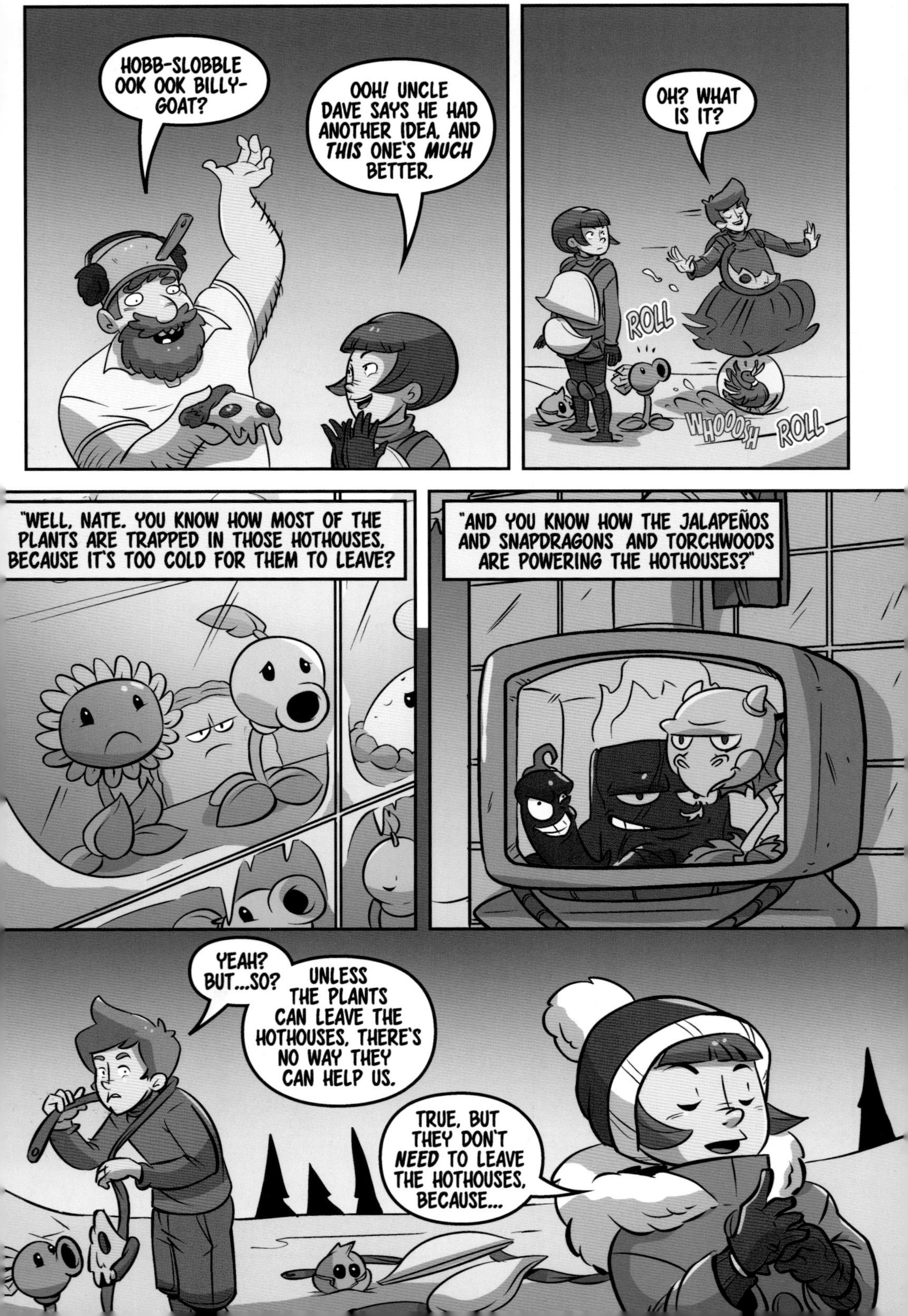
HOBB-SLOBBLE OOK OOK BILLY-GOAT?
OOH! UNCLE DAVE SAYS HE HAD ANOTHER IDEA, AND *THIS* ONE'S *MUCH* BETTER.
OH? WHAT IS IT?
ROLL
WHOOOSH
ROLL
"WELL, NATE. YOU KNOW HOW MOST OF THE PLANTS ARE TRAPPED IN THOSE HOTHOUSES, BECAUSE IT'S TOO COLD FOR THEM TO LEAVE?
"AND YOU KNOW HOW THE JALAPEÑOS AND SNAPDRAGONS AND TORCHWOODS ARE POWERING THE HOTHOUSES?"
YEAH? BUT...SO?
UNLESS THE PLANTS CAN LEAVE THE HOTHOUSES, THERE'S NO WAY THEY CAN HELP US.
TRUE, BUT THEY DON'T *NEED* TO LEAVE THE HOTHOUSES, BECAUSE...

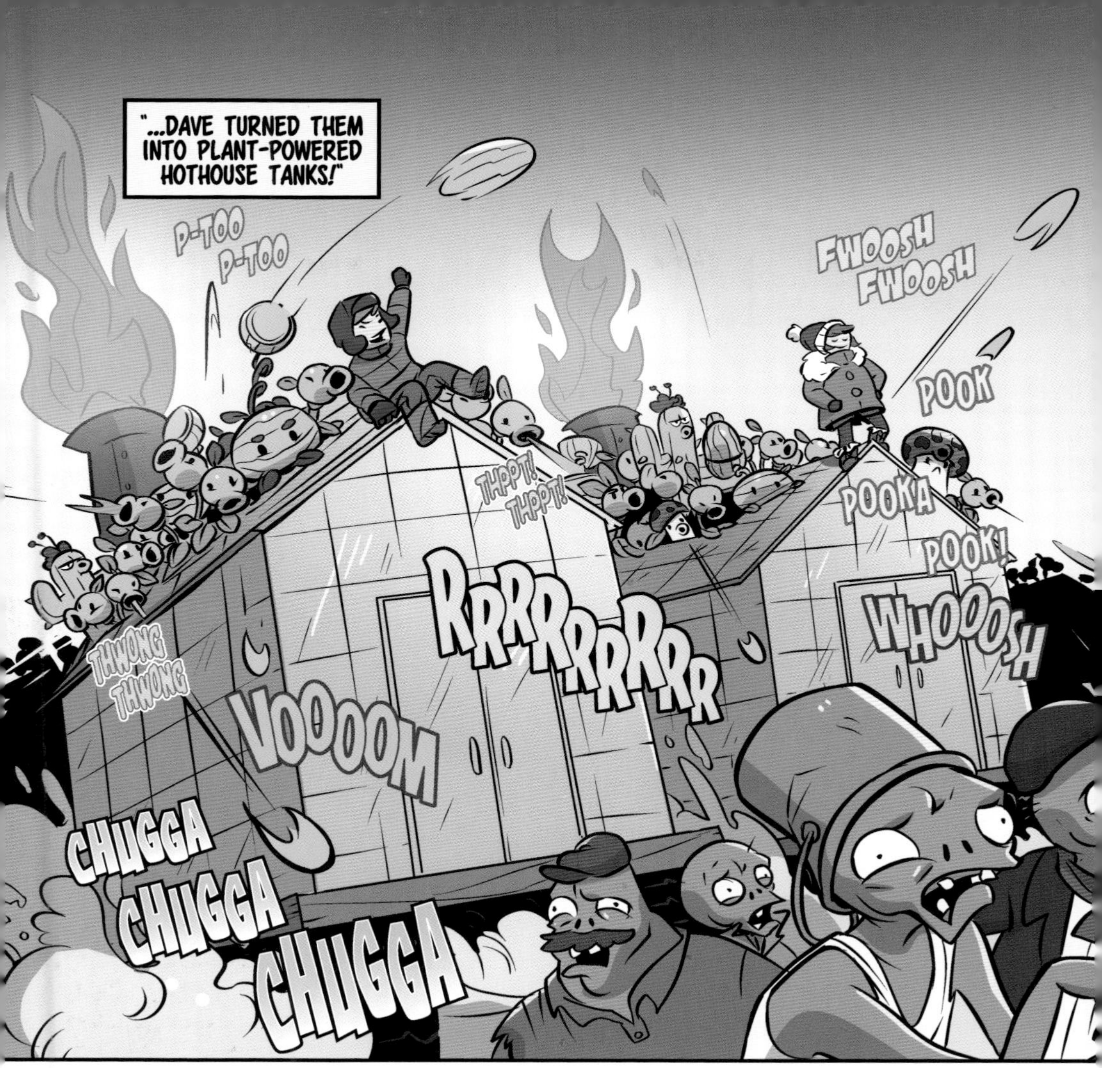
"...DAVE TURNED THEM INTO PLANT-POWERED HOTHOUSE TANKS!"
P-TOO P-TOO
FWOOSH FWOOSH
POOK
THPPT! THPPT!
POOKA POOK!
RRRRRRRRRR
WHOOOSH
THWONG THWONG
VOOOOM
CHUGGA CHUGGA CHUGGA

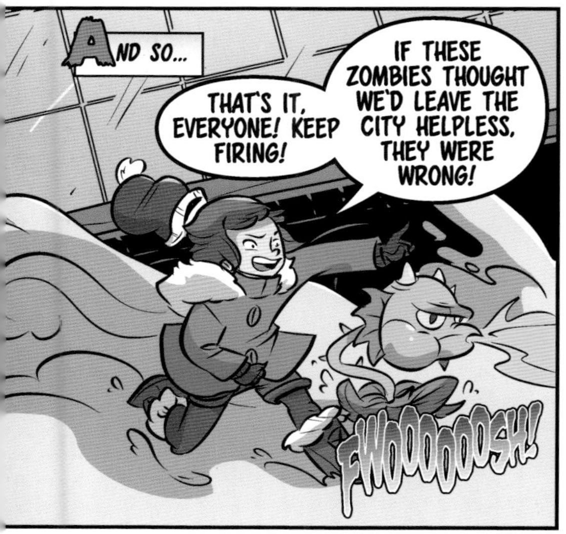
AND SO...
THAT'S IT, EVERYONE! KEEP FIRING!
IF THESE ZOMBIES THOUGHT WE'D LEAVE THE CITY HELPLESS, THEY WERE WRONG!
FWOOOOOOSH!

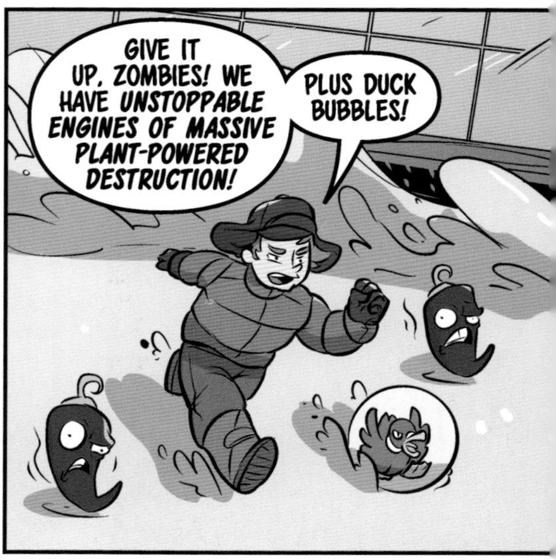
GIVE IT UP, ZOMBIES! WE HAVE UNSTOPPABLE ENGINES OF MASSIVE PLANT-POWERED DESTRUCTION!
PLUS DUCK BUBBLES!

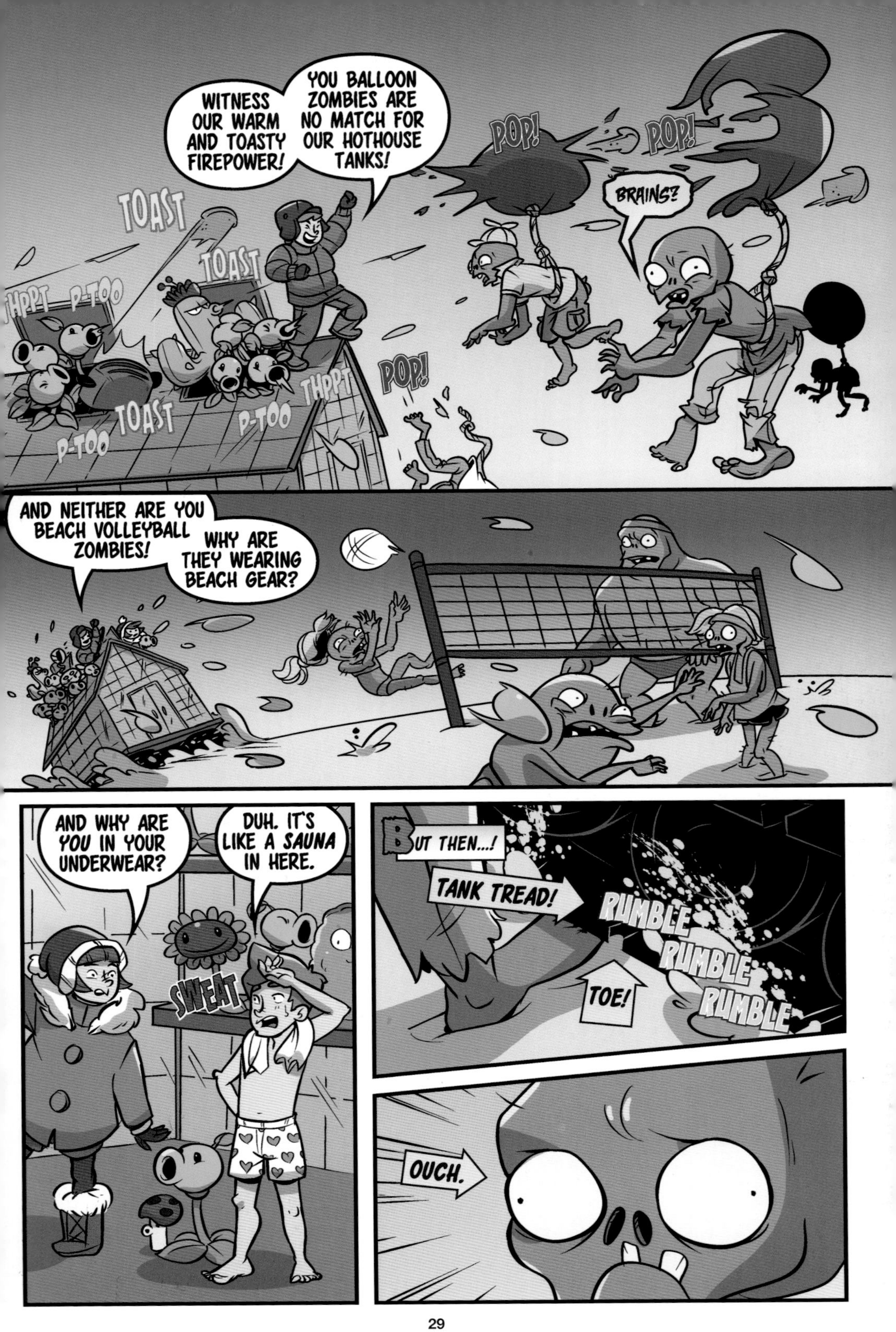
WITNESS OUR WARM AND TOASTY FIREPOWER!
YOU BALLOON ZOMBIES ARE NO MATCH FOR OUR HOTHOUSE TANKS!
POP!
POP!
BRAINS?
TOAST
TOAST
THPPT
P-TOO
TOAST
P-TOO
P-TOO
THPPT
POP!
AND NEITHER ARE YOU BEACH VOLLEYBALL ZOMBIES!
WHY ARE THEY WEARING BEACH GEAR?
AND WHY ARE YOU IN YOUR UNDERWEAR?
DUH. IT'S LIKE A SAUNA IN HERE.
SWEAT
BUT THEN...!
TANK TREAD!
RUMBLE
RUMBLE
RUMBLE
TOE!
OUCH.

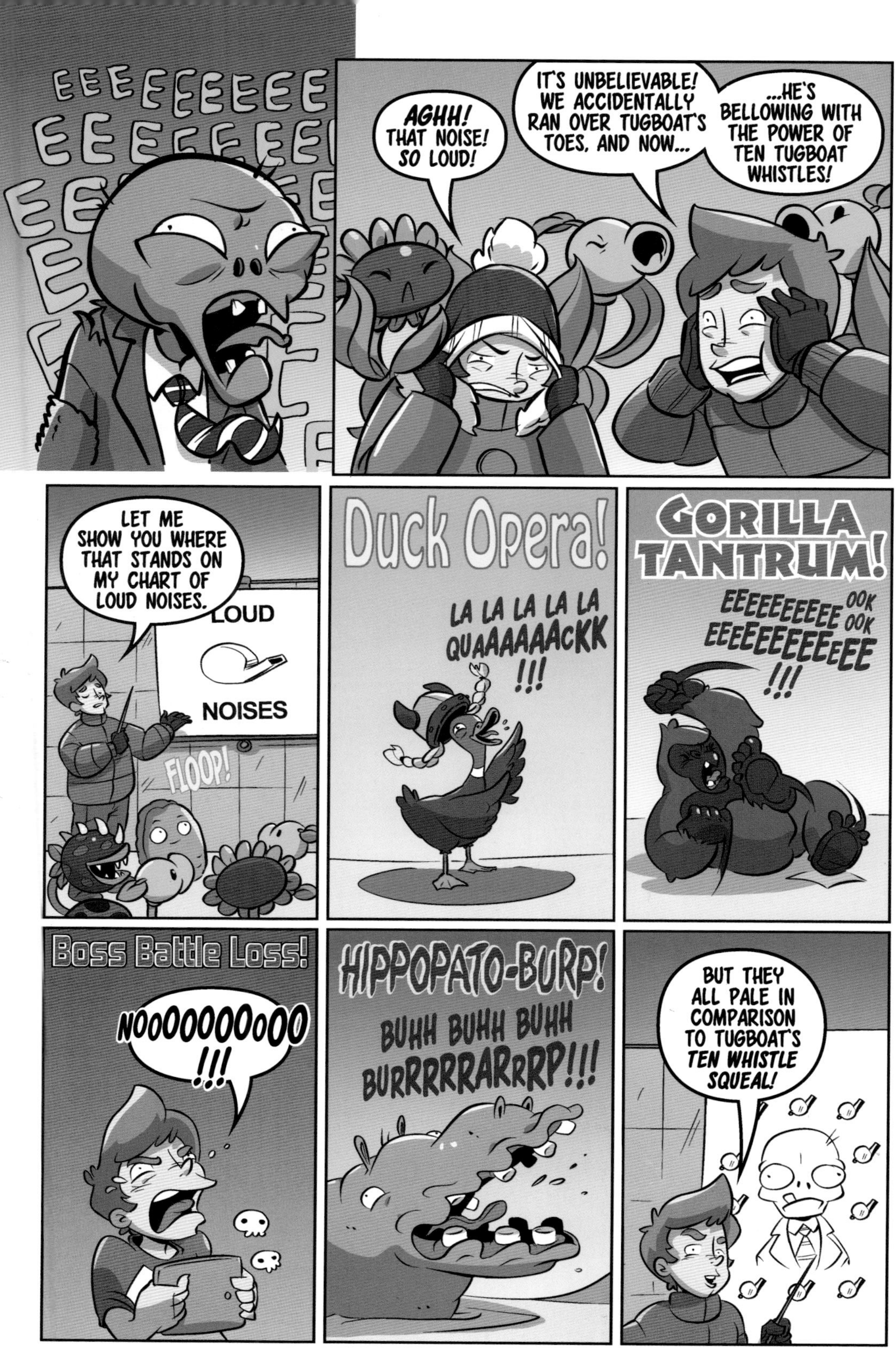
EEEEEEEEEE EEEEEEEEE EEE EE E E E E
AGHH! THAT NOISE! SO LOUD!
IT'S UNBELIEVABLE! WE ACCIDENTALLY RAN OVER TUGBOAT'S TOES, AND NOW...
...HE'S BELLOWING WITH THE POWER OF TEN TUGBOAT WHISTLES!
LET ME SHOW YOU WHERE THAT STANDS ON MY CHART OF LOUD NOISES.
LOUD
NOISES
FLOOP!
Duck Opera!
LA LA LA LA LA QUAAAAAACKK !!!
GORILLA TANTRUM!
EEEEEEEEEE OOK OOK EEEEEEEEEEEEE !!!
Boss Battle Loss!
NOOOOOOOOOO !!!
HIPPOPATO-BURP!
BUHH BUHH BUHH BURRRRRARRRP!!!
BUT THEY ALL PALE IN COMPARISON TO TUGBOAT'S TEN WHISTLE SQUEAL!

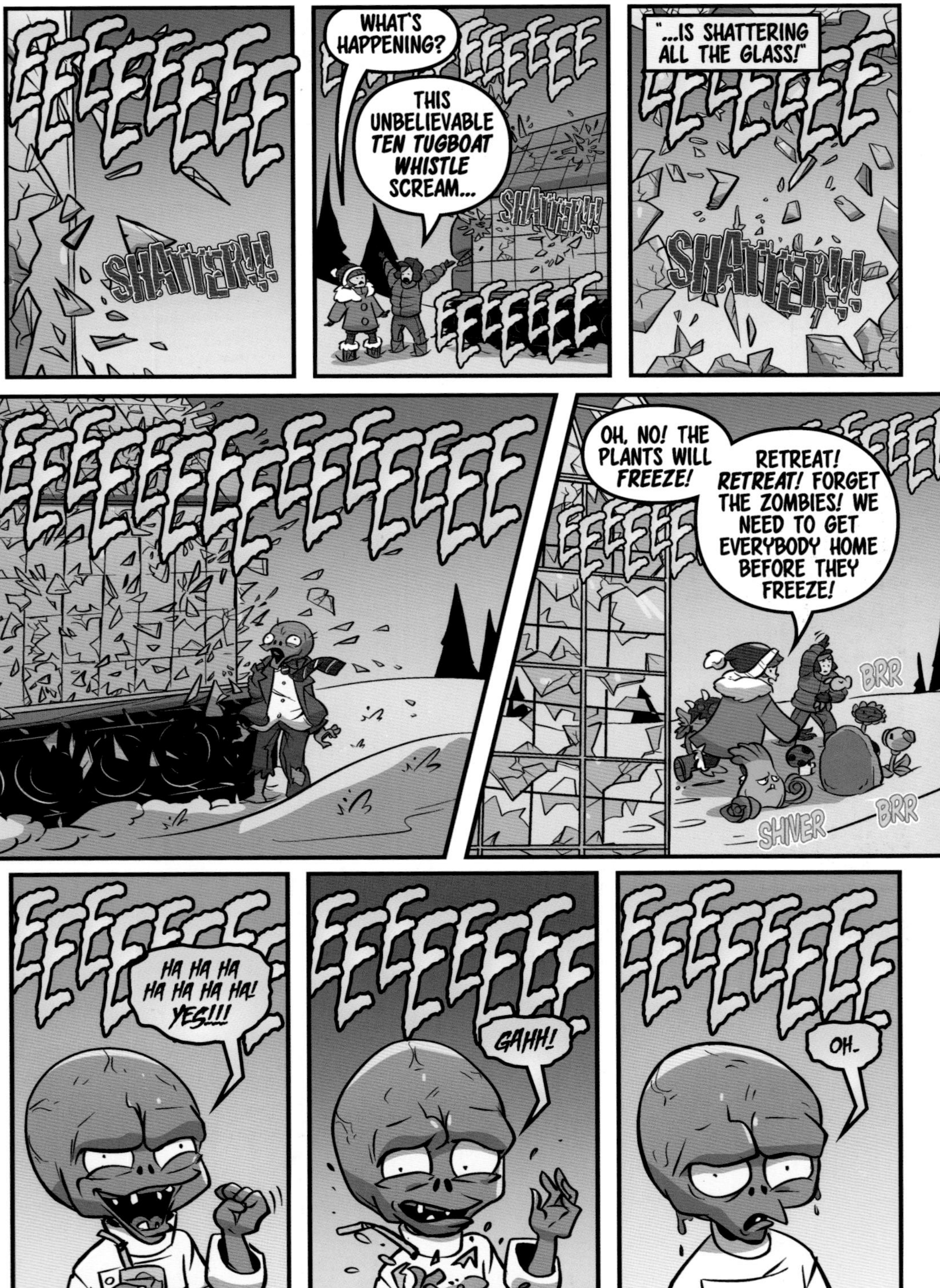
EEEEEEE
SHATTER!!!
WHAT'S HAPPENING?
EEEEEEE
THIS UNBELIEVABLE TEN TUGBOAT WHISTLE SCREAM...
SHATTER!!!
EEEEEE
"...IS SHATTERING ALL THE GLASS!"
EEEEEEE
SHATTER!!!
EEEEEEEEEEEEE
EEEEEE
OH, NO! THE PLANTS WILL FREEZE!
RETREAT! RETREAT! FORGET THE ZOMBIES! WE NEED TO GET EVERYBODY HOME BEFORE THEY FREEZE!
BRR
SHIVER
BRR
EEEEEEE
HA HA HA HA HA HA HA! YES!!!
FRESH GLASS OF ICED Z!
EEEEEEE
GAHH!
SHATTER!!!
EEEEEEE
OH.

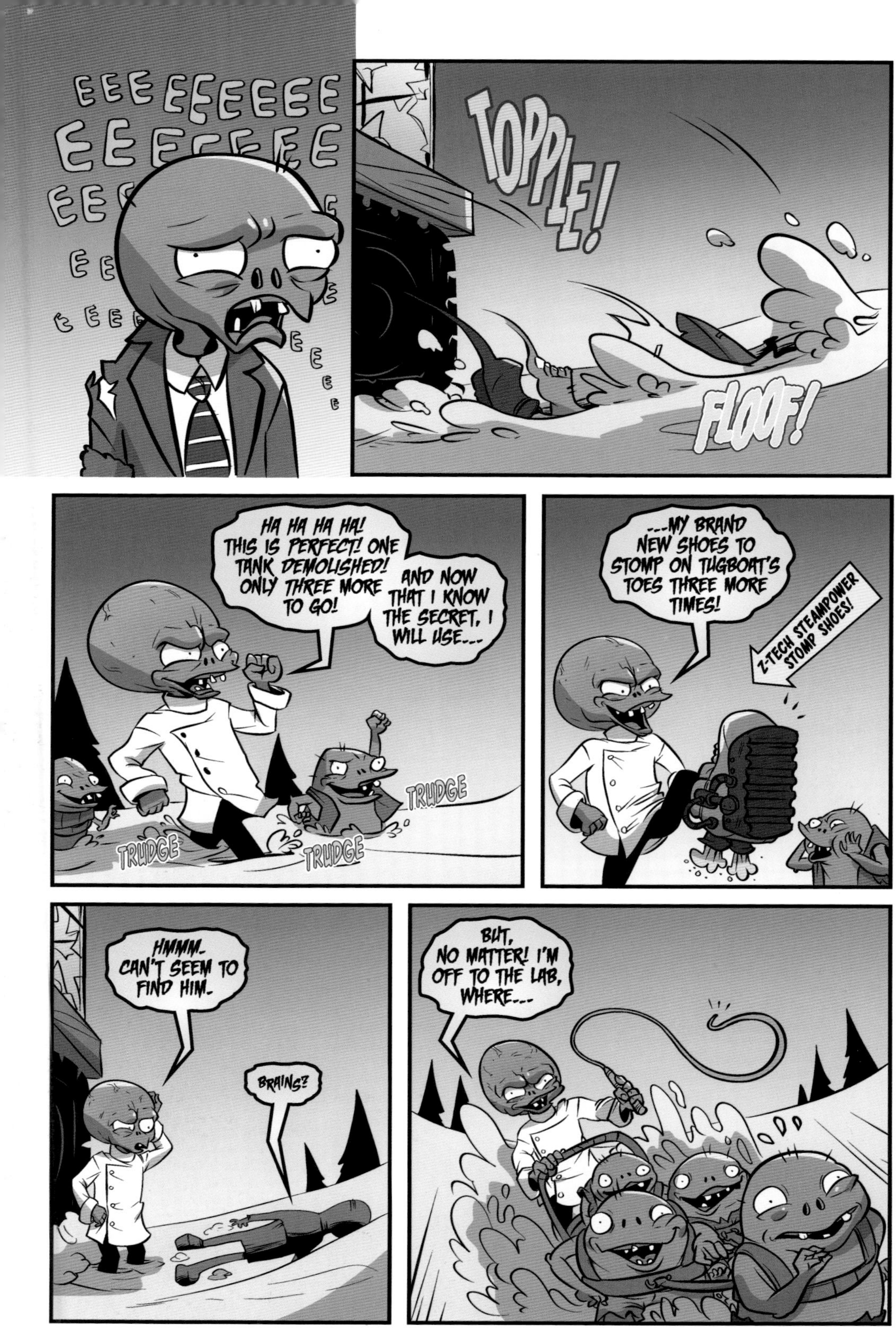
EEE EEEEEE EEEEEEEE EEE E EE E EEE E E E E
TOPPLE!
FLOOF!
HA HA HA HA! THIS IS PERFECT! ONE TANK DEMOLISHED! ONLY THREE MORE TO GO!
AND NOW THAT I KNOW THE SECRET, I WILL USE...
TRUDGE
TRUDGE
TRUDGE
...MY BRAND NEW SHOES TO STOMP ON TUGBOAT'S TOES THREE MORE TIMES!
Z-TECH STEAMPOWER STOMP SHOES!
HMMM... CAN'T SEEM TO FIND HIM...
BRAINS?
BUT, NO MATTER! I'M OFF TO THE LAB, WHERE...

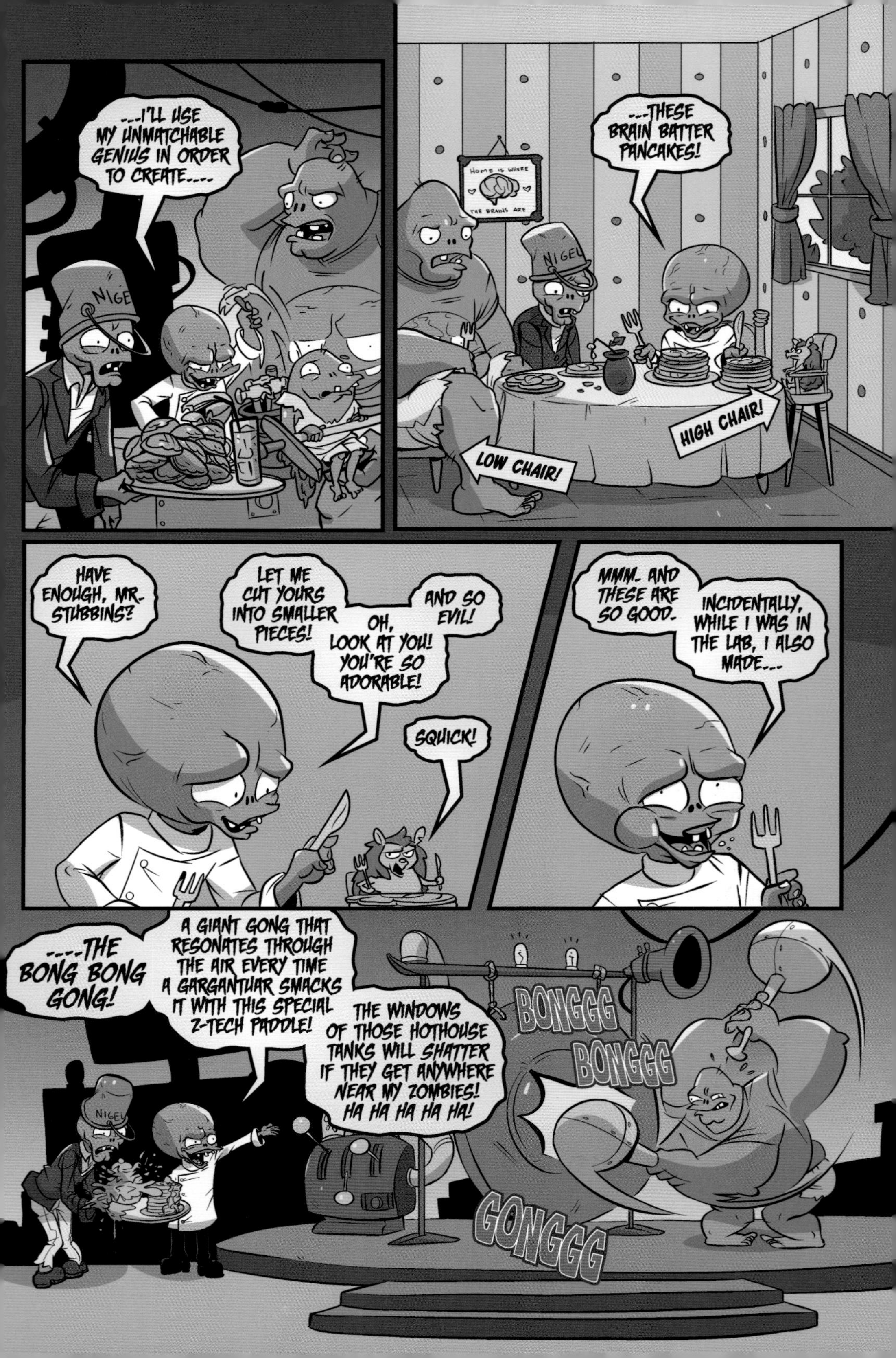
...I'LL USE MY UNMATCHABLE GENIUS IN ORDER TO CREATE....
...THESE BRAIN BATTER PANCAKES!
HOME IS WHERE THE BRAINS ARE
NIGEL
HIGH CHAIR!
LOW CHAIR!
HAVE ENOUGH, MR. STUBBINS?
LET ME CUT YOURS INTO SMALLER PIECES!
OH, LOOK AT YOU! YOU'RE SO ADORABLE!
AND SO EVIL!
SQUICK!
MMM. AND THESE ARE SO GOOD.
INCIDENTALLY, WHILE I WAS IN THE LAB, I ALSO MADE...
....THE BONG BONG GONG!
A GIANT GONG THAT RESONATES THROUGH THE AIR EVERY TIME A GARGANTUAR SMACKS IT WITH THIS SPECIAL Z-TECH PADDLE!
THE WINDOWS OF THOSE HOTHOUSE TANKS WILL SHATTER IF THEY GET ANYWHERE NEAR MY ZOMBIES! HA HA HA HA HA!
BONGGG
BONGGG
GONGGG

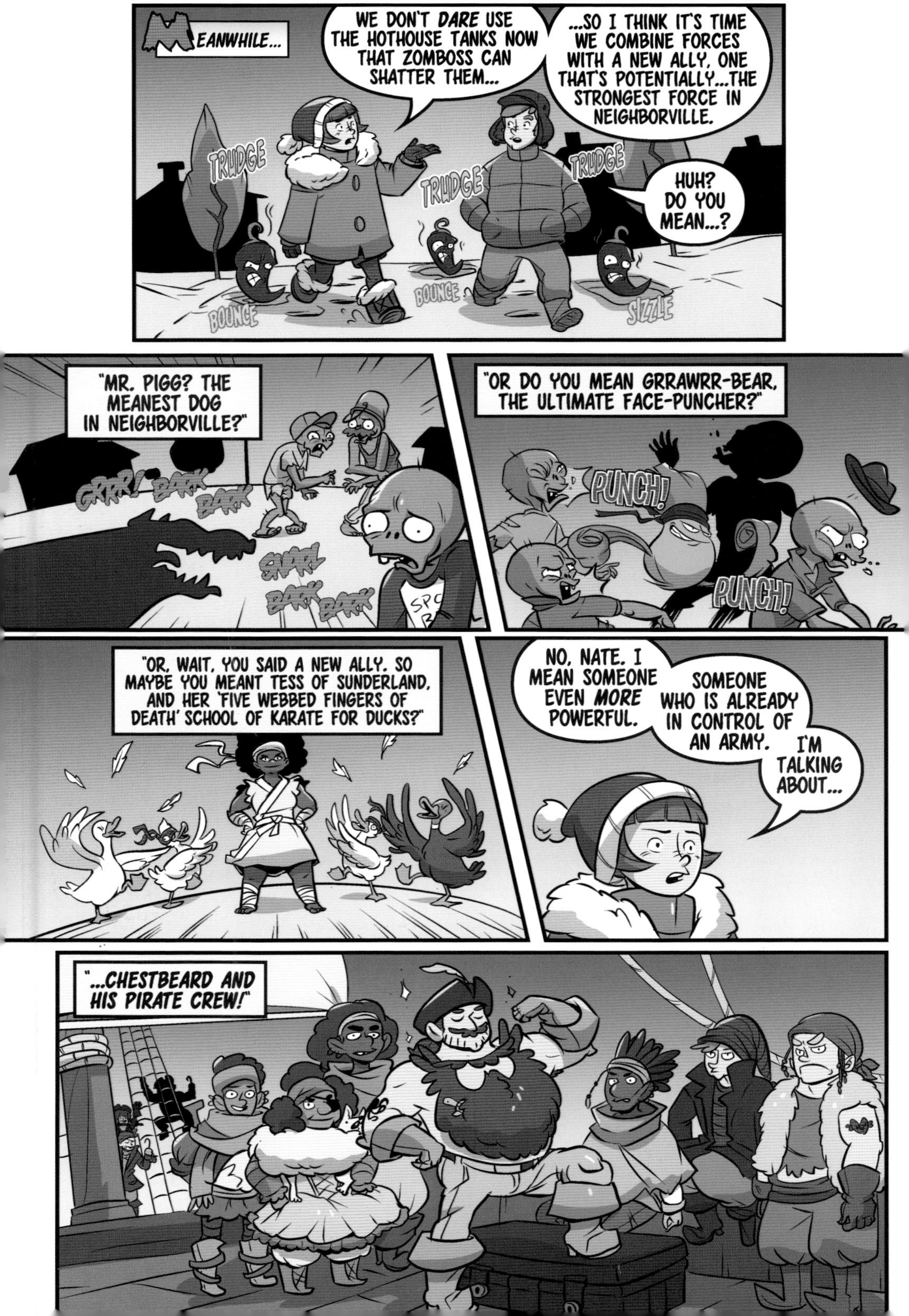
MEANWHILE...
WE DON'T *DARE* USE THE HOTHOUSE TANKS NOW THAT ZOMBOSS CAN SHATTER THEM...
...SO I THINK IT'S TIME WE COMBINE FORCES WITH A NEW ALLY, ONE THAT'S POTENTIALLY...THE STRONGEST FORCE IN NEIGHBORVILLE.
TRUDGE
TRUDGE
TRUDGE
HUH? DO YOU MEAN...?
BOUNCE
BOUNCE
SIZZLE
"MR. PIGG? THE MEANEST DOG IN NEIGHBORVILLE?"
GRRR! BARK BARK
SNARL
BARK BARK
"OR DO YOU MEAN GRRAWRR-BEAR, THE ULTIMATE FACE-PUNCHER?"
PUNCH!
PUNCH!
"OR, WAIT, YOU SAID A NEW ALLY. SO MAYBE YOU MEANT TESS OF SUNDERLAND, AND HER 'FIVE WEBBED FINGERS OF DEATH' SCHOOL OF KARATE FOR DUCKS?"
NO, NATE. I MEAN SOMEONE EVEN *MORE* POWERFUL.
SOMEONE WHO IS ALREADY IN CONTROL OF AN ARMY.
I'M TALKING ABOUT...
"...CHESTBEARD AND HIS PIRATE CREW!"

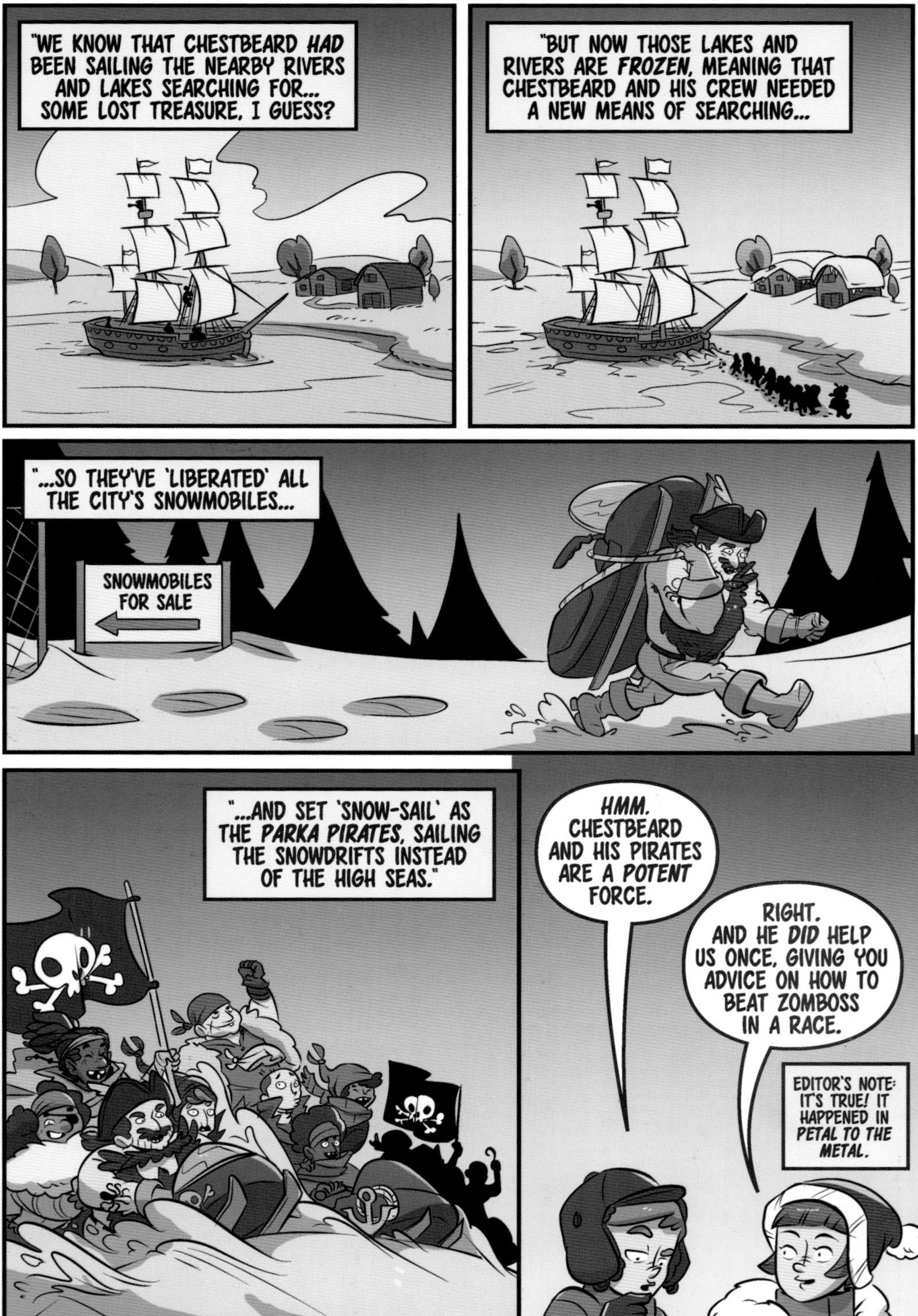
"WE KNOW THAT CHESTBEARD *HAD* BEEN SAILING THE NEARBY RIVERS AND LAKES SEARCHING FOR... SOME LOST TREASURE, I GUESS?
"BUT NOW THOSE LAKES AND RIVERS ARE *FROZEN*, MEANING THAT CHESTBEARD AND HIS CREW NEEDED A NEW MEANS OF SEARCHING...
"...SO THEY'VE 'LIBERATED' ALL THE CITY'S SNOWMOBILES...
SNOWMOBILES FOR SALE
"...AND SET 'SNOW-SAIL' AS THE *PARKA PIRATES*, SAILING THE SNOWDRIFTS INSTEAD OF THE HIGH SEAS."
HMM. CHESTBEARD AND HIS PIRATES ARE A *POTENT* FORCE.
RIGHT. AND HE *DID* HELP US ONCE, GIVING YOU ADVICE ON HOW TO BEAT ZOMBOSS IN A RACE.
EDITOR'S NOTE: IT'S TRUE! IT HAPPENED IN *PETAL TO THE METAL*.

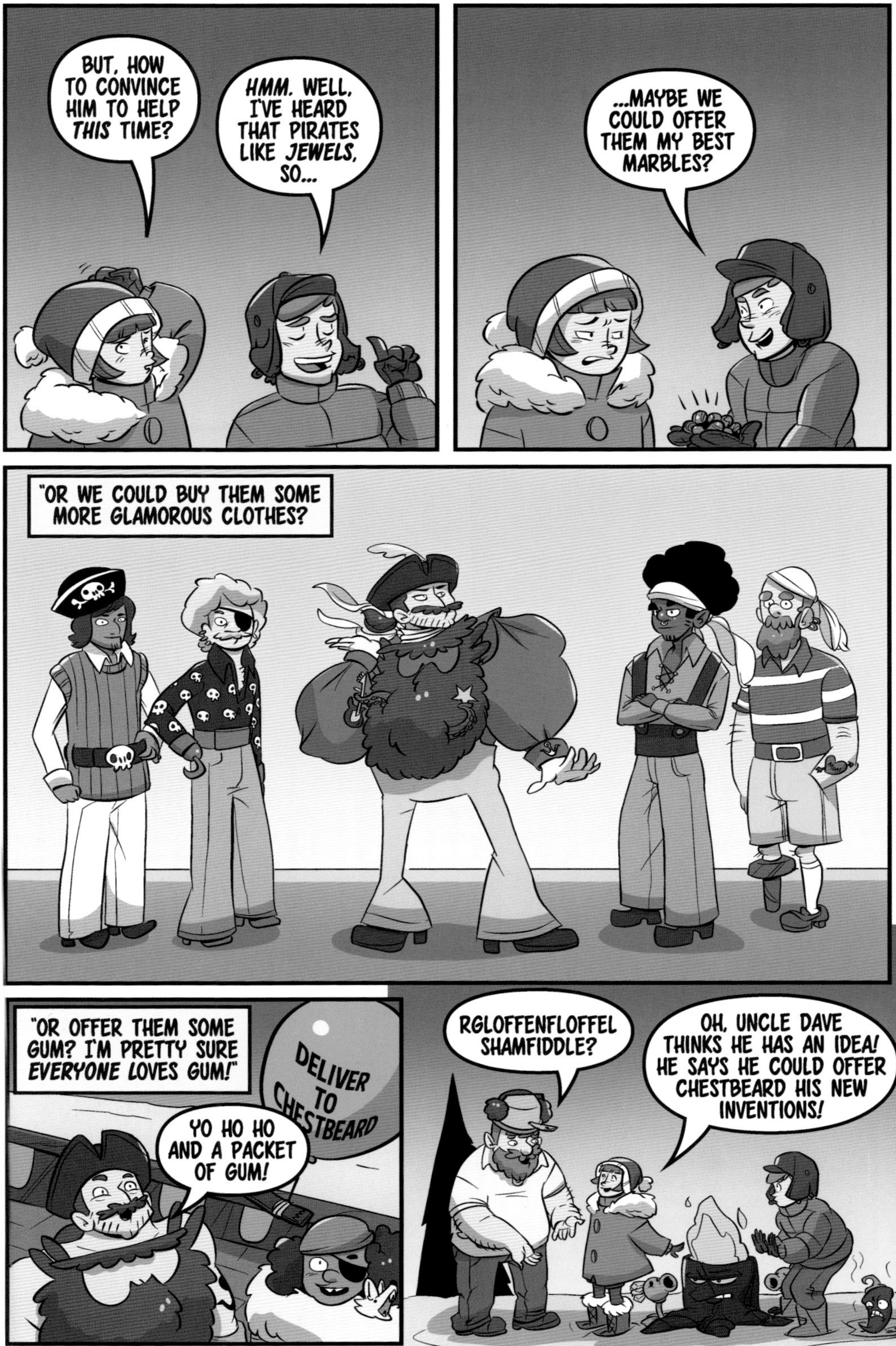
BUT, HOW TO CONVINCE HIM TO HELP *THIS* TIME?
HMM. WELL, I'VE HEARD THAT PIRATES LIKE *JEWELS,* SO...
...MAYBE WE COULD OFFER THEM MY BEST MARBLES?
"OR WE COULD BUY THEM SOME MORE GLAMOROUS CLOTHES?
"OR OFFER THEM SOME GUM? I'M PRETTY SURE *EVERYONE* LOVES GUM!"
DELIVER TO CHESTBEARD
YO HO HO AND A PACKET OF GUM!
RGLOFFENFLOFFEL SHAMFIDDLE?
OH, UNCLE DAVE THINKS HE HAS AN IDEA! HE SAYS HE COULD OFFER CHESTBEARD HIS NEW INVENTIONS!

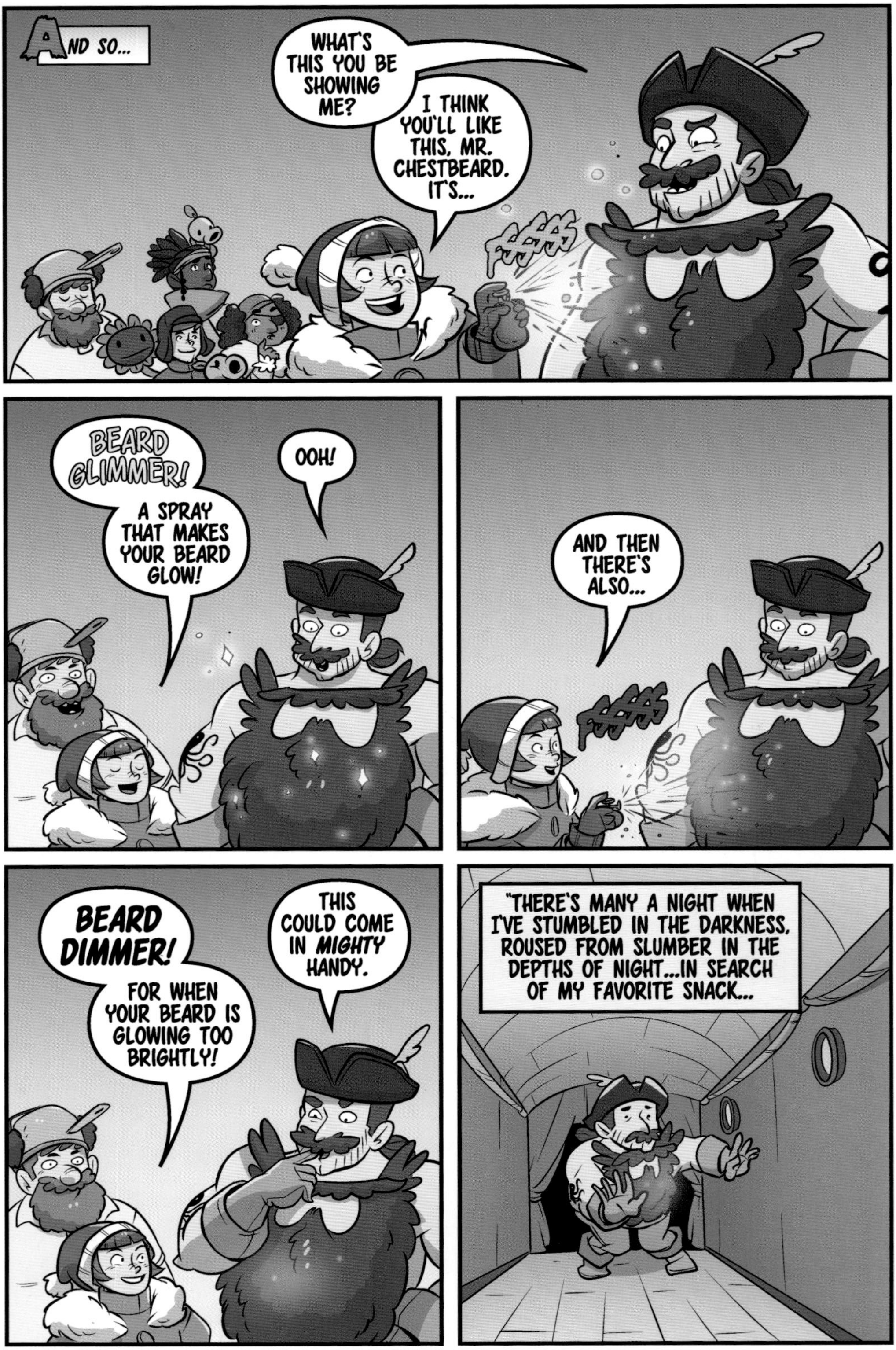

AND SO...
WHAT'S THIS YOU BE SHOWING ME?
I THINK YOU'LL LIKE THIS, MR. CHESTBEARD. IT'S...
BEARD GLIMMER!
A SPRAY THAT MAKES YOUR BEARD GLOW!
OOH!
AND THEN THERE'S ALSO...
BEARD DIMMER!
FOR WHEN YOUR BEARD IS GLOWING TOO BRIGHTLY!
THIS COULD COME IN *MIGHTY* HANDY.
"THERE'S MANY A NIGHT WHEN I'VE STUMBLED IN THE DARKNESS, ROUSED FROM SLUMBER IN THE DEPTHS OF NIGHT...IN SEARCH OF MY FAVORITE SNACK...

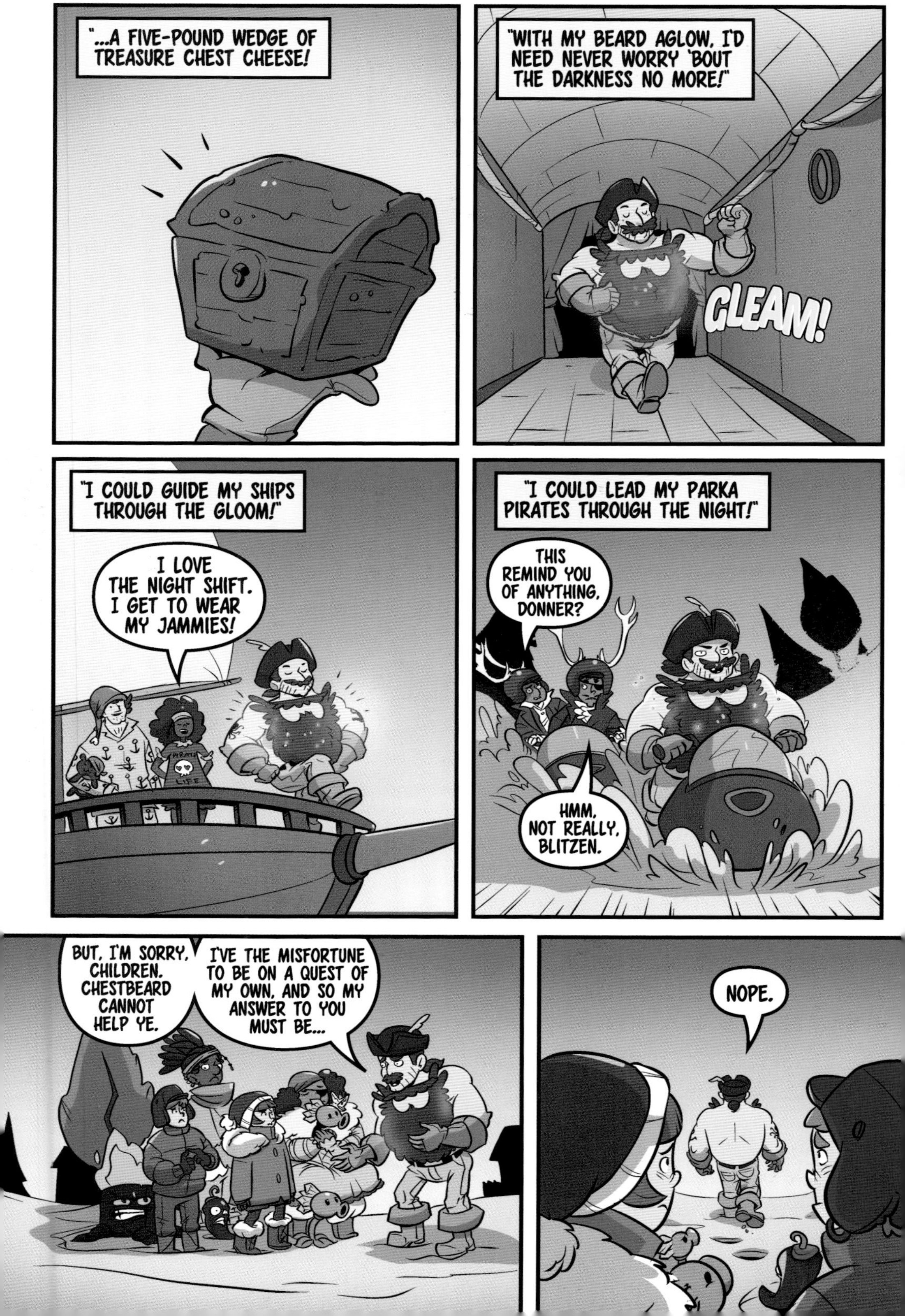
"...A FIVE-POUND WEDGE OF TREASURE CHEST CHEESE!
"WITH MY BEARD AGLOW, I'D NEED NEVER WORRY 'BOUT THE DARKNESS NO MORE!"
GLEAM!
"I COULD GUIDE MY SHIPS THROUGH THE GLOOM!"
I LOVE THE NIGHT SHIFT. I GET TO WEAR MY JAMMIES!
PIRATE LIFE
"I COULD LEAD MY PARKA PIRATES THROUGH THE NIGHT!"
THIS REMIND YOU OF ANYTHING, DONNER?
HMM, NOT REALLY, BLITZEN.
BUT, I'M SORRY, CHILDREN. CHESTBEARD CANNOT HELP YE.
I'VE THE MISFORTUNE TO BE ON A QUEST OF MY OWN, AND SO MY ANSWER TO YOU MUST BE...
NOPE.

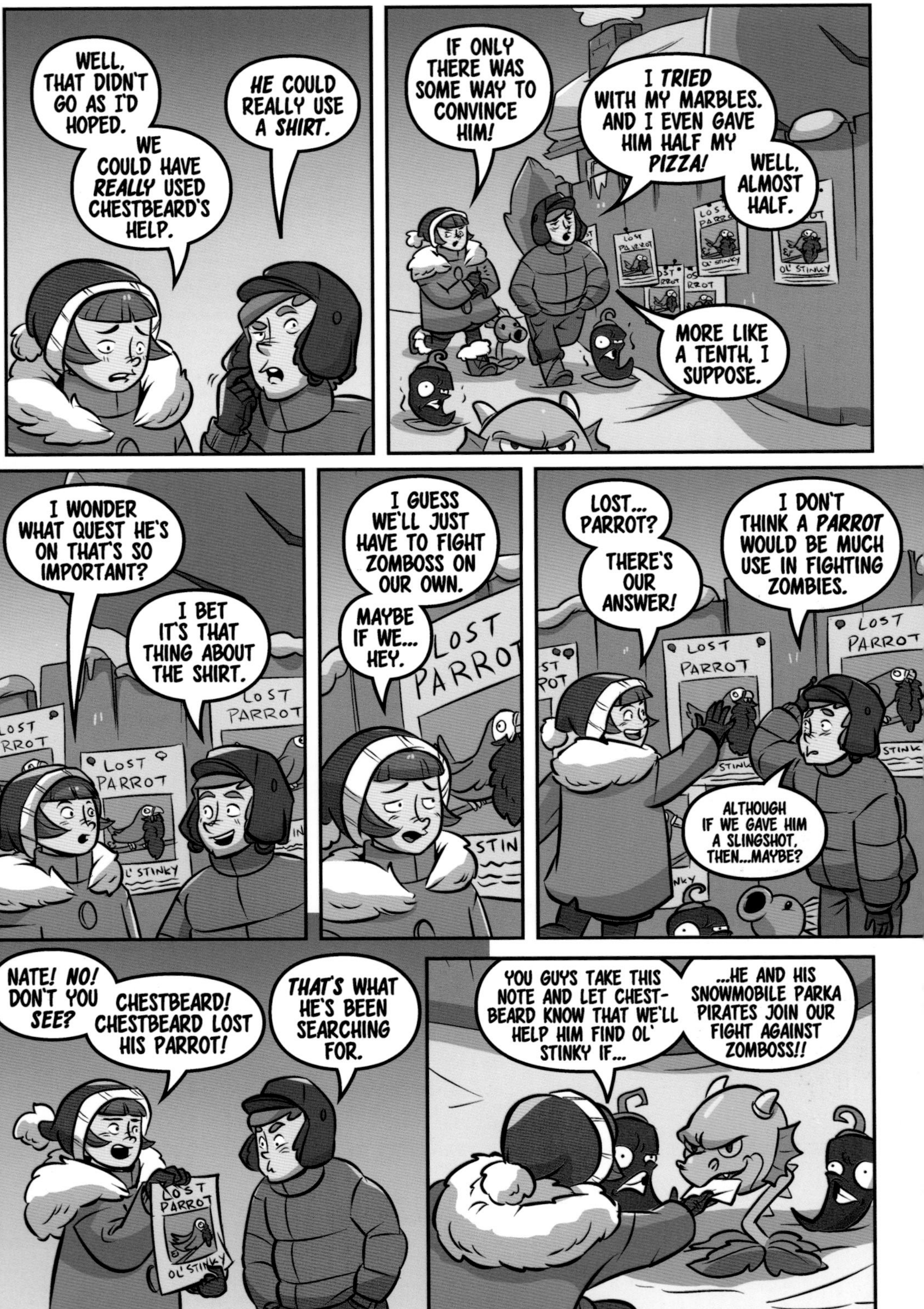

WELL, THAT DIDN'T GO AS I'D HOPED.
WE COULD HAVE *REALLY* USED CHESTBEARD'S HELP.
HE COULD REALLY USE A *SHIRT*.
IF ONLY THERE WAS SOME WAY TO CONVINCE HIM!
I *TRIED* WITH MY MARBLES. AND I EVEN GAVE HIM HALF MY *PIZZA!*
WELL, ALMOST HALF.
MORE LIKE A TENTH, I SUPPOSE.
I WONDER WHAT QUEST HE'S ON THAT'S SO IMPORTANT?
I BET IT'S THAT THING ABOUT THE SHIRT.
I GUESS WE'LL JUST HAVE TO FIGHT ZOMBOSS ON OUR OWN.
MAYBE IF WE... HEY.
LOST PARROT
LOST... PARROT?
THERE'S OUR ANSWER!
I DON'T THINK A *PARROT* WOULD BE MUCH USE IN FIGHTING ZOMBIES.
ALTHOUGH IF WE GAVE HIM A SLINGSHOT, THEN...MAYBE?
NATE! *NO!* DON'T YOU *SEE?*
CHESTBEARD! CHESTBEARD LOST HIS PARROT!
THAT'S WHAT HE'S BEEN SEARCHING FOR.
LOST PARROT
OL' STINKY
YOU GUYS TAKE THIS NOTE AND LET CHEST-BEARD KNOW THAT WE'LL HELP HIM FIND OL' STINKY IF...
...HE AND HIS SNOWMOBILE PARKA PIRATES JOIN OUR FIGHT AGAINST ZOMBOSS!!

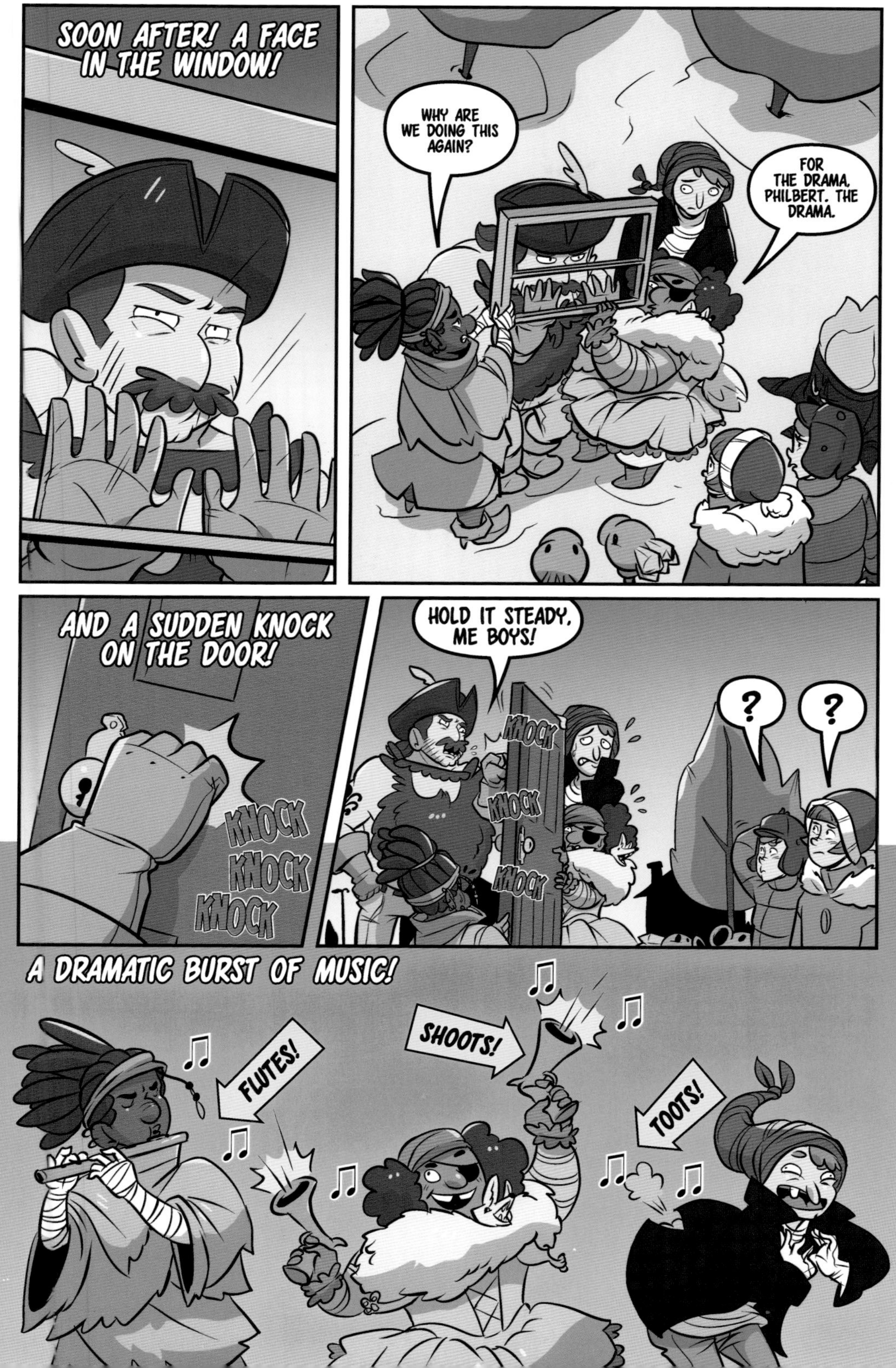
SOON AFTER! A FACE IN THE WINDOW!
WHY ARE WE DOING THIS AGAIN?
FOR THE DRAMA, PHILBERT. THE DRAMA.
AND A SUDDEN KNOCK ON THE DOOR!
KNOCK
KNOCK
KNOCK
HOLD IT STEADY, ME BOYS!
KNOCK
KNOCK
KNOCK
?
?
A DRAMATIC BURST OF MUSIC!
FLUTES!
SHOOTS!
TOOTS!

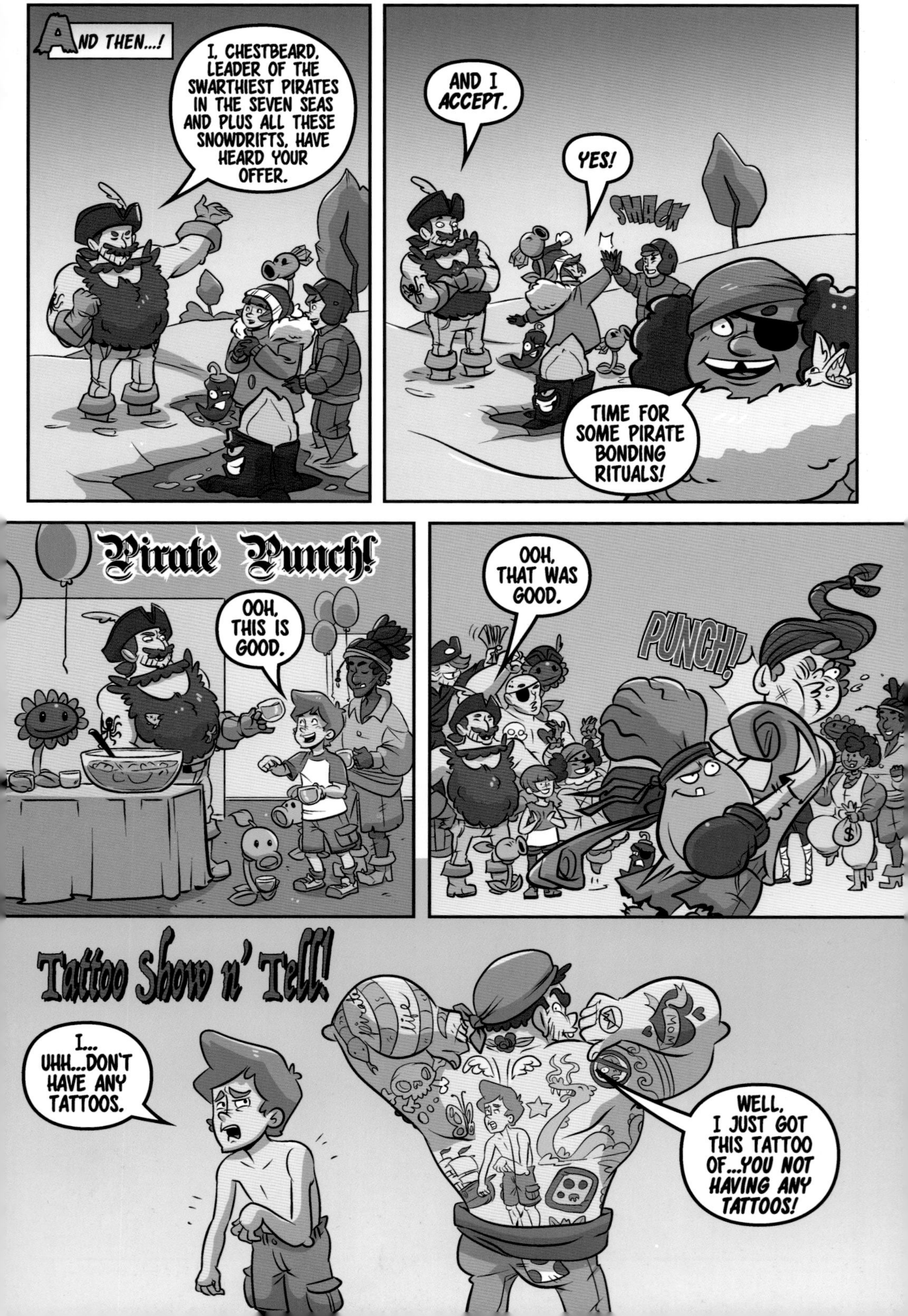
AND THEN...!
I, CHESTBEARD, LEADER OF THE SWARTHIEST PIRATES IN THE SEVEN SEAS AND PLUS ALL THESE SNOWDRIFTS, HAVE HEARD YOUR OFFER.
AND I ACCEPT.
YES!
SMACK
TIME FOR SOME PIRATE BONDING RITUALS!
Pirate Punch!
OOH, THIS IS GOOD.
OOH, THAT WAS GOOD.
PUNCH!
Tattoo Show n' Tell!
I... UHH...DON'T HAVE ANY TATTOOS.
WELL, I JUST GOT THIS TATTOO OF...YOU NOT HAVING ANY TATTOOS!

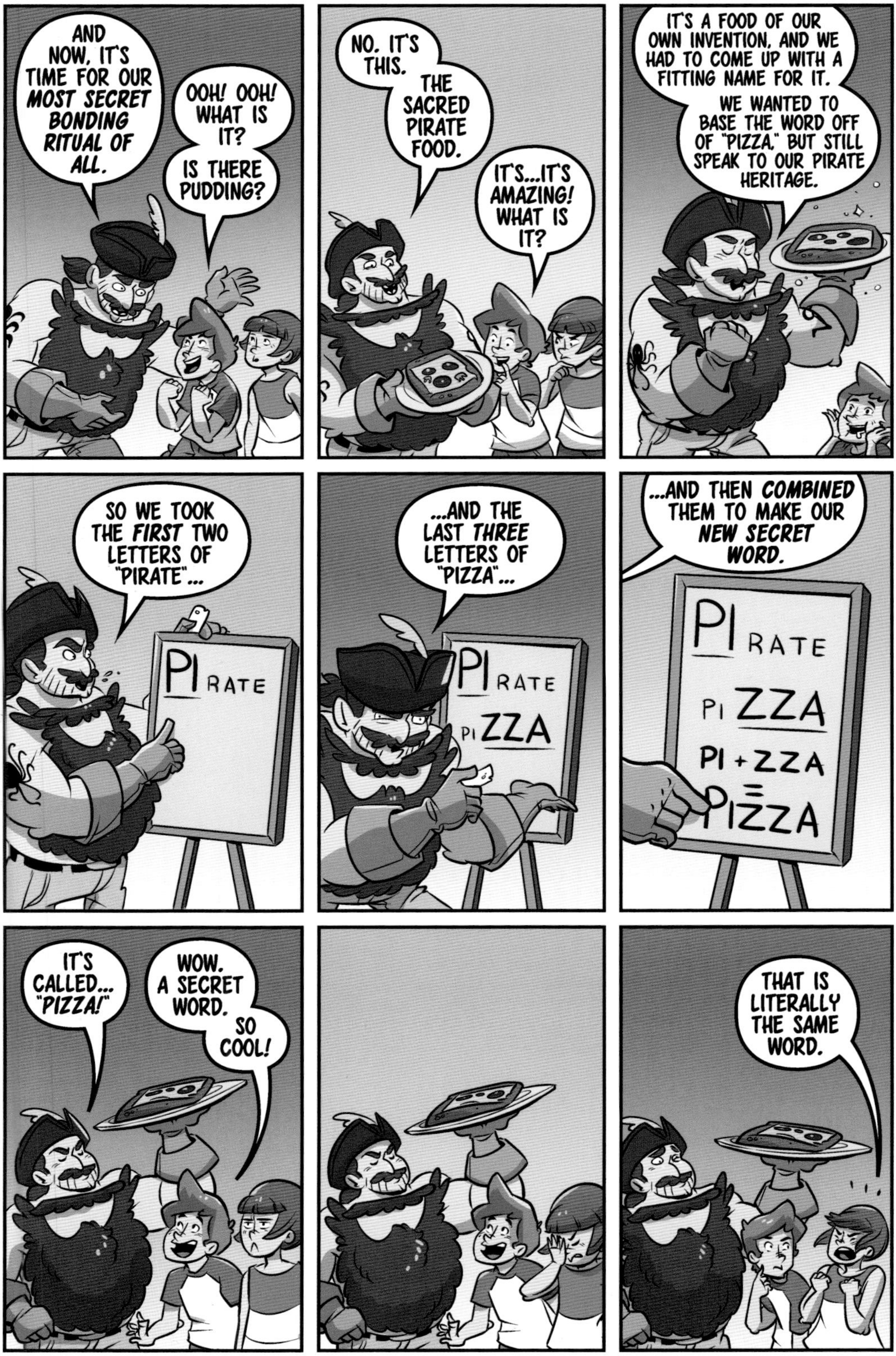
AND NOW, IT'S TIME FOR OUR MOST SECRET BONDING RITUAL OF ALL.
OOH! OOH! WHAT IS IT?
IS THERE PUDDING?
NO. IT'S THIS.
THE SACRED PIRATE FOOD.
IT'S...IT'S AMAZING! WHAT IS IT?
IT'S A FOOD OF OUR OWN INVENTION, AND WE HAD TO COME UP WITH A FITTING NAME FOR IT.
WE WANTED TO BASE THE WORD OFF OF "PIZZA," BUT STILL SPEAK TO OUR PIRATE HERITAGE.
SO WE TOOK THE FIRST TWO LETTERS OF "PIRATE"...
PI RATE
...AND THE LAST THREE LETTERS OF "PIZZA"...
PI RATE
PI ZZA
...AND THEN COMBINED THEM TO MAKE OUR NEW SECRET WORD.
PI RATE
PI ZZA
PI + ZZA
=
PIZZA
IT'S CALLED... "PIZZA!"
WOW. A SECRET WORD.
SO COOL!
THAT IS LITERALLY THE SAME WORD.

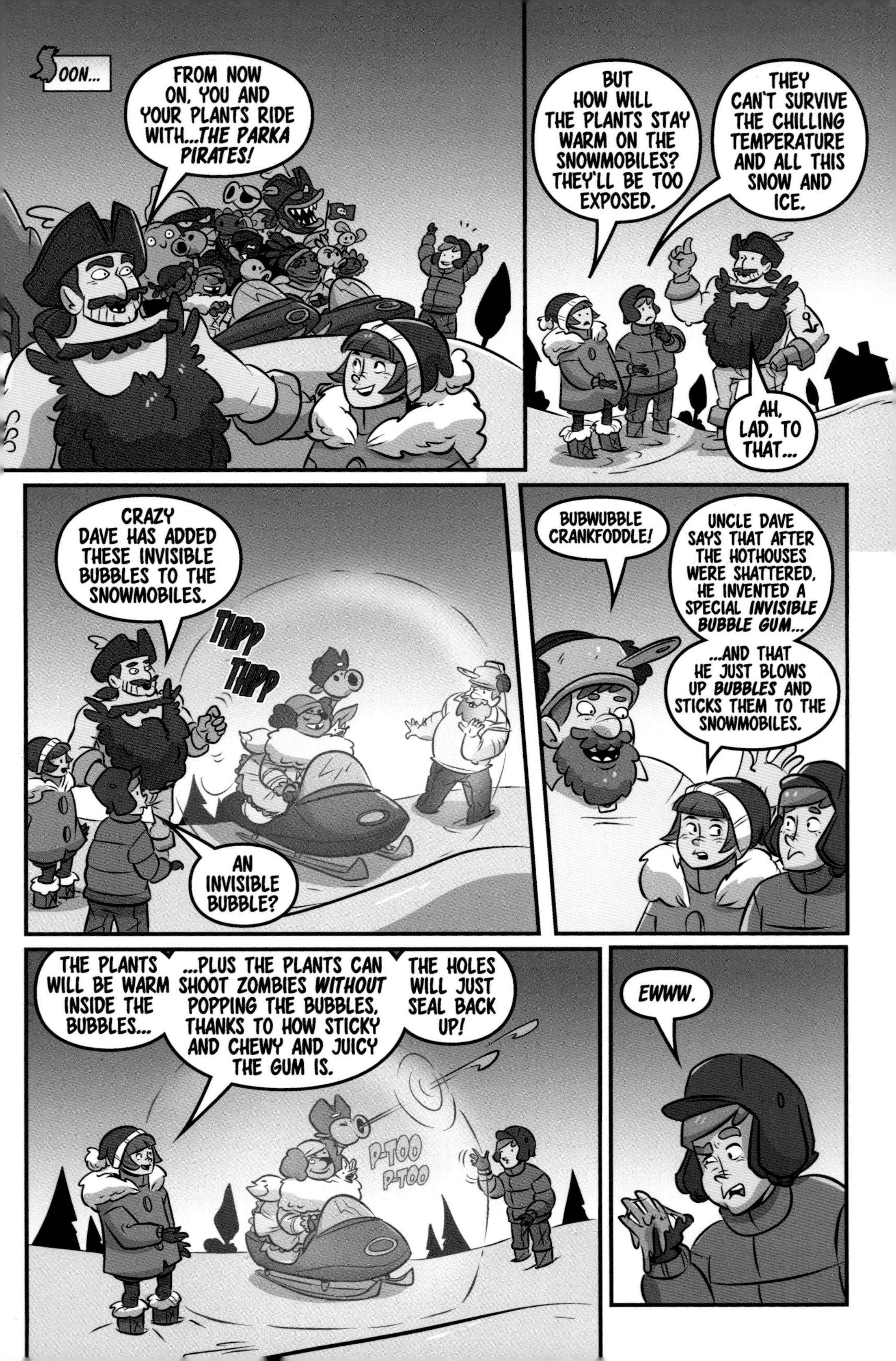
SOON...
FROM NOW ON, YOU AND YOUR PLANTS RIDE WITH...THE PARKA PIRATES!
BUT HOW WILL THE PLANTS STAY WARM ON THE SNOWMOBILES? THEY'LL BE TOO EXPOSED.
THEY CAN'T SURVIVE THE CHILLING TEMPERATURE AND ALL THIS SNOW AND ICE.
AH, LAD, TO THAT...
CRAZY DAVE HAS ADDED THESE INVISIBLE BUBBLES TO THE SNOWMOBILES.
THPP THPP
AN INVISIBLE BUBBLE?
BUBWUBBLE CRANKFODDLE!
UNCLE DAVE SAYS THAT AFTER THE HOTHOUSES WERE SHATTERED, HE INVENTED A SPECIAL INVISIBLE BUBBLE GUM...
...AND THAT HE JUST BLOWS UP BUBBLES AND STICKS THEM TO THE SNOWMOBILES.
THE PLANTS WILL BE WARM INSIDE THE BUBBLES...
...PLUS THE PLANTS CAN SHOOT ZOMBIES WITHOUT POPPING THE BUBBLES, THANKS TO HOW STICKY AND CHEWY AND JUICY THE GUM IS.
THE HOLES WILL JUST SEAL BACK UP!
P-TOO P-TOO
EWWW.

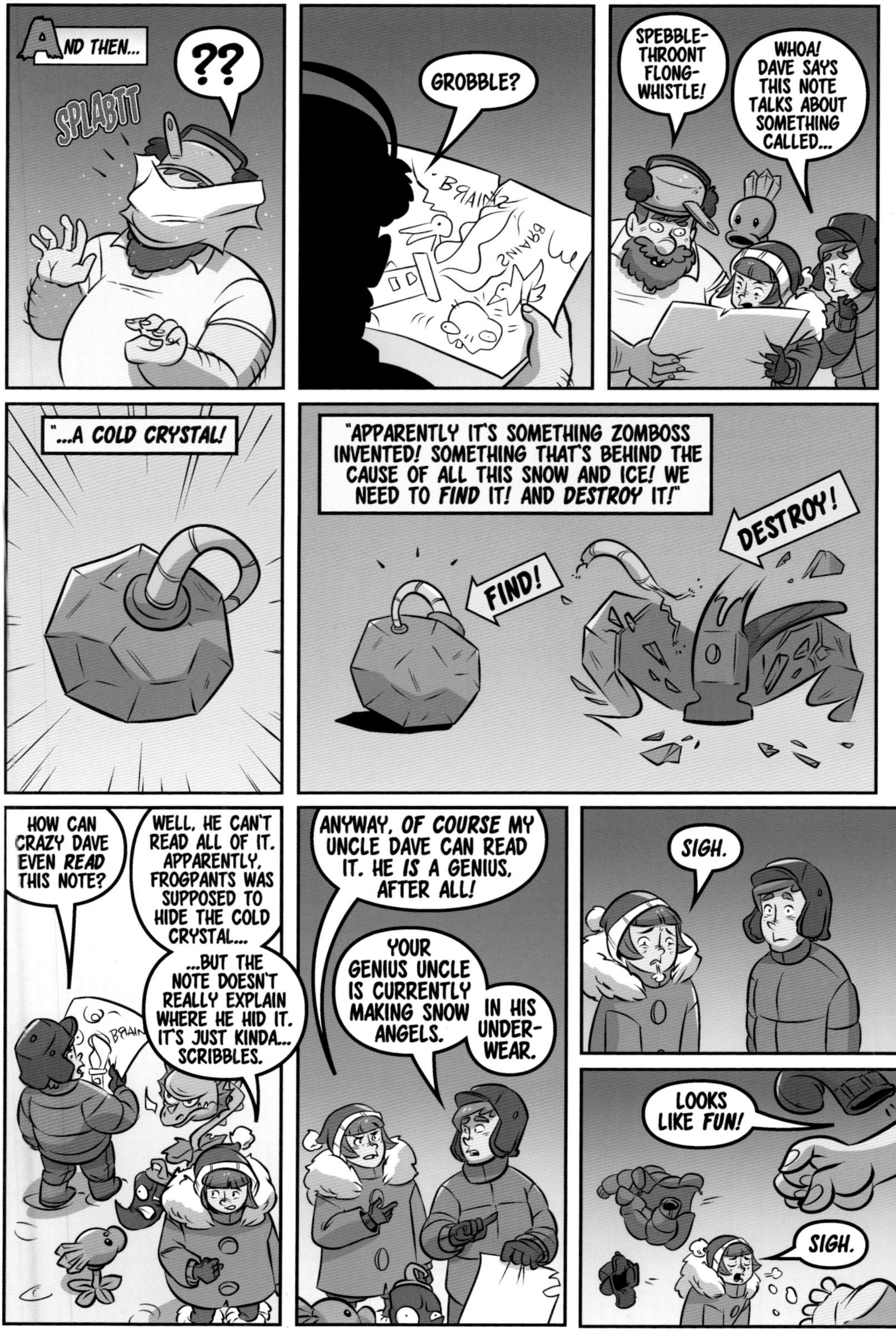
AND THEN...
??
SPLABTT
GROBBLE?
BRAINZ
BRAINS
SPEBBLE-THROONT FLONG-WHISTLE!
WHOA! DAVE SAYS THIS NOTE TALKS ABOUT SOMETHING CALLED...
"...A COLD CRYSTAL!
"APPARENTLY IT'S SOMETHING ZOMBOSS INVENTED! SOMETHING THAT'S BEHIND THE CAUSE OF ALL THIS SNOW AND ICE! WE NEED TO FIND IT! AND DESTROY IT!"
FIND!
DESTROY!
HOW CAN CRAZY DAVE EVEN READ THIS NOTE?
WELL, HE CAN'T READ ALL OF IT. APPARENTLY, FROGPANTS WAS SUPPOSED TO HIDE THE COLD CRYSTAL...
...BUT THE NOTE DOESN'T REALLY EXPLAIN WHERE HE HID IT. IT'S JUST KINDA... SCRIBBLES.
ANYWAY, OF COURSE MY UNCLE DAVE CAN READ IT. HE IS A GENIUS, AFTER ALL!
YOUR GENIUS UNCLE IS CURRENTLY MAKING SNOW ANGELS.
IN HIS UNDER-WEAR.
SIGH.
LOOKS LIKE FUN!
SIGH.

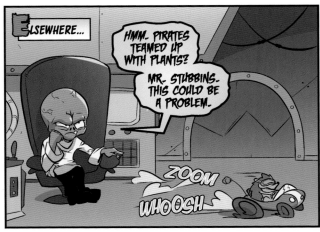

ELSEWHERE...

HMM. PIRATES TEAMED UP WITH PLANTS?

MR. STUBBINS. THIS COULD BE A PROBLEM.

ZOOM

WHOOSH

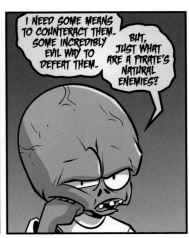

I NEED SOME MEANS TO COUNTERACT THEM. SOME INCREDIBLY EVIL WAY TO DEFEAT THEM.

BUT, JUST WHAT ARE A PIRATE'S NATURAL ENEMIES?

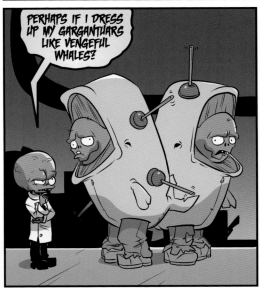

PERHAPS IF I DRESS UP MY GARGANTUARS LIKE VENGEFUL WHALES?

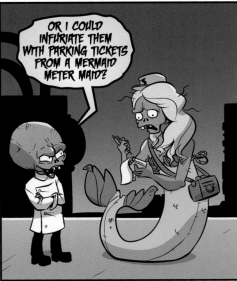

OR I COULD INFURIATE THEM WITH PARKING TICKETS FROM A MERMAID METER MAID?

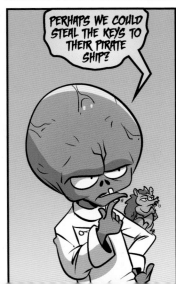

PERHAPS WE COULD STEAL THE KEYS TO THEIR PIRATE SHIP?

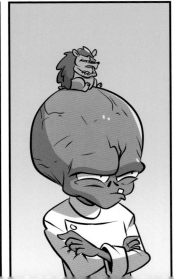

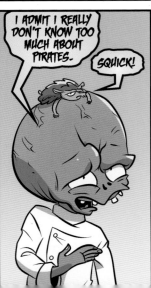

I ADMIT I REALLY DON'T KNOW TOO MUCH ABOUT PIRATES.

SQUICK!

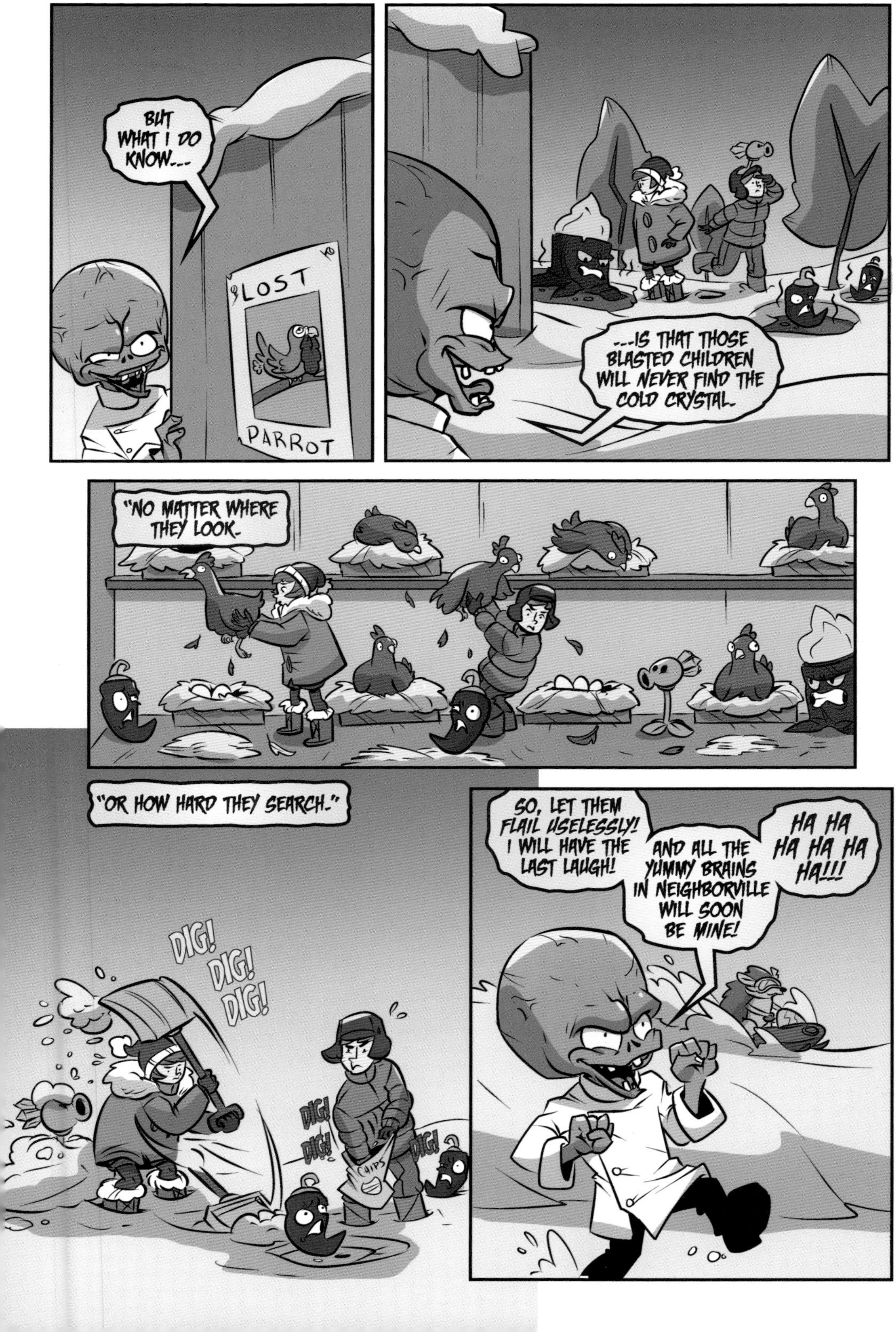

BUT WHAT I DO KNOW...
LOST
PARROT
...IS THAT THOSE BLASTED CHILDREN WILL NEVER FIND THE COLD CRYSTAL.
"NO MATTER WHERE THEY LOOK.
"OR HOW HARD THEY SEARCH."
DIG! DIG! DIG!
DIG! DIG!
DIG!
CHIPS
SO, LET THEM FLAIL USELESSLY! I WILL HAVE THE LAST LAUGH!
AND ALL THE YUMMY BRAINS IN NEIGHBORVILLE WILL SOON BE MINE!
HA HA HA HA HA HA!!!

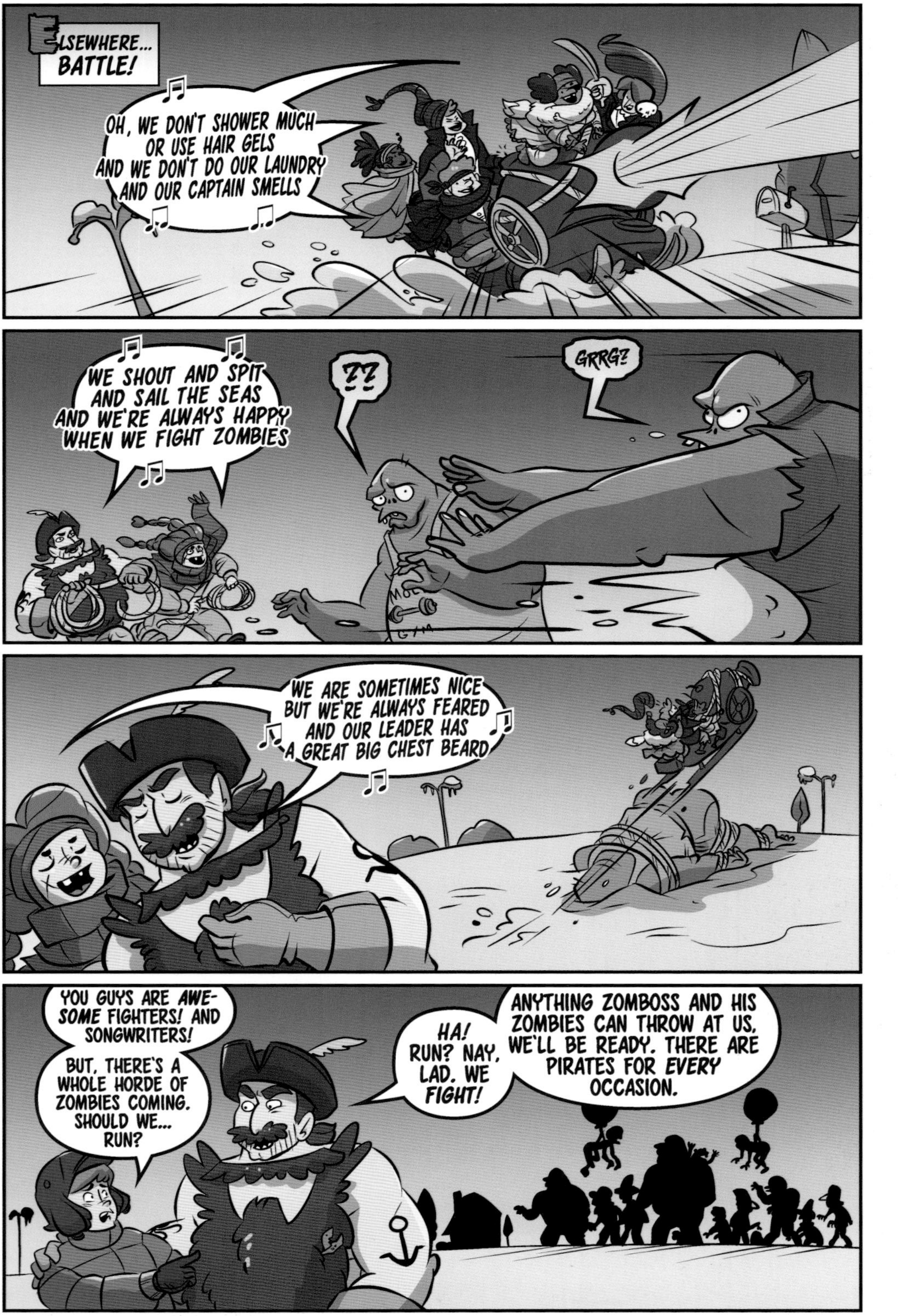
ELSEWHERE... BATTLE!
OH, WE DON'T SHOWER MUCH OR USE HAIR GELS AND WE DON'T DO OUR LAUNDRY AND OUR CAPTAIN SMELLS
WE SHOUT AND SPIT AND SAIL THE SEAS AND WE'RE ALWAYS HAPPY WHEN WE FIGHT ZOMBIES
??
GRRG?
WE ARE SOMETIMES NICE BUT WE'RE ALWAYS FEARED AND OUR LEADER HAS A GREAT BIG CHEST BEARD
YOU GUYS ARE AWESOME FIGHTERS! AND SONGWRITERS!
BUT, THERE'S A WHOLE HORDE OF ZOMBIES COMING. SHOULD WE... RUN?
HA! RUN? NAY, LAD. WE FIGHT!
ANYTHING ZOMBOSS AND HIS ZOMBIES CAN THROW AT US, WE'LL BE READY. THERE ARE PIRATES FOR EVERY OCCASION.

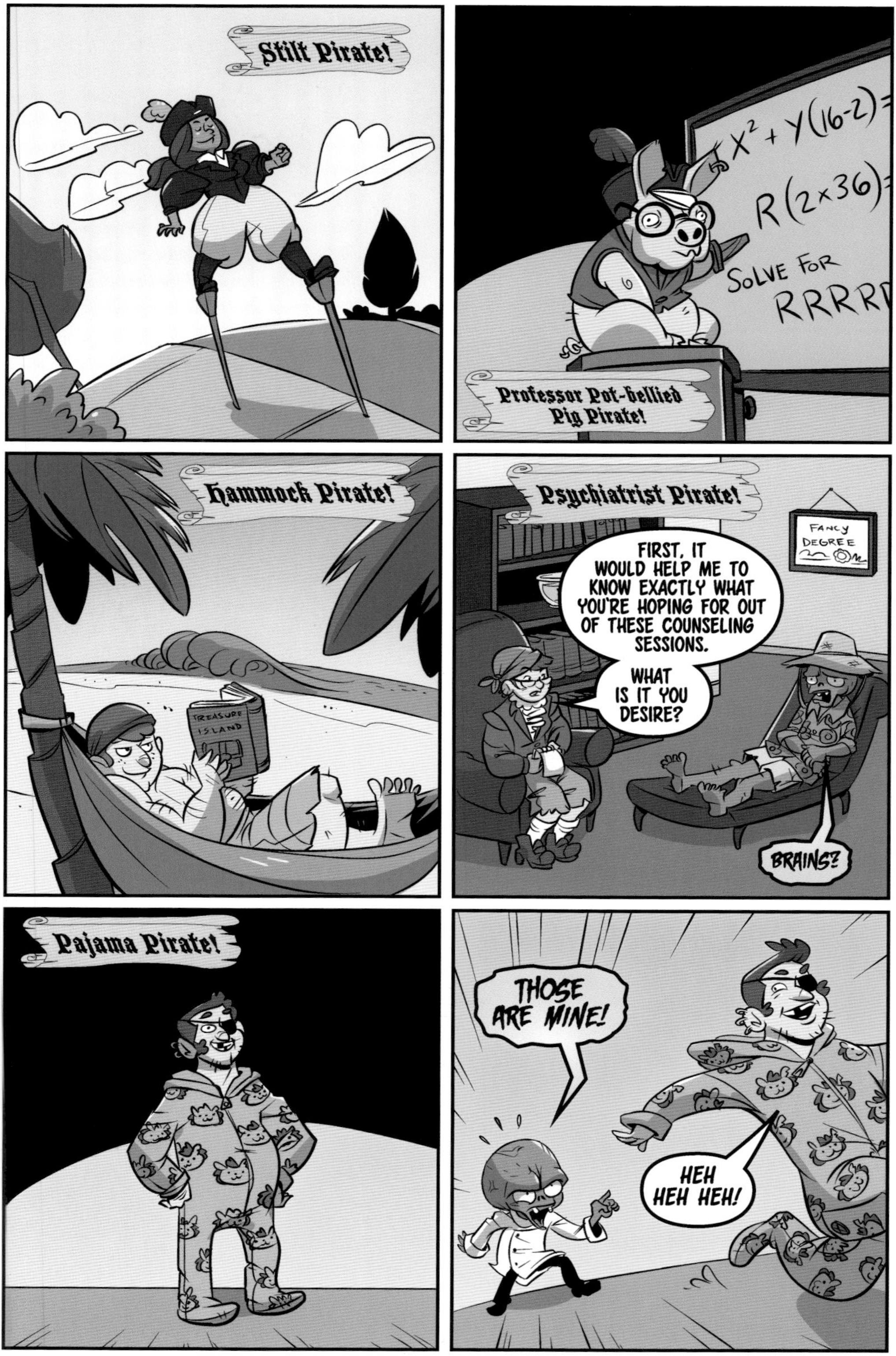
Stilt Pirate!
X² + Y(16-2)=
R(2x36)=
SOLVE FOR
RRRR
Professor Pot-bellied Pig Pirate!
Hammock Pirate!
TREASURE ISLAND
Psychiatrist Pirate!
FANCY DEGREE
FIRST, IT WOULD HELP ME TO KNOW EXACTLY WHAT YOU'RE HOPING FOR OUT OF THESE COUNSELING SESSIONS.
WHAT IS IT YOU DESIRE?
BRAINS?
Pajama Pirate!
THOSE ARE MINE!
HEH HEH HEH!

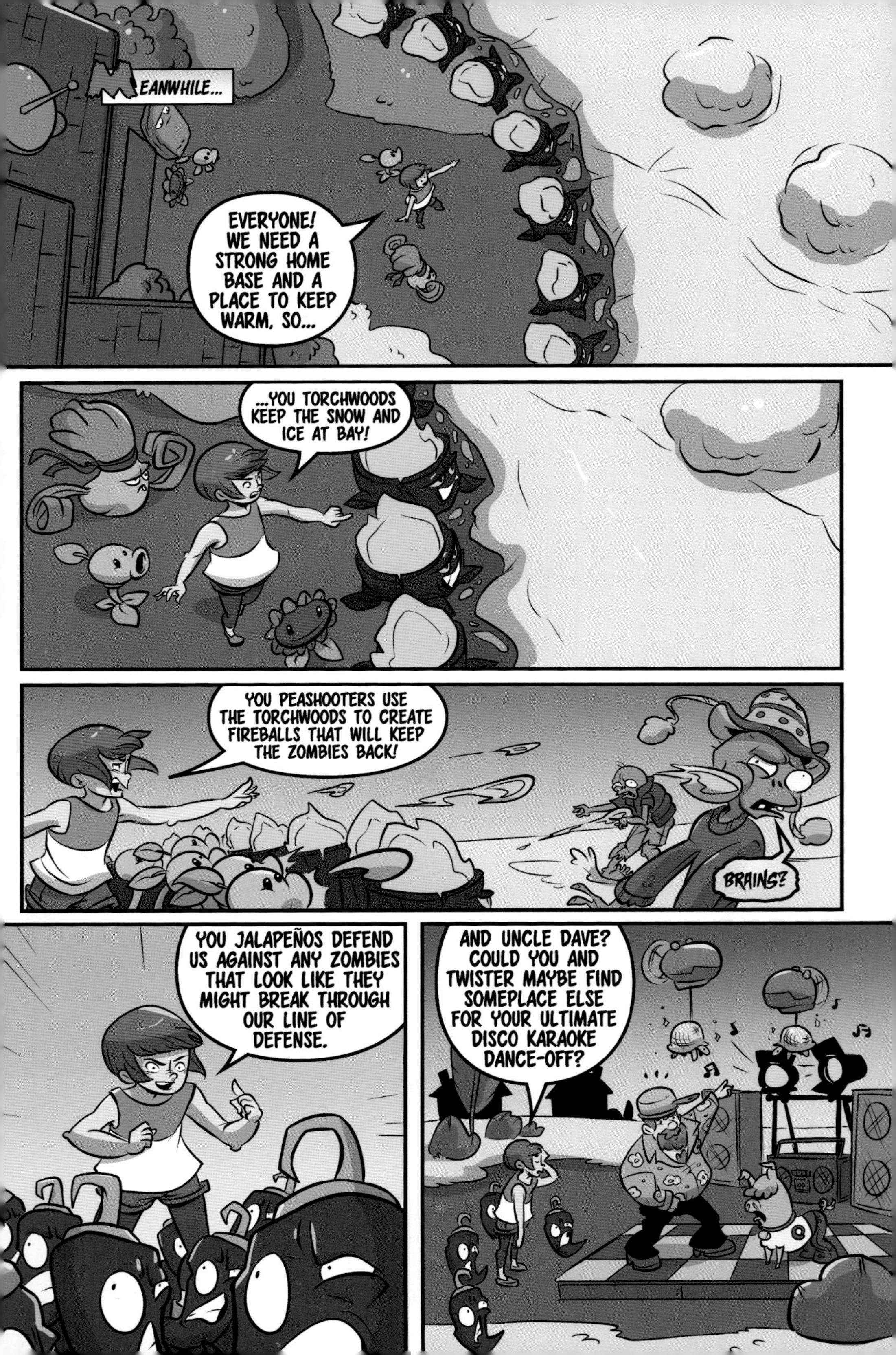
MEANWHILE...
EVERYONE! WE NEED A STRONG HOME BASE AND A PLACE TO KEEP WARM, SO...
...YOU TORCHWOODS KEEP THE SNOW AND ICE AT BAY!
YOU PEASHOOTERS USE THE TORCHWOODS TO CREATE FIREBALLS THAT WILL KEEP THE ZOMBIES BACK!
BRAINS?
YOU JALAPEÑOS DEFEND US AGAINST ANY ZOMBIES THAT LOOK LIKE THEY MIGHT BREAK THROUGH OUR LINE OF DEFENSE.
AND UNCLE DAVE? COULD YOU AND TWISTER MAYBE FIND SOMEPLACE ELSE FOR YOUR ULTIMATE DISCO KARAOKE DANCE-OFF?

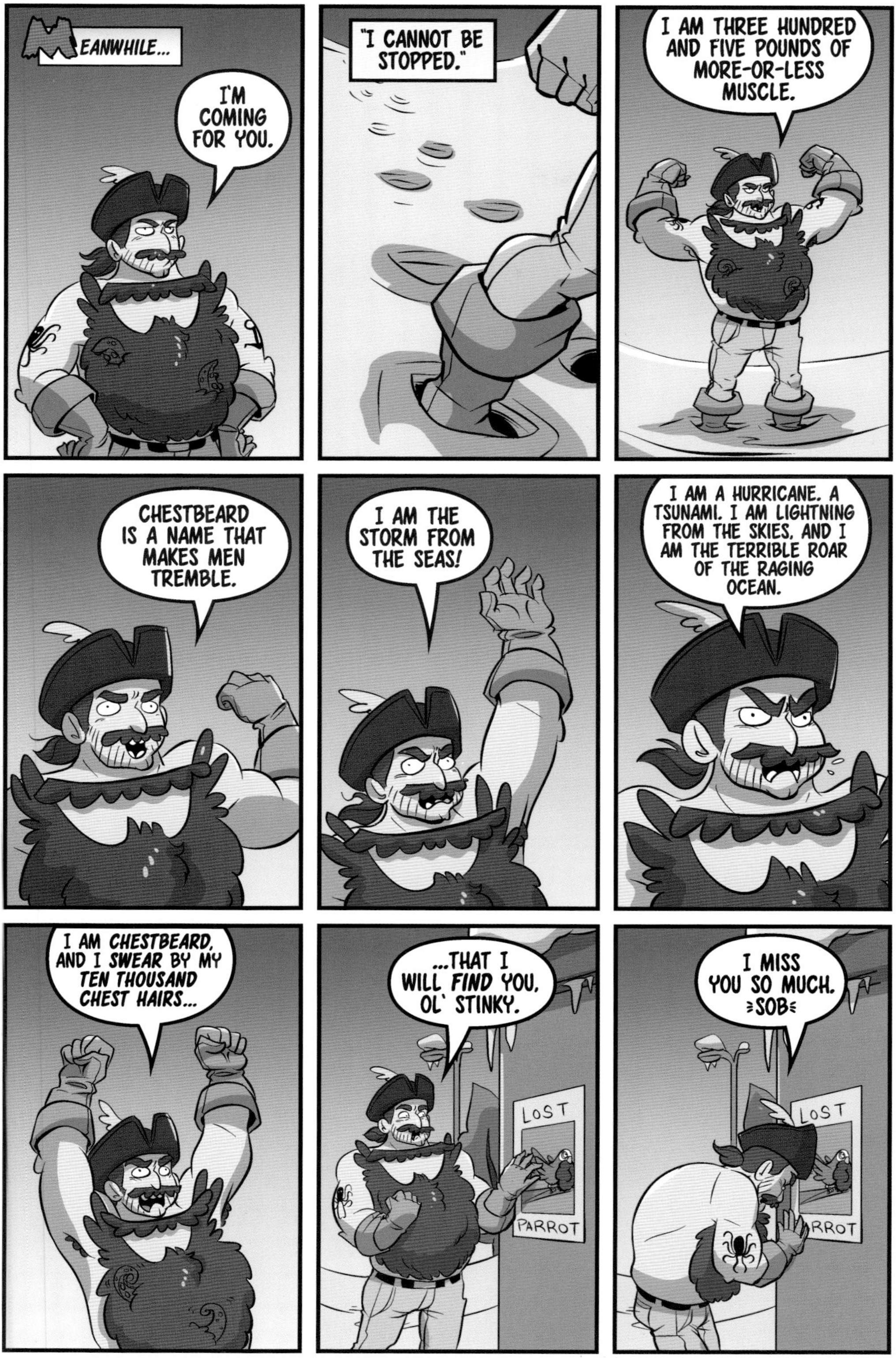
MEANWHILE...
I'M COMING FOR YOU.
"I CANNOT BE STOPPED."
I AM THREE HUNDRED AND FIVE POUNDS OF MORE-OR-LESS MUSCLE.
CHESTBEARD IS A NAME THAT MAKES MEN TREMBLE.
I AM THE STORM FROM THE SEAS!
I AM A HURRICANE. A TSUNAMI. I AM LIGHTNING FROM THE SKIES, AND I AM THE TERRIBLE ROAR OF THE RAGING OCEAN.
I AM *CHESTBEARD*, AND I *SWEAR* BY MY *TEN THOUSAND* CHEST HAIRS...
...THAT I WILL *FIND* YOU, OL' STINKY.
LOST
PARROT
I MISS YOU SO MUCH. SOB
LOST
PARROT

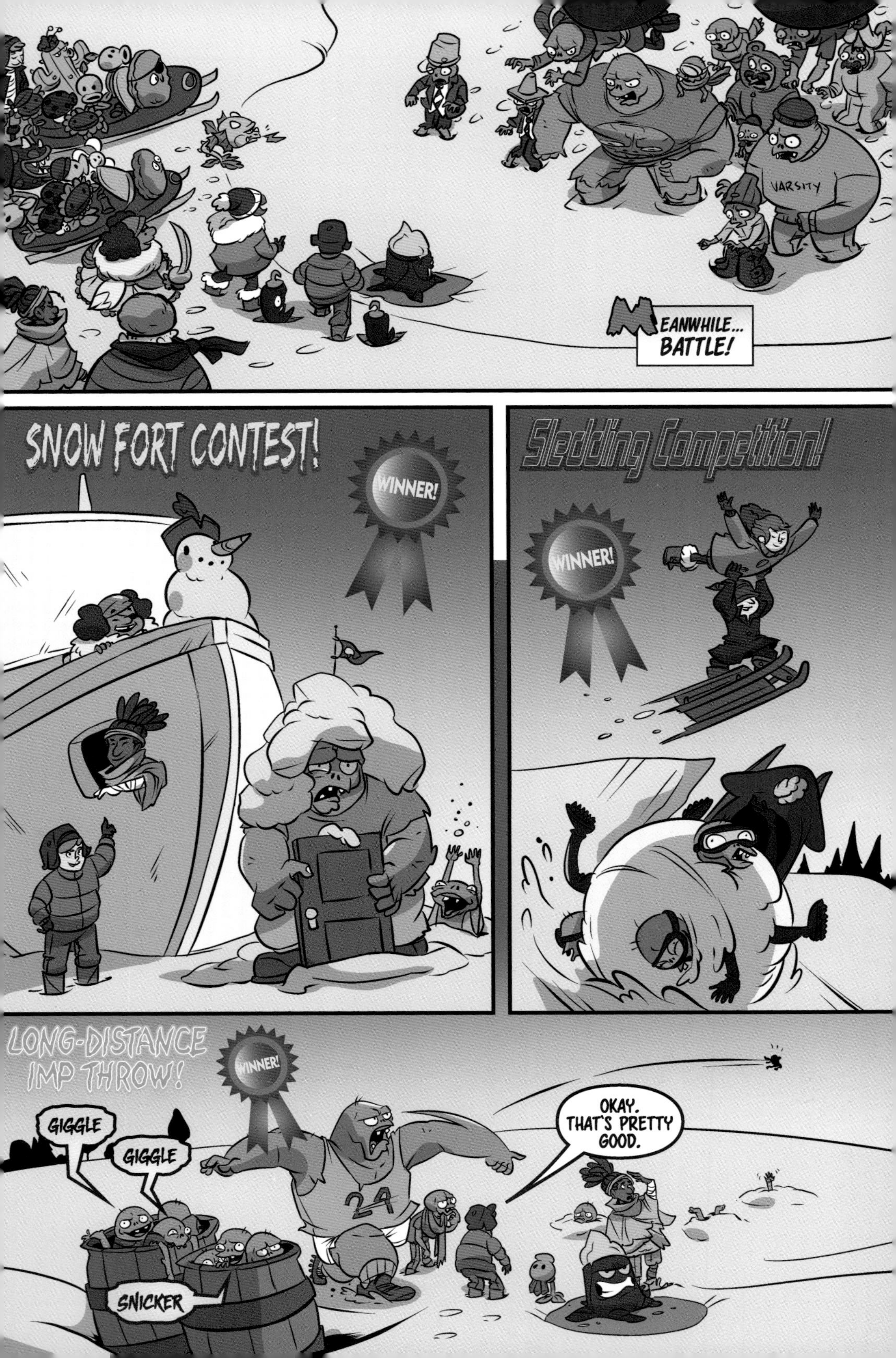
MEANWHILE... BATTLE!
VARSITY
SNOW FORT CONTEST!
WINNER!
Sledding Competition!
WINNER!
LONG-DISTANCE IMP THROW!
WINNER!
GIGGLE
GIGGLE
SNICKER
OKAY. THAT'S PRETTY GOOD.

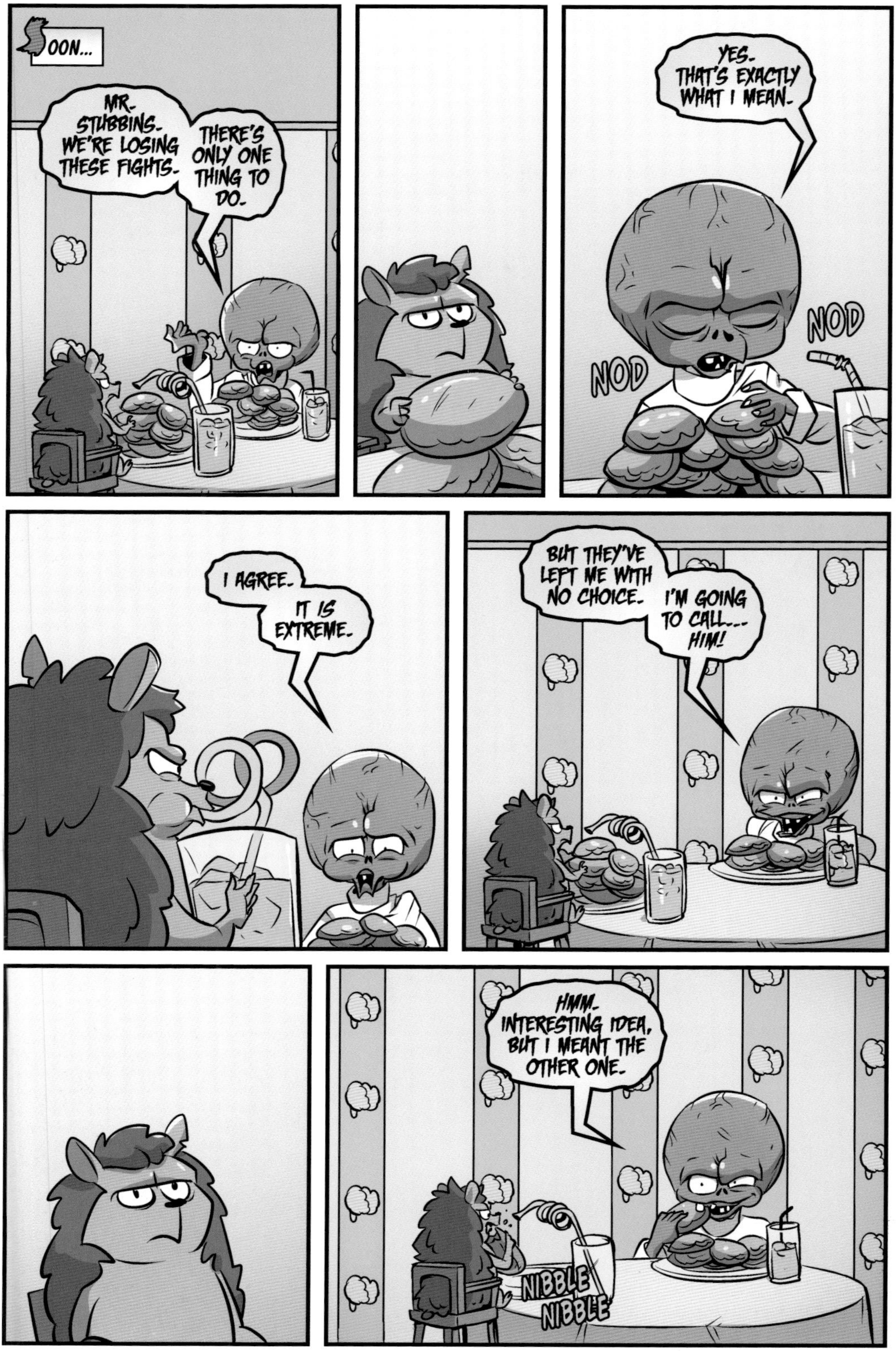
SOON...
MR. STUBBINS. WE'RE LOSING THESE FIGHTS.
THERE'S ONLY ONE THING TO DO.
YES. THAT'S EXACTLY WHAT I MEAN.
NOD
NOD
I AGREE.
IT IS EXTREME.
BUT THEY'VE LEFT ME WITH NO CHOICE.
I'M GOING TO CALL... HIM!
HMM. INTERESTING IDEA, BUT I MEANT THE OTHER ONE.
NIBBLE NIBBLE

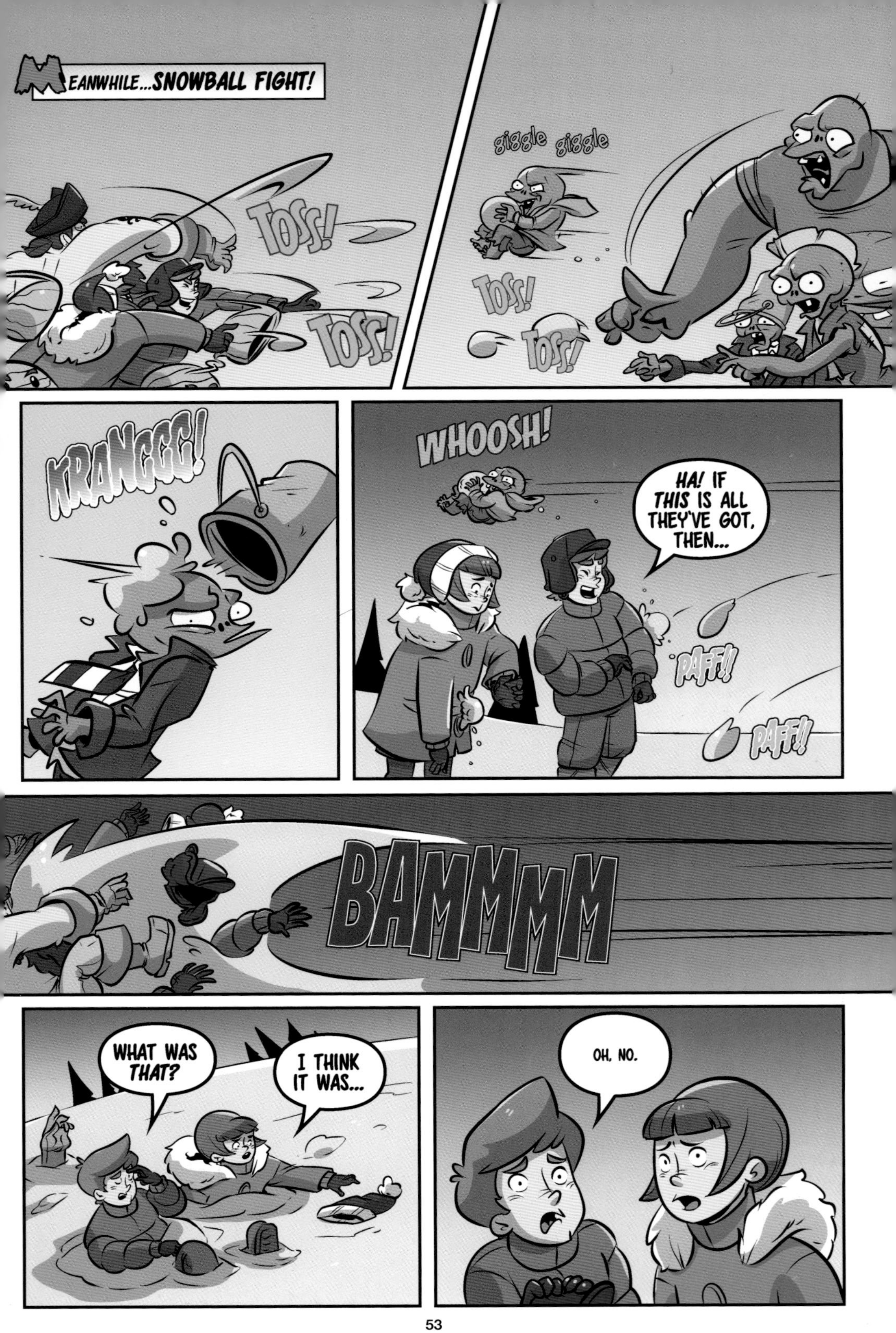
MEANWHILE...SNOWBALL FIGHT!
TOSS!
TOSS!
giggle giggle
TOSS!
TOSS!
KRANGGG!
WHOOSH!
HA! IF THIS IS ALL THEY'VE GOT, THEN...
PAFF!!
PAFF!!
BAMMMMM
WHAT WAS THAT?
I THINK IT WAS...
OH, NO.

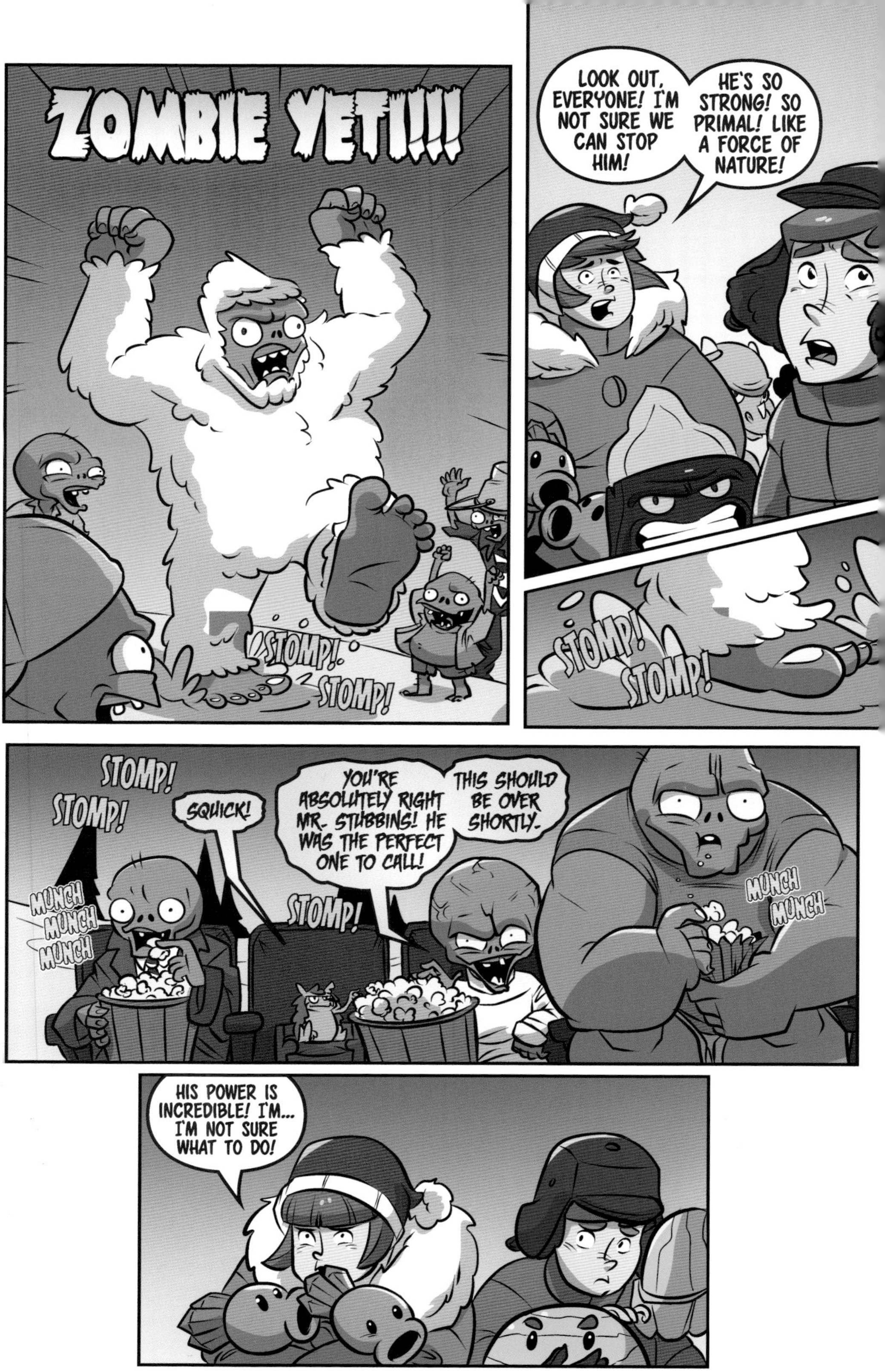
ZOMBIE YETI!!!!
STOMP!
STOMP!
LOOK OUT, EVERYONE! I'M NOT SURE WE CAN STOP HIM!
HE'S SO STRONG! SO PRIMAL! LIKE A FORCE OF NATURE!
STOMP!
STOMP!
STOMP!
STOMP!
SQUICK!
MUNCH MUNCH MUNCH
YOU'RE ABSOLUTELY RIGHT MR. STUBBINS! HE WAS THE PERFECT ONE TO CALL!
STOMP!
THIS SHOULD BE OVER SHORTLY.
MUNCH MUNCH
HIS POWER IS INCREDIBLE! I'M... I'M NOT SURE WHAT TO DO!

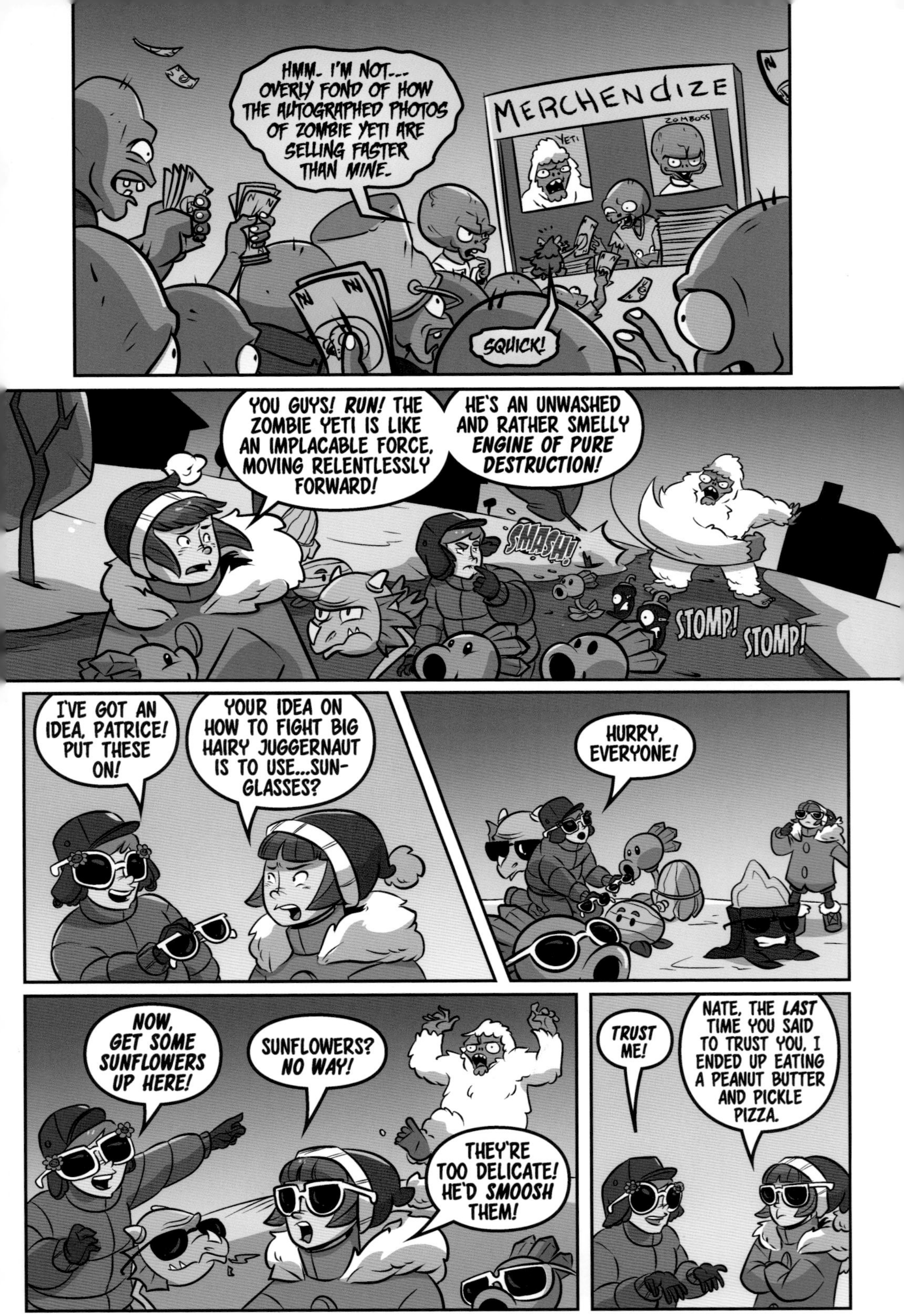

MERCHENdIZE
YETI
ZOMBOSS
HMM. I'M NOT... OVERLY FOND OF HOW THE AUTOGRAPHED PHOTOS OF ZOMBIE YETI ARE SELLING FASTER THAN MINE.
SQUICK!
YOU GUYS! RUN! THE ZOMBIE YETI IS LIKE AN IMPLACABLE FORCE, MOVING RELENTLESSLY FORWARD!
HE'S AN UNWASHED AND RATHER SMELLY ENGINE OF PURE DESTRUCTION!
SMASH!
STOMP!
STOMP!
I'VE GOT AN IDEA, PATRICE! PUT THESE ON!
YOUR IDEA ON HOW TO FIGHT BIG HAIRY JUGGERNAUT IS TO USE...SUNGLASSES?
HURRY, EVERYONE!
NOW, GET SOME SUNFLOWERS UP HERE!
SUNFLOWERS? NO WAY!
THEY'RE TOO DELICATE! HE'D SMOOSH THEM!
TRUST ME!
NATE, THE LAST TIME YOU SAID TO TRUST YOU, I ENDED UP EATING A PEANUT BUTTER AND PICKLE PIZZA.

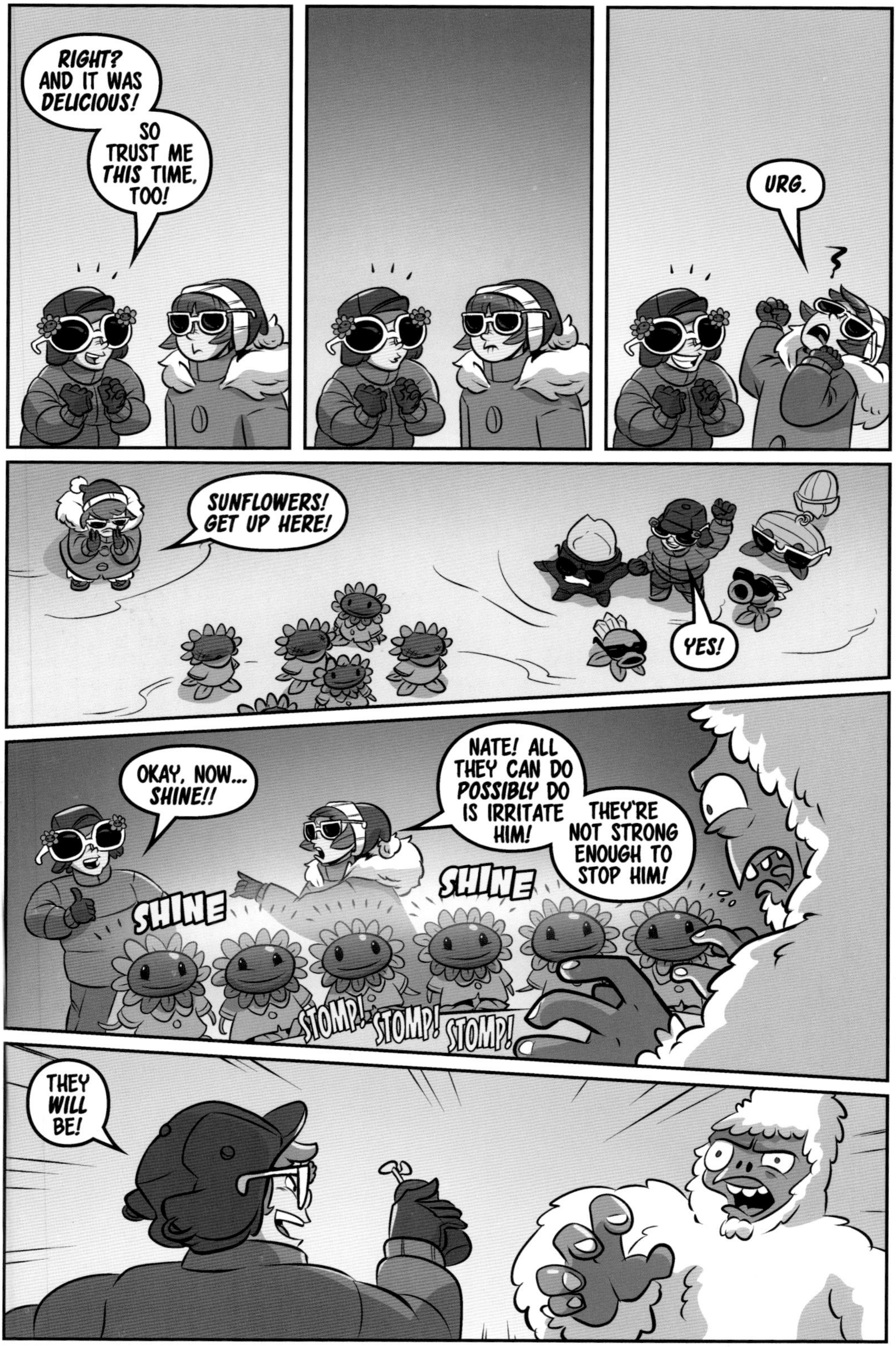
RIGHT? AND IT WAS DELICIOUS!
SO TRUST ME THIS TIME, TOO!
URG.
SUNFLOWERS! GET UP HERE!
YES!
OKAY, NOW... SHINE!!
NATE! ALL THEY CAN DO POSSIBLY DO IS IRRITATE HIM!
THEY'RE NOT STRONG ENOUGH TO STOP HIM!
SHINE
SHINE
STOMP! STOMP! STOMP!
THEY WILL BE!

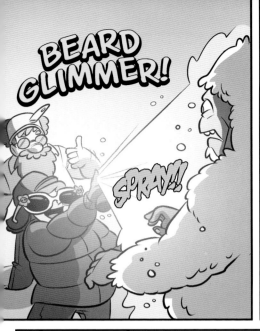

BEARD GLIMMER!

SPRAY!

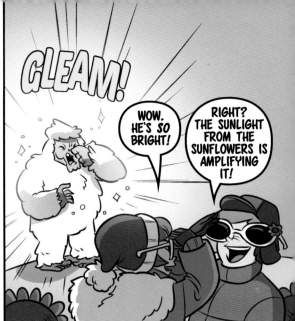

GLEAM!

WOW. HE'S SO BRIGHT!

RIGHT? THE SUNLIGHT FROM THE SUNFLOWERS IS AMPLIFYING IT!

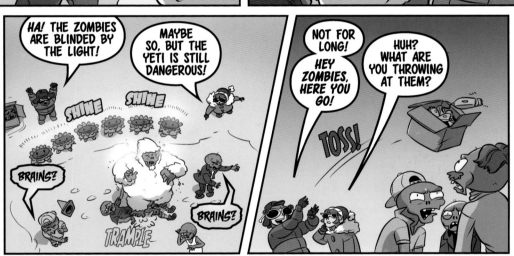

HA! THE ZOMBIES ARE BLINDED BY THE LIGHT!

MAYBE SO, BUT THE YETI IS STILL DANGEROUS!

SHINE   SHINE

BRAINS?

TRAMPLE

BRAINS?

NOT FOR LONG!

HEY ZOMBIES, HERE YOU GO!

HUH? WHAT ARE YOU THROWING AT THEM?

TOSS!

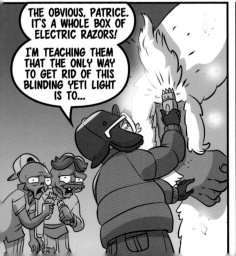

THE OBVIOUS, PATRICE. IT'S A WHOLE BOX OF ELECTRIC RAZORS!

I'M TEACHING THEM THAT THE ONLY WAY TO GET RID OF THIS BLINDING YETI LIGHT IS TO...

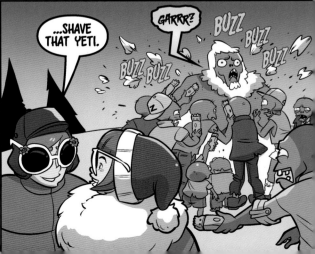

...SHAVE THAT YETI.

GARRR?

BUZZ   BUZZ   BUZZ

BUZZ BUZZ

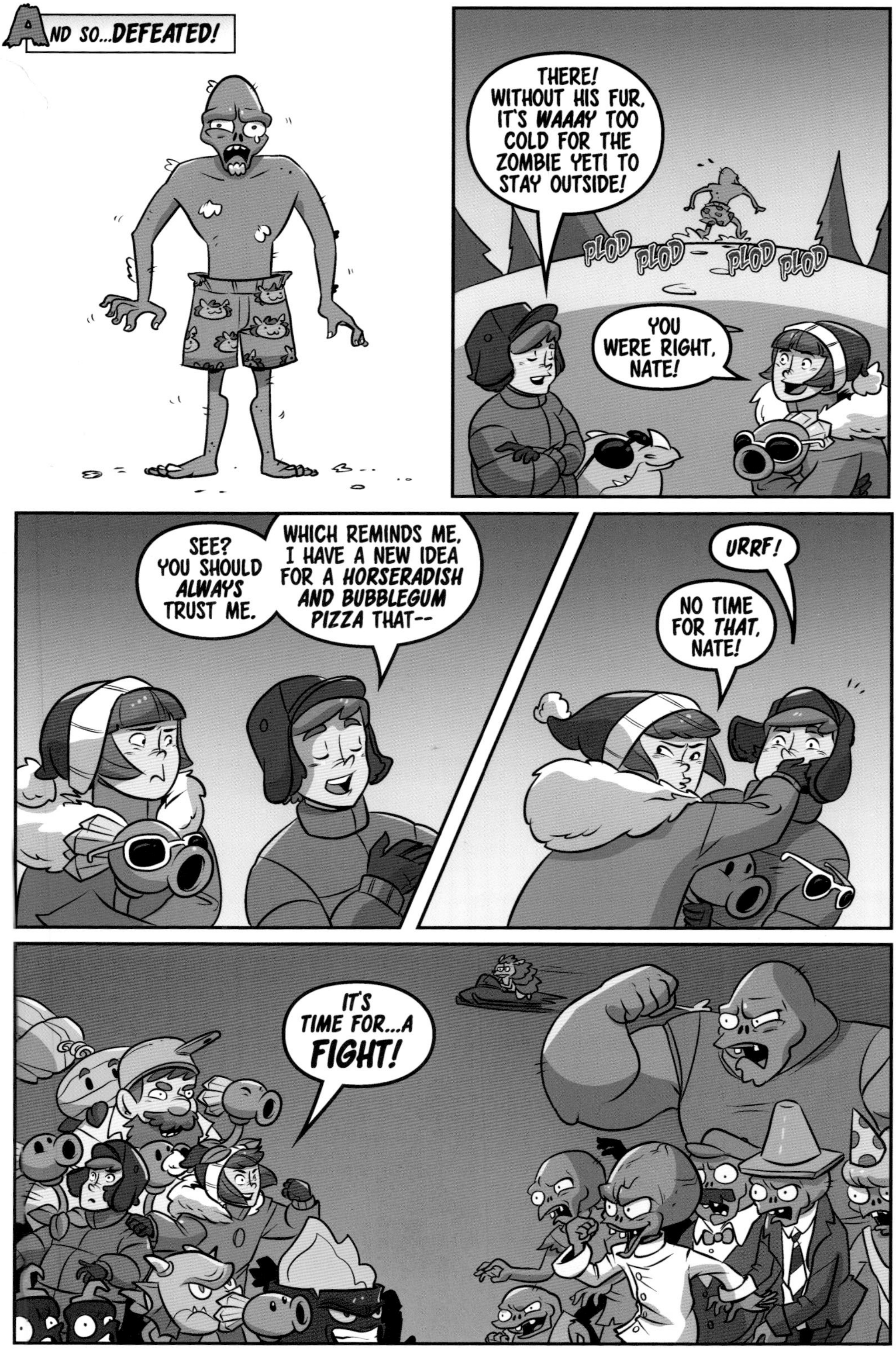
AND SO...DEFEATED!
THERE! WITHOUT HIS FUR, IT'S WAAAY TOO COLD FOR THE ZOMBIE YETI TO STAY OUTSIDE!
PLOD PLOD PLOD PLOD
YOU WERE RIGHT, NATE!
SEE? YOU SHOULD ALWAYS TRUST ME.
WHICH REMINDS ME, I HAVE A NEW IDEA FOR A HORSERADISH AND BUBBLEGUM PIZZA THAT--
URRF!
NO TIME FOR THAT, NATE!
IT'S TIME FOR...A FIGHT!

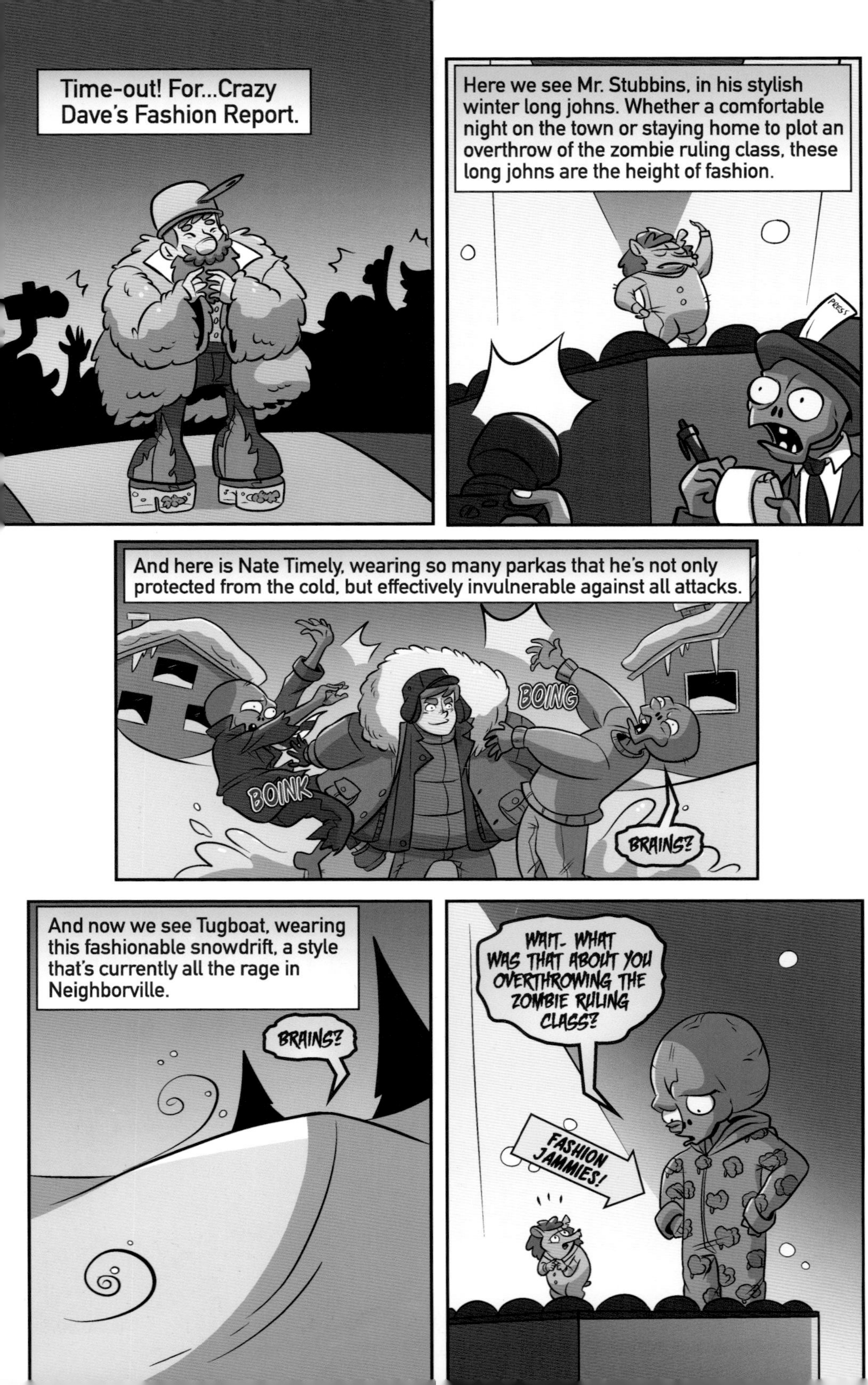
Time-out! For...Crazy Dave's Fashion Report.
Here we see Mr. Stubbins, in his stylish winter long johns. Whether a comfortable night on the town or staying home to plot an overthrow of the zombie ruling class, these long johns are the height of fashion.
PRESS
And here is Nate Timely, wearing so many parkas that he's not only protected from the cold, but effectively invulnerable against all attacks.
BOING
BOINK
BRAINS?
And now we see Tugboat, wearing this fashionable snowdrift, a style that's currently all the rage in Neighborville.
BRAINS?
WAIT- WHAT WAS THAT ABOUT YOU OVERTHROWING THE ZOMBIE RULING CLASS?
FASHION JAMMIES!

Check out this *elegant* headwear!

Six quart capacity!

Stainless steel, with solid aluminum core!

Dishwasher and shower safe!

Stainless steel handle: riveted for strength!

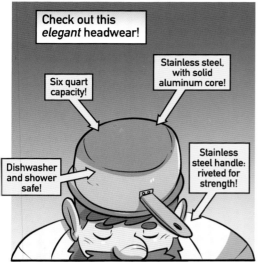

And here is Tabor the Gargantuar, struggling to get into one of Zomboss' shirts!

TAKE THAT OFF! TAKE THAT OFF! YOU'LL RUIN IT!

URFF!

ZOMBO

STRUGGLE STRUGGLE

YANK

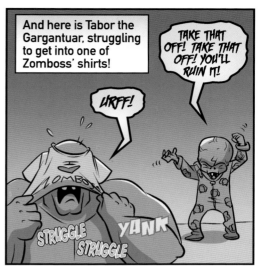

And here is Patrice Blazing in her specially-made *beard-coat*, made from Chestbeard's hairs!

I PLUCKED THEM MYSELF!

OH. EWWW!

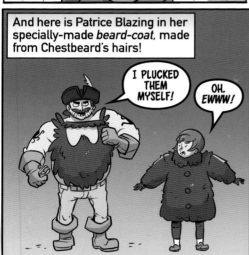

This fashion allows the young Patrice to command the fire plants on their missions to push back the snow and ice from Crazy Dave's garage, since the shirt is the only thing that's impervious to the terrible cold AND also flame-resistant, so she can handle the plants!

OH, THIS IS *SO* GROSS!

The full "Chest-Hair" ensemble comes not only with the full coat, but with matching hat and gloves!

WHICH I AM *NOT* PUTTING ON.

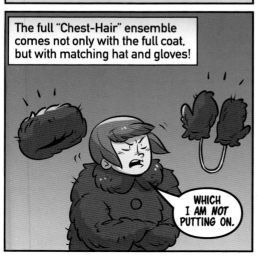

And here is the recently shaved Yeti Zombie, wearing a selection of toupees super-glued to his body. Looking *good*, yeti!

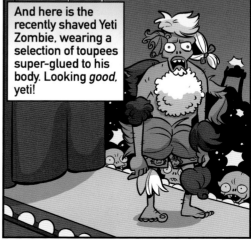

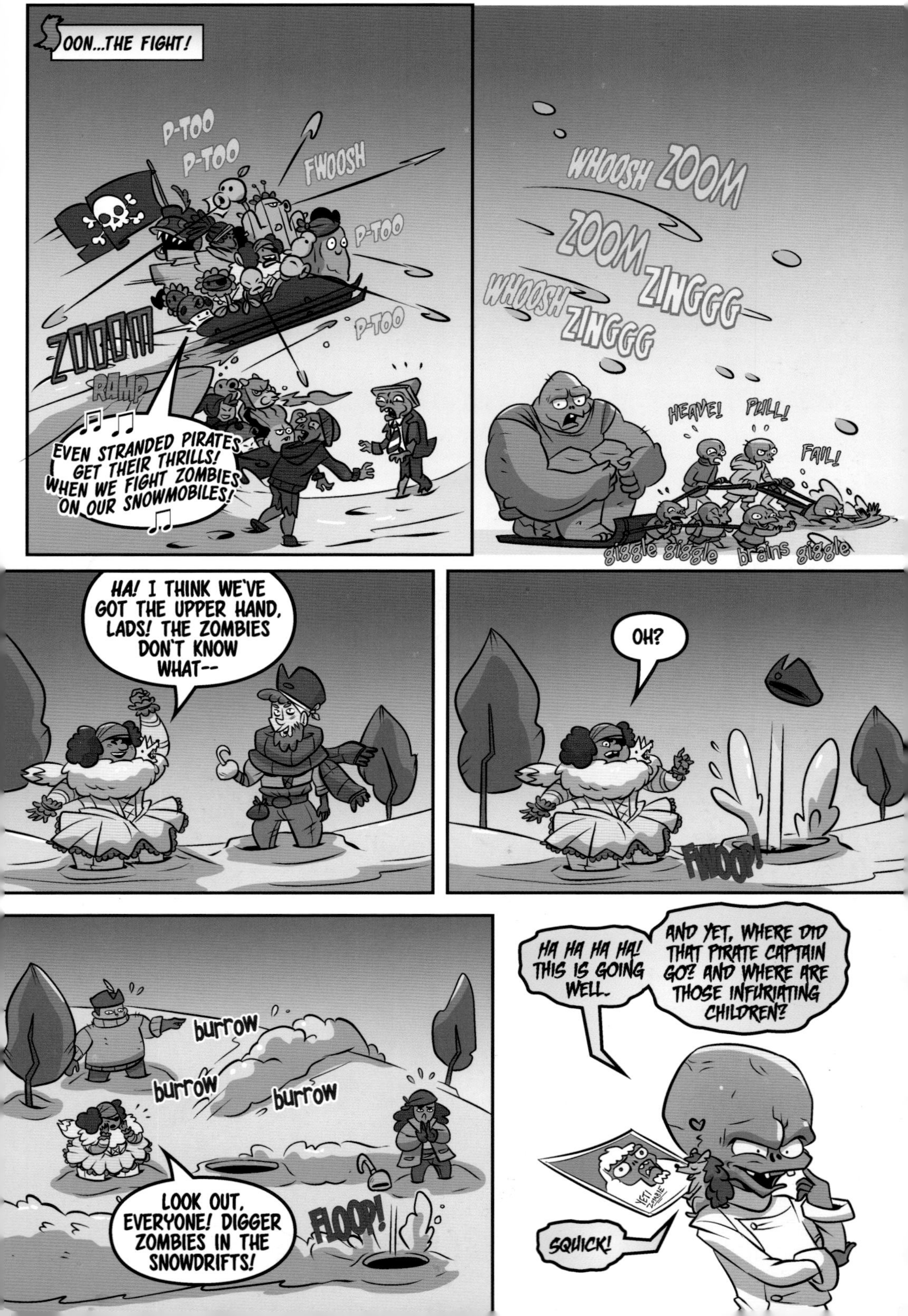
SOON...THE FIGHT!
P-TOO
P-TOO
FWOOSH
P-TOO
P-TOO
ZOOOM
RAMP
EVEN STRANDED PIRATES GET THEIR THRILLS! WHEN WE FIGHT ZOMBIES ON OUR SNOWMOBILES!
WHOOSH ZOOM
ZOOM
ZINGGG
WHOOSH
ZINGGG
HEAVE!
PULL!
FAIL!
giggle giggle brains giggle
HA! I THINK WE'VE GOT THE UPPER HAND, LADS! THE ZOMBIES DON'T KNOW WHAT--
OH?
FWOOP!
burrow
burrow
burrow
LOOK OUT, EVERYONE! DIGGER ZOMBIES IN THE SNOWDRIFTS!
FLOOP!
HA HA HA HA! THIS IS GOING WELL.
AND YET, WHERE DID THAT PIRATE CAPTAIN GO? AND WHERE ARE THOSE INFURIATING CHILDREN?
YETI ZOMBIE
SQUICK!

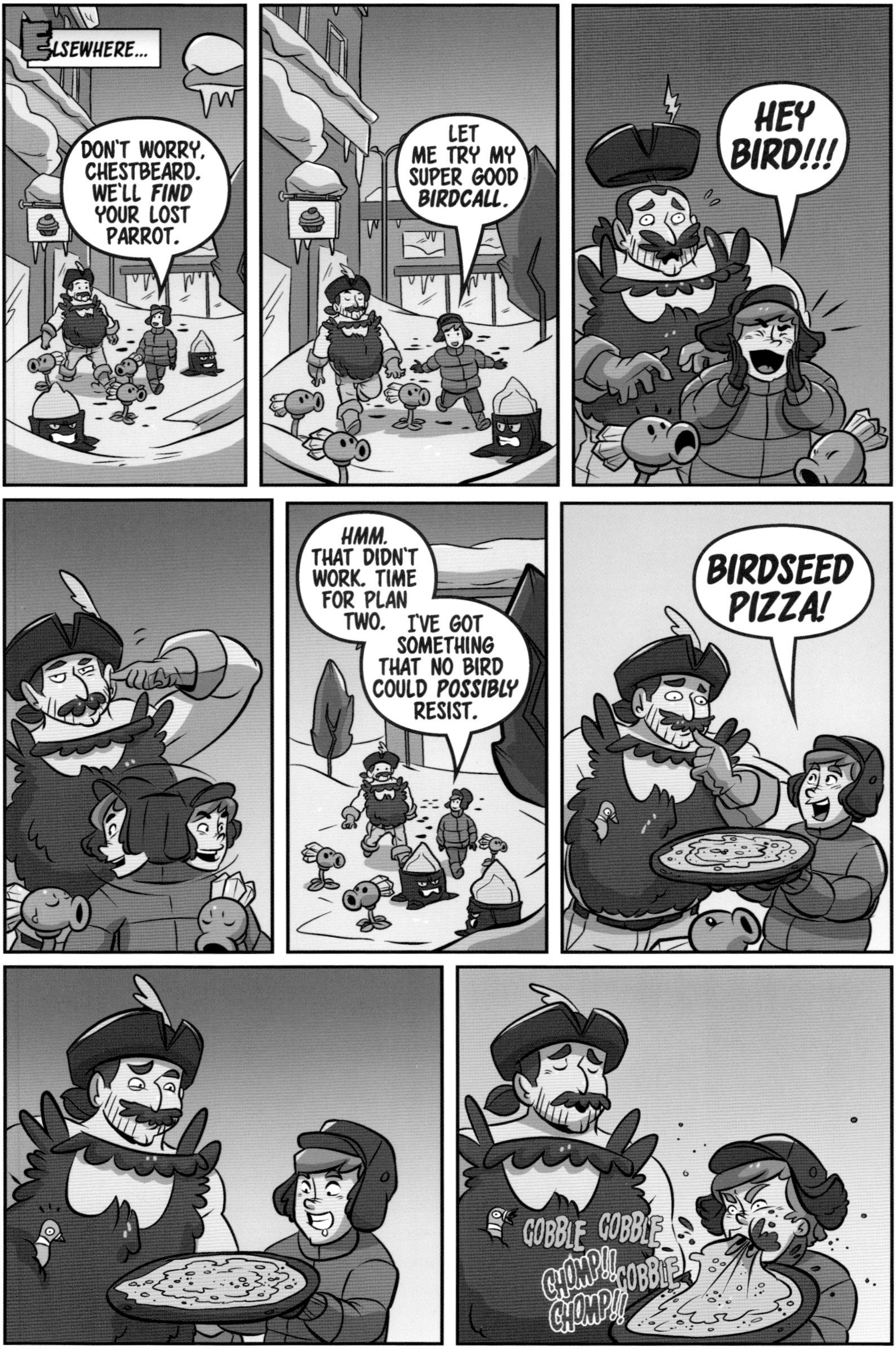
ELSEWHERE...
DON'T WORRY, CHESTBEARD. WE'LL FIND YOUR LOST PARROT.
LET ME TRY MY SUPER GOOD BIRDCALL.
HEY BIRD!!!
HMM. THAT DIDN'T WORK. TIME FOR PLAN TWO.
I'VE GOT SOMETHING THAT NO BIRD COULD POSSIBLY RESIST.
BIRDSEED PIZZA!
GOBBLE GOBBLE
CHOMP!! CHOMP!!
GOBBLE

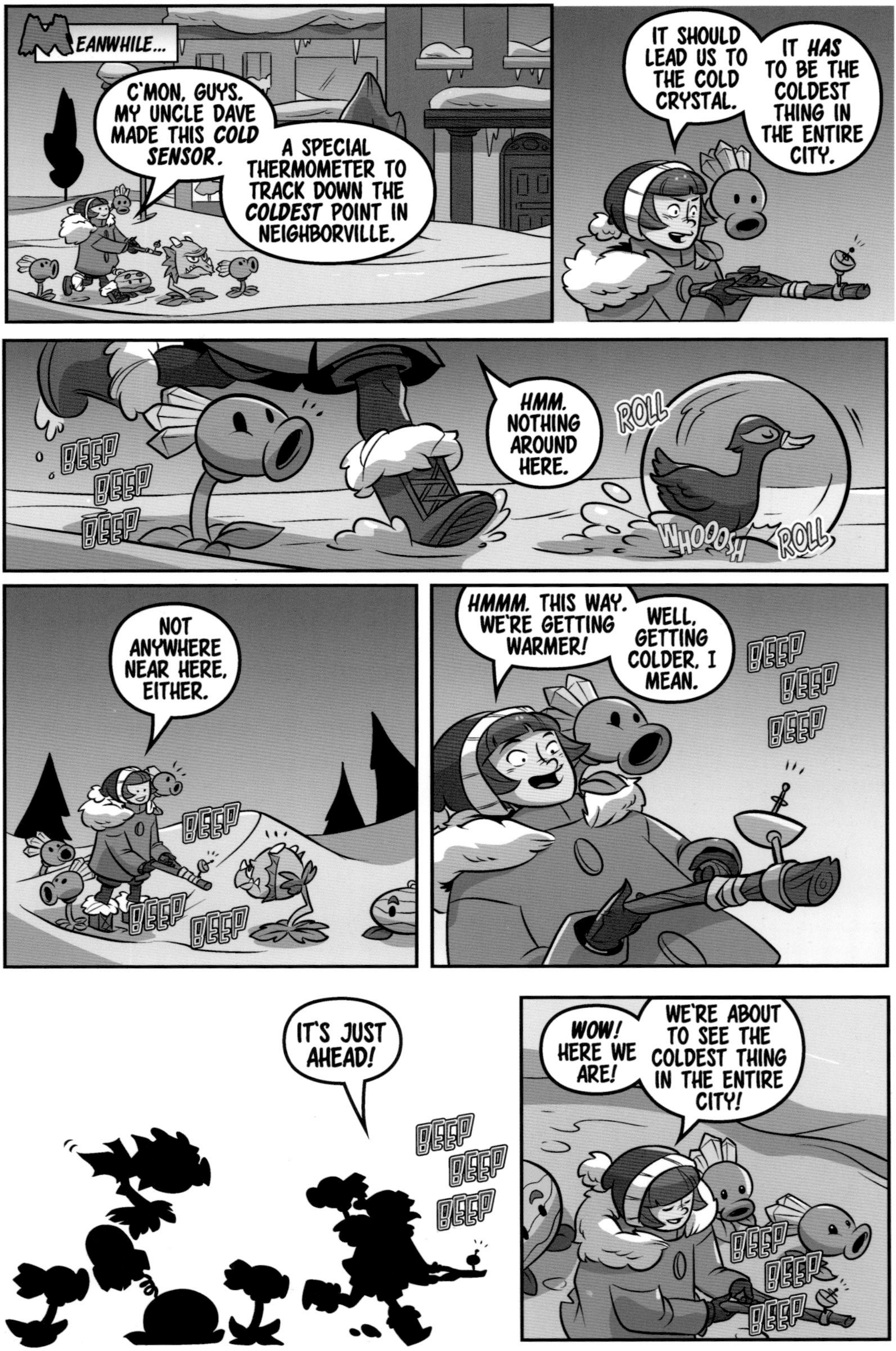
MEANWHILE...
C'MON, GUYS. MY UNCLE DAVE MADE THIS COLD SENSOR.
A SPECIAL THERMOMETER TO TRACK DOWN THE COLDEST POINT IN NEIGHBORVILLE.
IT SHOULD LEAD US TO THE COLD CRYSTAL.
IT HAS TO BE THE COLDEST THING IN THE ENTIRE CITY.
BEEP BEEP BEEP
HMM. NOTHING AROUND HERE.
ROLL
WHOOOSH
ROLL
NOT ANYWHERE NEAR HERE, EITHER.
BEEP
BEEP
BEEP
HMMM. THIS WAY. WE'RE GETTING WARMER!
WELL, GETTING COLDER, I MEAN.
BEEP BEEP BEEP
IT'S JUST AHEAD!
BEEP BEEP BEEP
WOW! HERE WE ARE!
WE'RE ABOUT TO SEE THE COLDEST THING IN THE ENTIRE CITY!
BEEP BEEP BEEP

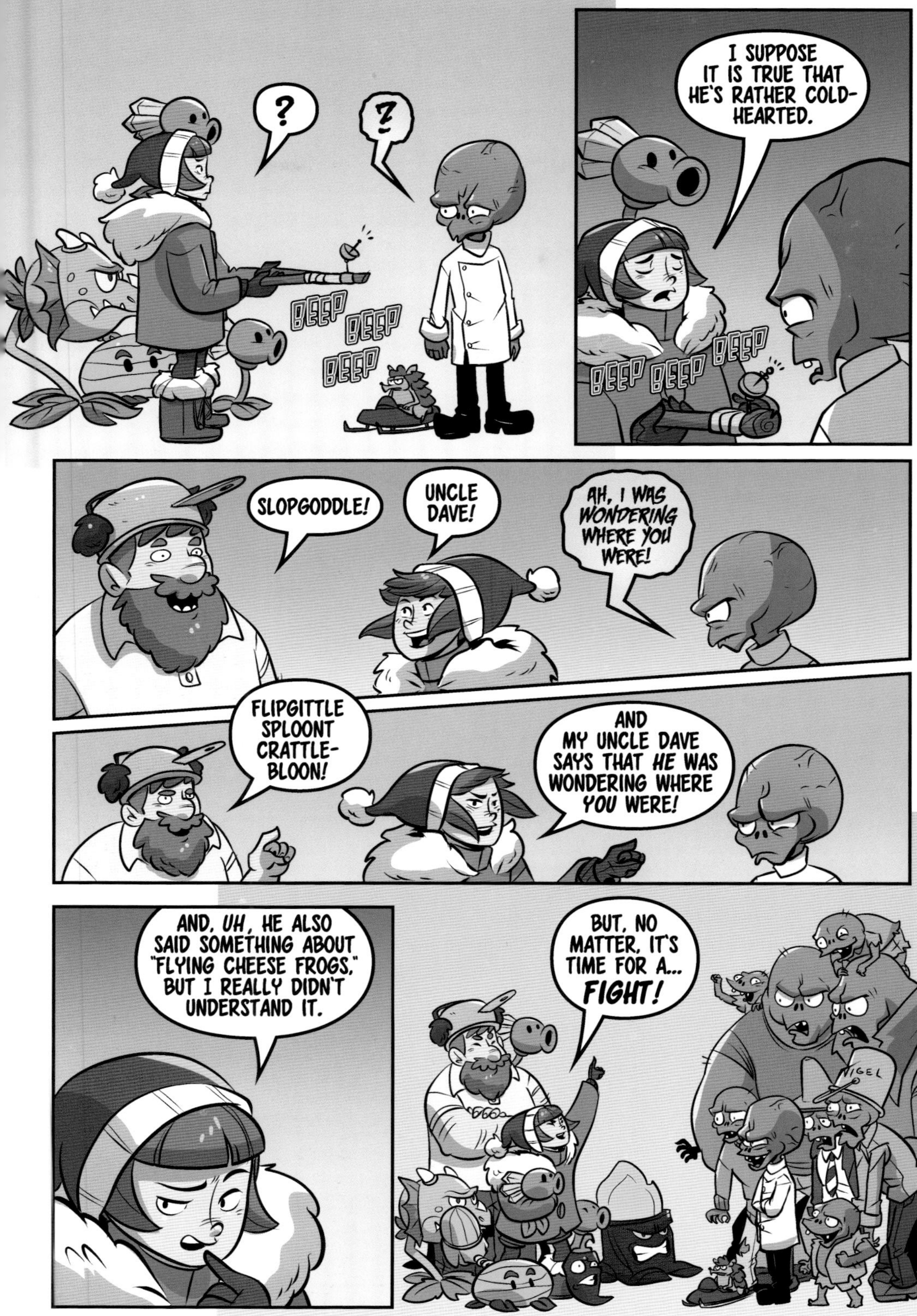
?
?
BEEP BEEP BEEP
I SUPPOSE IT IS TRUE THAT HE'S RATHER COLD-HEARTED.
BEEP BEEP BEEP
SLOPGODDLE!
UNCLE DAVE!
AH, I WAS WONDERING WHERE YOU WERE!
FLIPGITTLE SPLOONT CRATTLE-BLOON!
AND MY UNCLE DAVE SAYS THAT HE WAS WONDERING WHERE YOU WERE!
AND, UH, HE ALSO SAID SOMETHING ABOUT "FLYING CHEESE FROGS," BUT I REALLY DIDN'T UNDERSTAND IT.
BUT, NO MATTER, IT'S TIME FOR A... FIGHT!
NIGEL

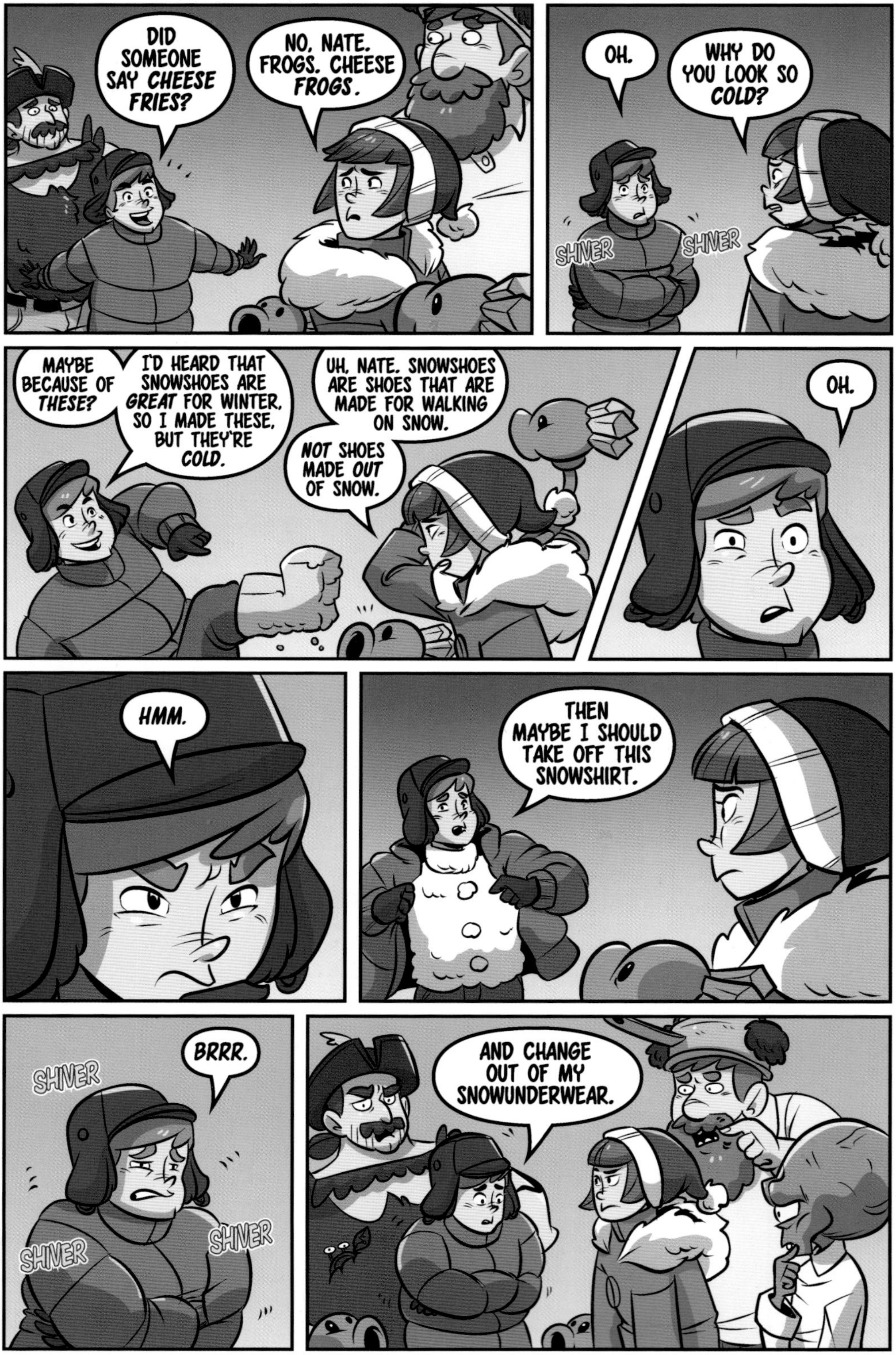

DID SOMEONE SAY CHEESE FRIES?
NO, NATE. FROGS. CHEESE FROGS.
OH.
WHY DO YOU LOOK SO COLD?
SHIVER
SHIVER
MAYBE BECAUSE OF THESE?
I'D HEARD THAT SNOWSHOES ARE GREAT FOR WINTER, SO I MADE THESE, BUT THEY'RE COLD.
UH, NATE. SNOWSHOES ARE SHOES THAT ARE MADE FOR WALKING ON SNOW.
NOT SHOES MADE OUT OF SNOW.
OH.
HMM.
THEN MAYBE I SHOULD TAKE OFF THIS SNOWSHIRT.
SHIVER
BRRR.
SHIVER
SHIVER
AND CHANGE OUT OF MY SNOWUNDERWEAR.

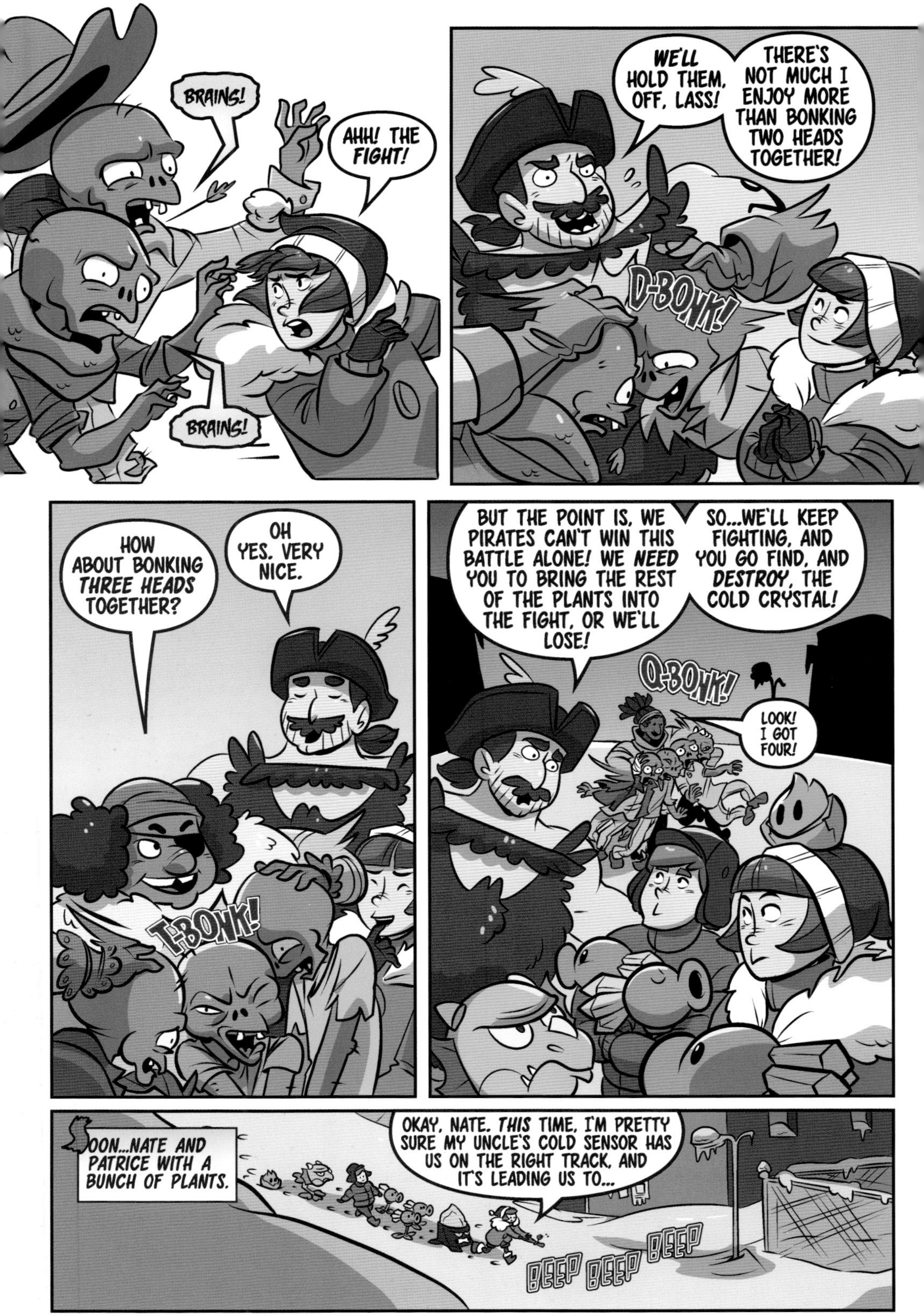
BRAINS!
AHH! THE FIGHT!
BRAINS!
WE'LL HOLD THEM, OFF, LASS!
THERE'S NOT MUCH I ENJOY MORE THAN BONKING TWO HEADS TOGETHER!
D-BONK!
HOW ABOUT BONKING *THREE HEADS* TOGETHER?
OH YES. VERY NICE.
T-BONK!
BUT THE POINT IS, WE PIRATES CAN'T WIN THIS BATTLE ALONE! WE *NEED* YOU TO BRING THE REST OF THE PLANTS INTO THE FIGHT, OR WE'LL LOSE!
SO...WE'LL KEEP FIGHTING, AND YOU GO FIND, AND *DESTROY*, THE COLD CRYSTAL!
Q-BONK!
LOOK! I GOT FOUR!
OON...NATE AND PATRICE WITH A BUNCH OF PLANTS.
OKAY, NATE. *THIS* TIME, I'M PRETTY SURE MY UNCLE'S COLD SENSOR HAS US ON THE RIGHT TRACK, AND IT'S LEADING US TO...
BEEP BEEP BEEP

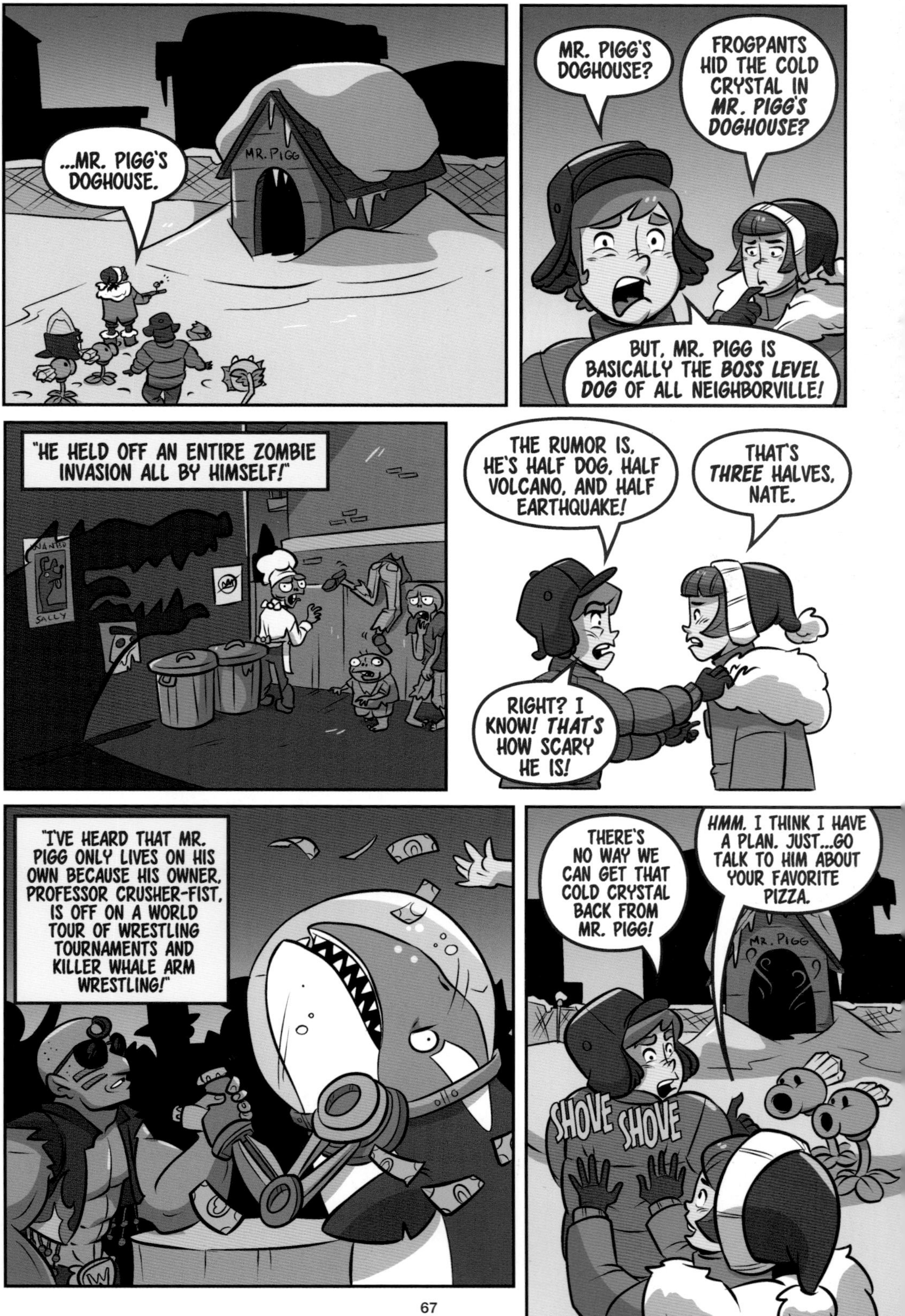

...MR. PIGG'S DOGHOUSE.
MR. PIGG
MR. PIGG'S DOGHOUSE?
FROGPANTS HID THE COLD CRYSTAL IN *MR. PIGG'S DOGHOUSE?*
BUT, MR. PIGG IS BASICALLY THE *BOSS LEVEL DOG* OF ALL NEIGHBORVILLE!
"HE HELD OFF AN ENTIRE ZOMBIE INVASION ALL BY HIMSELF!"
SALLY
THE RUMOR IS, HE'S HALF DOG, HALF VOLCANO, AND HALF EARTHQUAKE!
THAT'S *THREE* HALVES, NATE.
RIGHT? I KNOW! *THAT'S* HOW SCARY HE IS!
"I'VE HEARD THAT MR. PIGG ONLY LIVES ON HIS OWN BECAUSE HIS OWNER, PROFESSOR CRUSHER-FIST, IS OFF ON A WORLD TOUR OF WRESTLING TOURNAMENTS AND KILLER WHALE ARM WRESTLING!"
THERE'S NO WAY WE CAN GET THAT COLD CRYSTAL BACK FROM MR. PIGG!
HMM. I THINK I HAVE A PLAN. JUST...GO TALK TO HIM ABOUT YOUR FAVORITE PIZZA.
MR. PIGG
SHOVE SHOVE

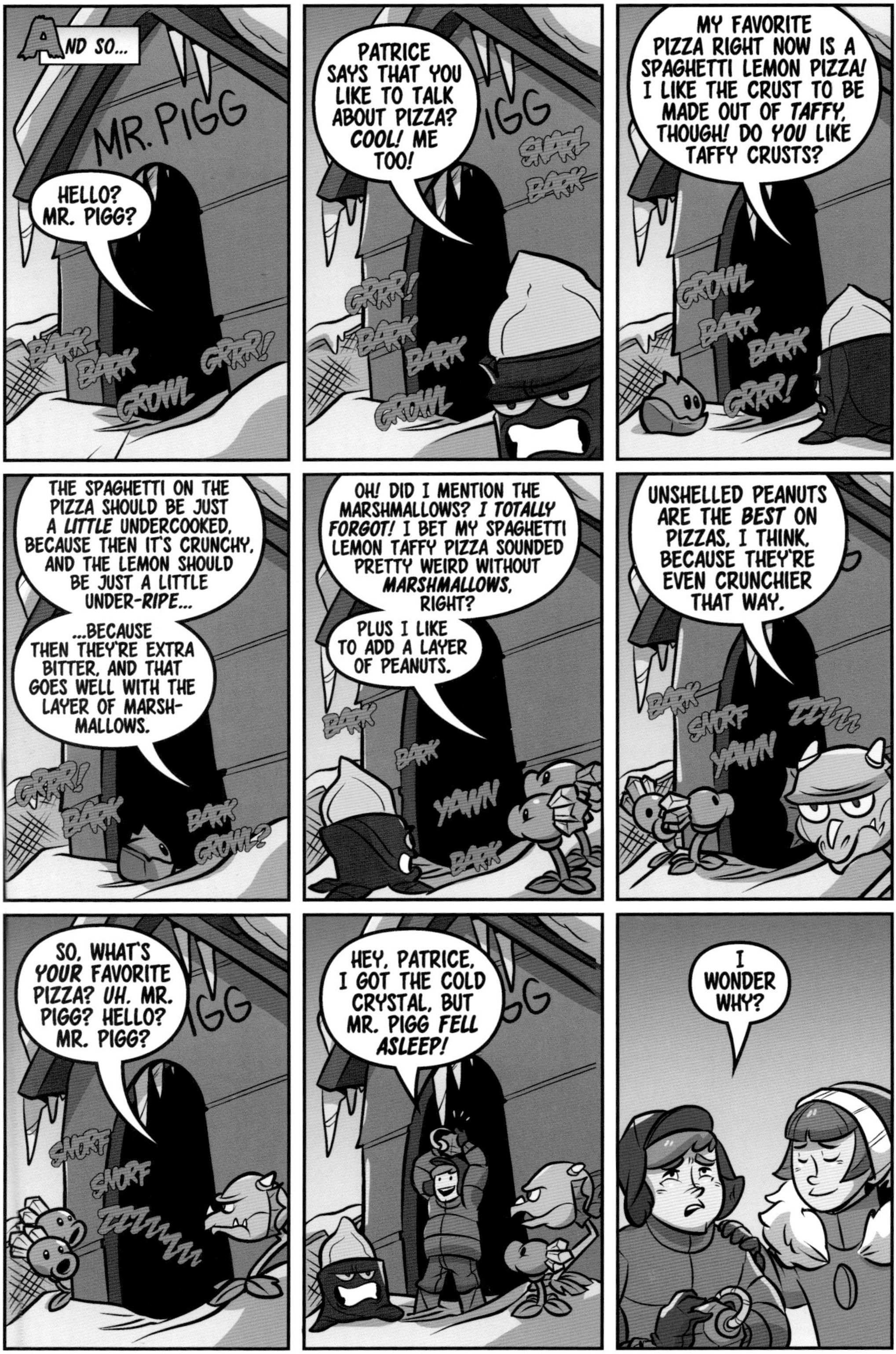
AND SO...
MR. PIGG
HELLO? MR. PIGG?
BARK
BARK
GROWL
GRRR!
PATRICE SAYS THAT YOU LIKE TO TALK ABOUT PIZZA? COOL! ME TOO!
SNARL
BARK
GRRR!
BARK
BARK
GROWL
MY FAVORITE PIZZA RIGHT NOW IS A SPAGHETTI LEMON PIZZA! I LIKE THE CRUST TO BE MADE OUT OF TAFFY, THOUGH! DO YOU LIKE TAFFY CRUSTS?
GROWL
BARK
BARK
GRRR!
THE SPAGHETTI ON THE PIZZA SHOULD BE JUST A LITTLE UNDERCOOKED, BECAUSE THEN IT'S CRUNCHY, AND THE LEMON SHOULD BE JUST A LITTLE UNDER-RIPE...
...BECAUSE THEN THEY'RE EXTRA BITTER, AND THAT GOES WELL WITH THE LAYER OF MARSH-MALLOWS.
GRRR!
BARK
BARK
GROWL?
OH! DID I MENTION THE MARSHMALLOWS? I TOTALLY FORGOT! I BET MY SPAGHETTI LEMON TAFFY PIZZA SOUNDED PRETTY WEIRD WITHOUT MARSHMALLOWS, RIGHT?
PLUS I LIKE TO ADD A LAYER OF PEANUTS.
BARK
BARK
YAWN
BARK
UNSHELLED PEANUTS ARE THE BEST ON PIZZAS, I THINK, BECAUSE THEY'RE EVEN CRUNCHIER THAT WAY.
BARK
SNORF
ZZZzz
YAWN
SO, WHAT'S YOUR FAVORITE PIZZA? UH. MR. PIGG? HELLO? MR. PIGG?
SNORF
SNORF
ZZZZzzzz
HEY, PATRICE, I GOT THE COLD CRYSTAL, BUT MR. PIGG FELL ASLEEP!
I WONDER WHY?

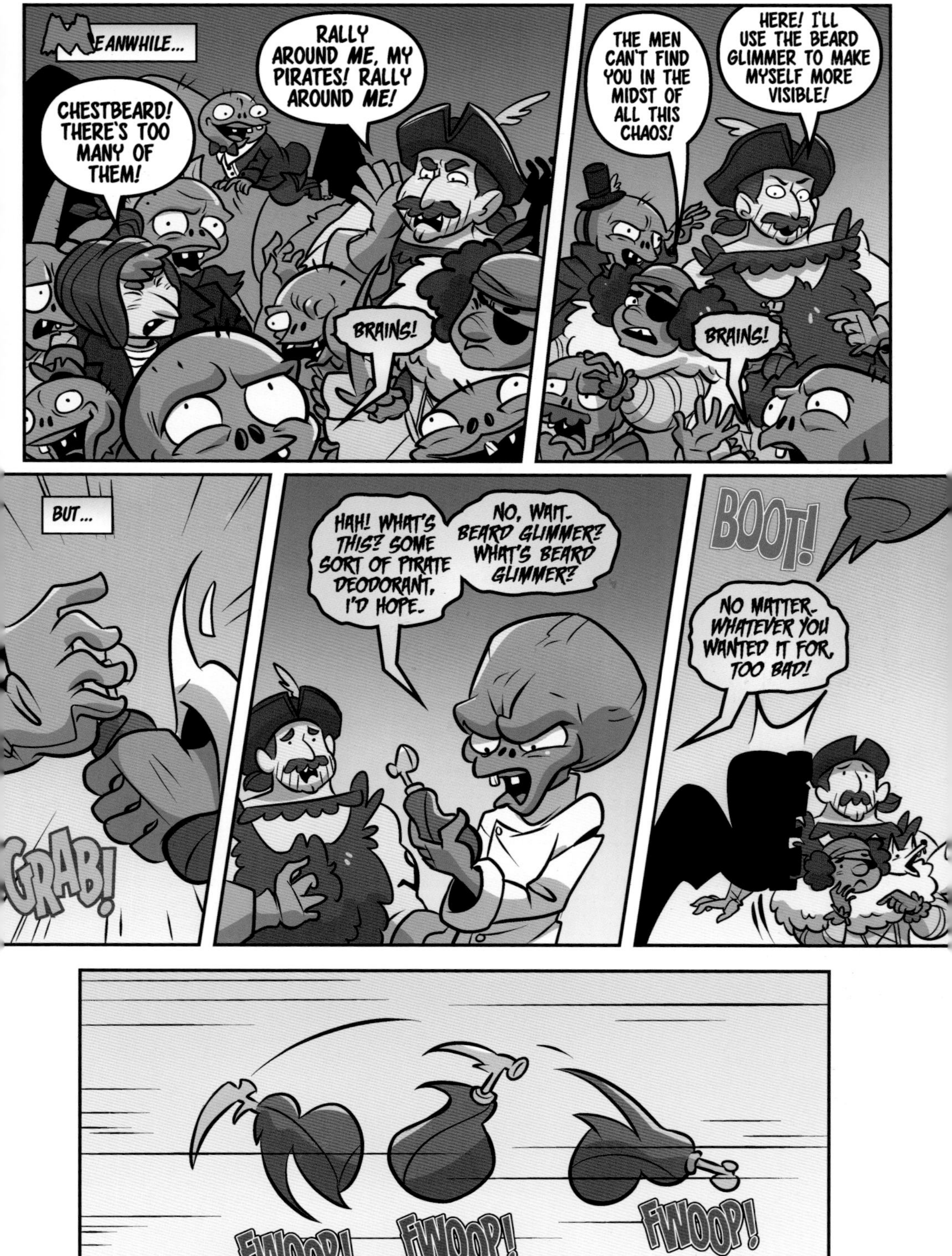
MEANWHILE...
CHESTBEARD! THERE'S TOO MANY OF THEM!
RALLY AROUND ME, MY PIRATES! RALLY AROUND ME!
BRAINS!
THE MEN CAN'T FIND YOU IN THE MIDST OF ALL THIS CHAOS!
HERE! I'LL USE THE BEARD GLIMMER TO MAKE MYSELF MORE VISIBLE!
BRAINS!
BUT...
GRAB!
HAH! WHAT'S THIS? SOME SORT OF PIRATE DEODORANT, I'D HOPE.
NO, WAIT. BEARD GLIMMER? WHAT'S BEARD GLIMMER?
BOOT!
NO MATTER. WHATEVER YOU WANTED IT FOR, TOO BAD!
FWOOP!
FWOOP!
FWOOP!

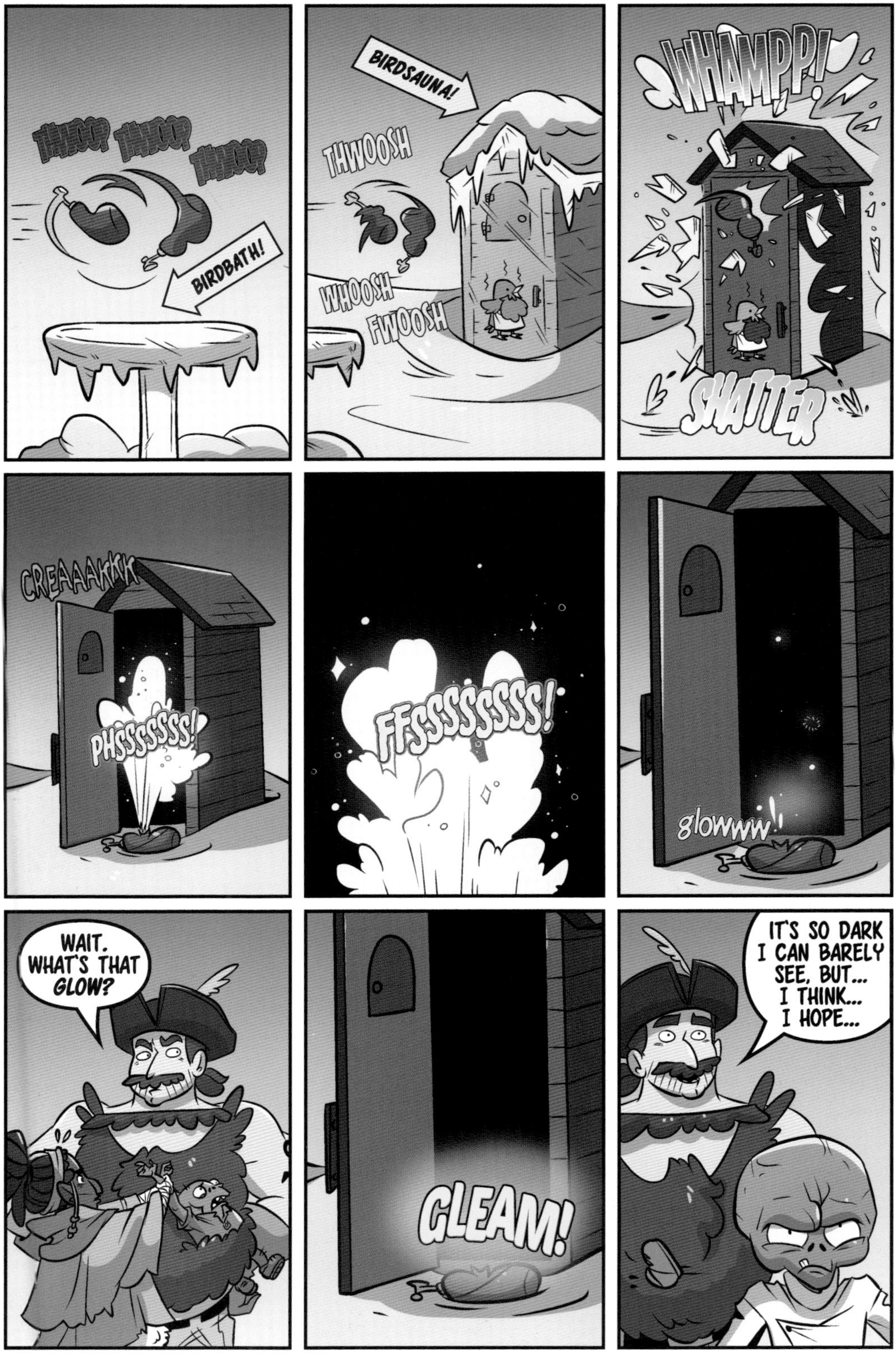
THWOOP THWOOP THWOOP
BIRDBATH!
BIRDSAUNA!
THWOOSH
WHOOSH
FWOOSH
WHAMPP!
SHATTER
CREAAAKKK
PHSSSSSSS!
FFSSSSSSSS!
glowww!
WAIT. WHAT'S THAT GLOW?
GLEAM!
IT'S SO DARK I CAN BARELY SEE, BUT... I THINK... I HOPE...

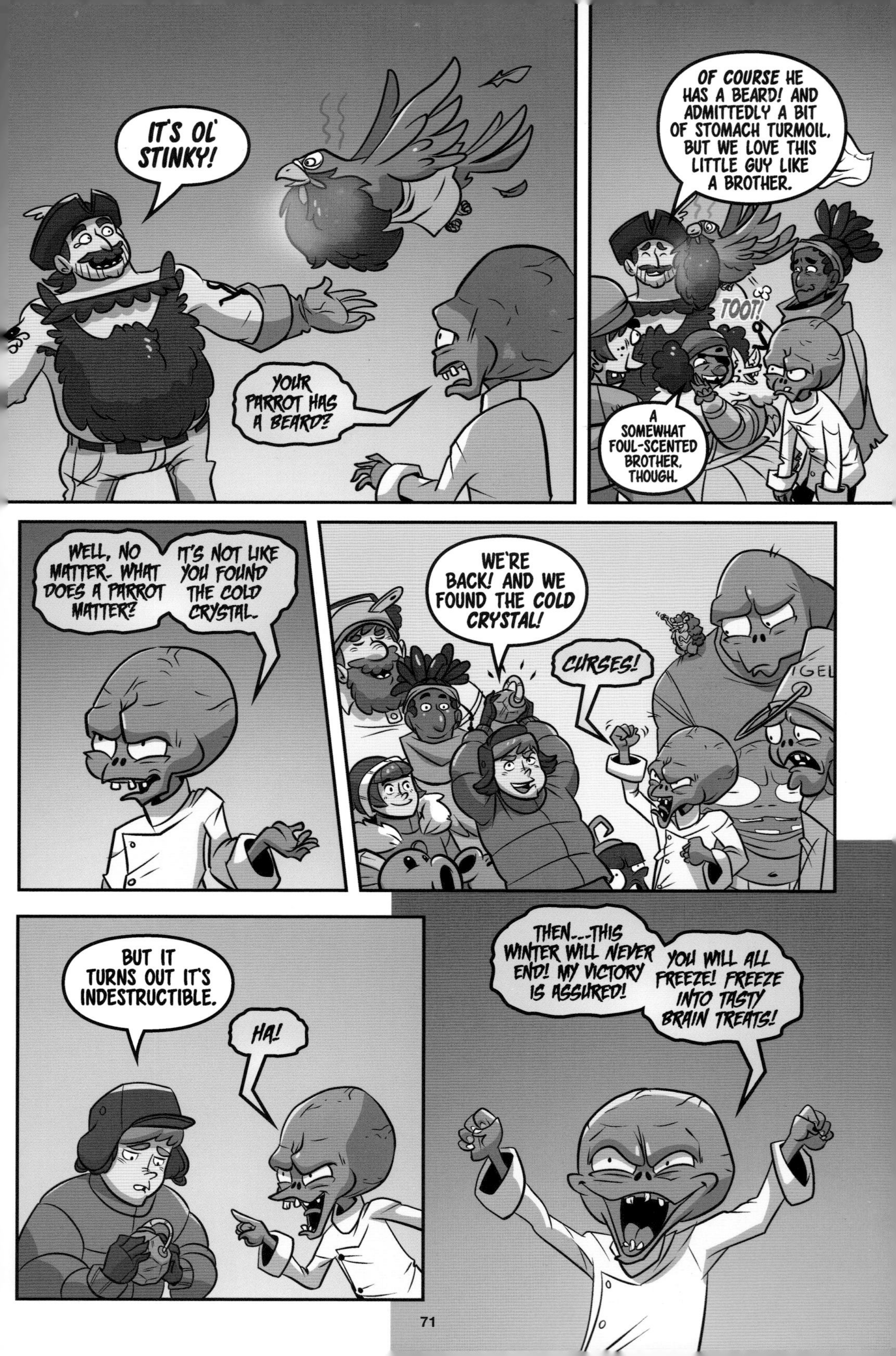
IT'S OL' STINKY!
YOUR PARROT HAS A BEARD?
OF COURSE HE HAS A BEARD! AND ADMITTEDLY A BIT OF STOMACH TURMOIL, BUT WE LOVE THIS LITTLE GUY LIKE A BROTHER.
TOOT!
A SOMEWHAT FOUL-SCENTED BROTHER, THOUGH.
WELL, NO MATTER. WHAT DOES A PARROT MATTER?
IT'S NOT LIKE YOU FOUND THE COLD CRYSTAL.
WE'RE BACK! AND WE FOUND THE COLD CRYSTAL!
CURSES!
BUT IT TURNS OUT IT'S INDESTRUCTIBLE.
HA!
THEN...THIS WINTER WILL NEVER END! MY VICTORY IS ASSURED!
YOU WILL ALL FREEZE! FREEZE INTO TASTY BRAIN TREATS!

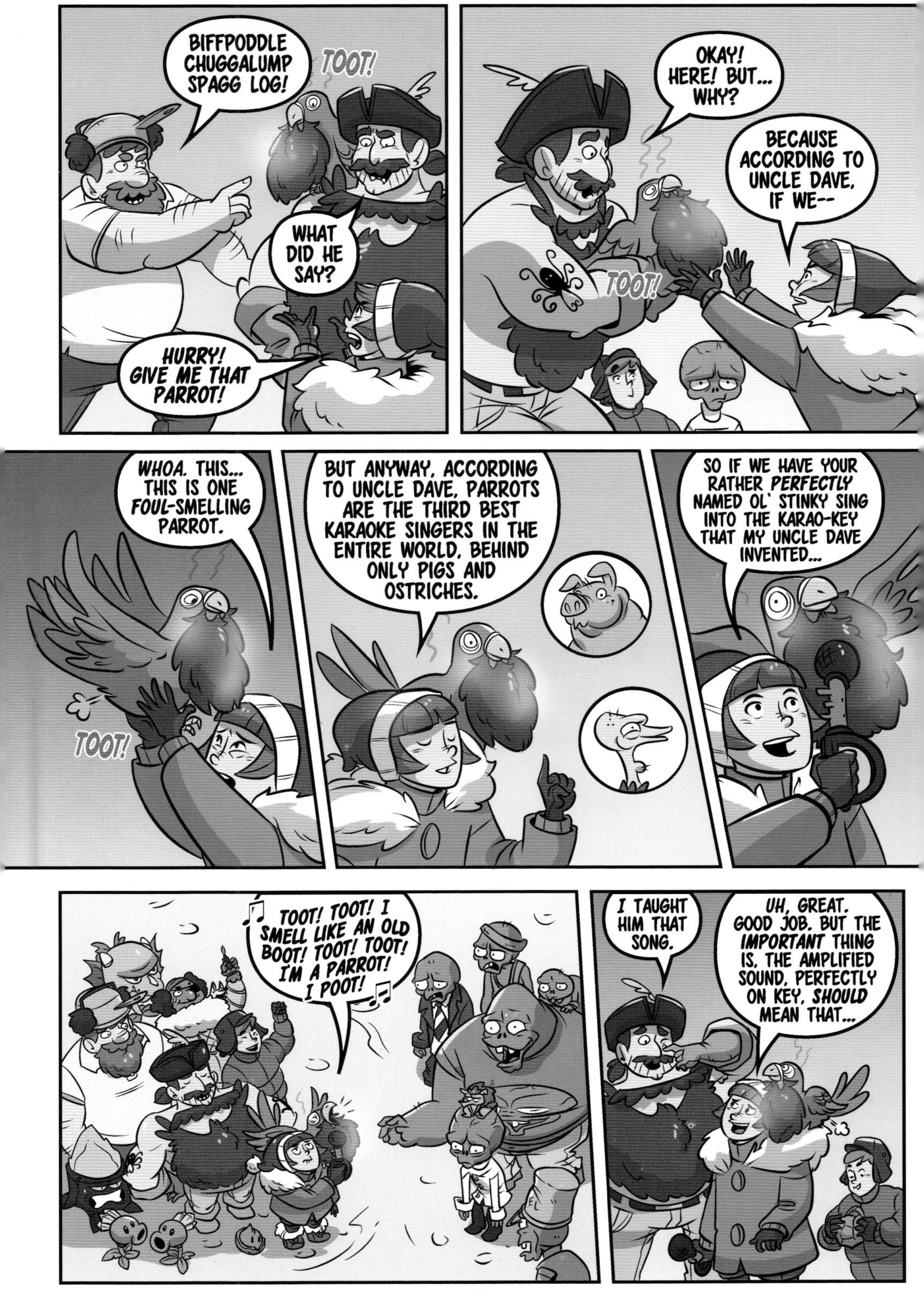
BIFFPODDLE CHUGGALUMP SPAGG LOG!
TOOT!
WHAT DID HE SAY?
HURRY! GIVE ME THAT PARROT!
OKAY! HERE! BUT... WHY?
BECAUSE ACCORDING TO UNCLE DAVE, IF WE--
TOOT!
WHOA. THIS... THIS IS ONE FOUL-SMELLING PARROT.
TOOT!
BUT ANYWAY, ACCORDING TO UNCLE DAVE, PARROTS ARE THE THIRD BEST KARAOKE SINGERS IN THE ENTIRE WORLD, BEHIND ONLY PIGS AND OSTRICHES.
SO IF WE HAVE YOUR RATHER PERFECTLY NAMED OL' STINKY SING INTO THE KARAO-KEY THAT MY UNCLE DAVE INVENTED...
TOOT! TOOT! I SMELL LIKE AN OLD BOOT! TOOT! TOOT! I'M A PARROT! I POOT!
I TAUGHT HIM THAT SONG.
UH, GREAT. GOOD JOB. BUT THE IMPORTANT THING IS, THE AMPLIFIED SOUND, PERFECTLY ON KEY, SHOULD MEAN THAT...

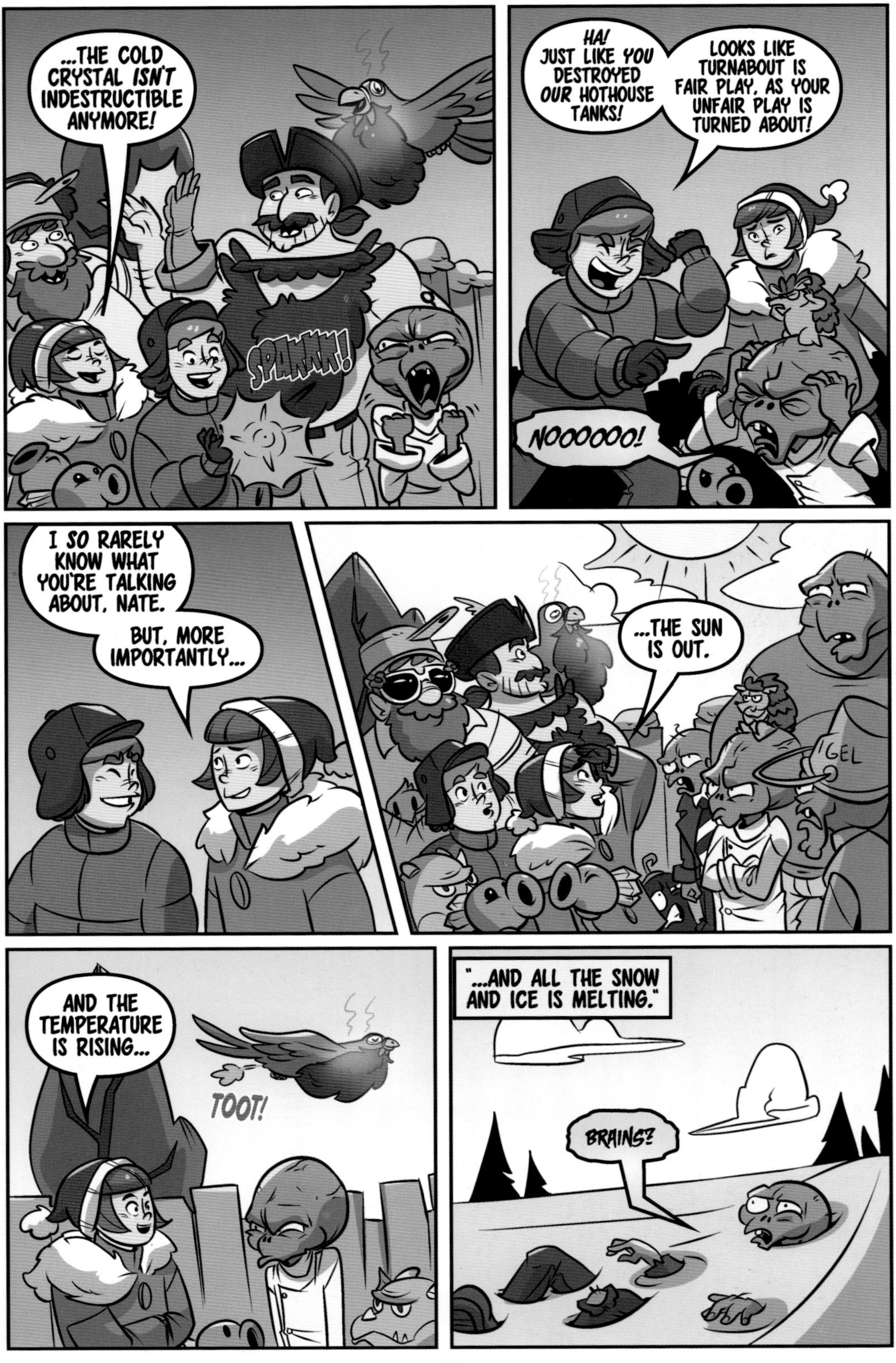
...THE COLD CRYSTAL ISN'T INDESTRUCTIBLE ANYMORE!
SPANKK!
HA! JUST LIKE YOU DESTROYED OUR HOTHOUSE TANKS!
LOOKS LIKE TURNABOUT IS FAIR PLAY, AS YOUR UNFAIR PLAY IS TURNED ABOUT!
NOOOOOO!
I SO RARELY KNOW WHAT YOU'RE TALKING ABOUT, NATE.
BUT, MORE IMPORTANTLY...
...THE SUN IS OUT.
GEL
AND THE TEMPERATURE IS RISING...
TOOT!
"...AND ALL THE SNOW AND ICE IS MELTING."
BRAINS?

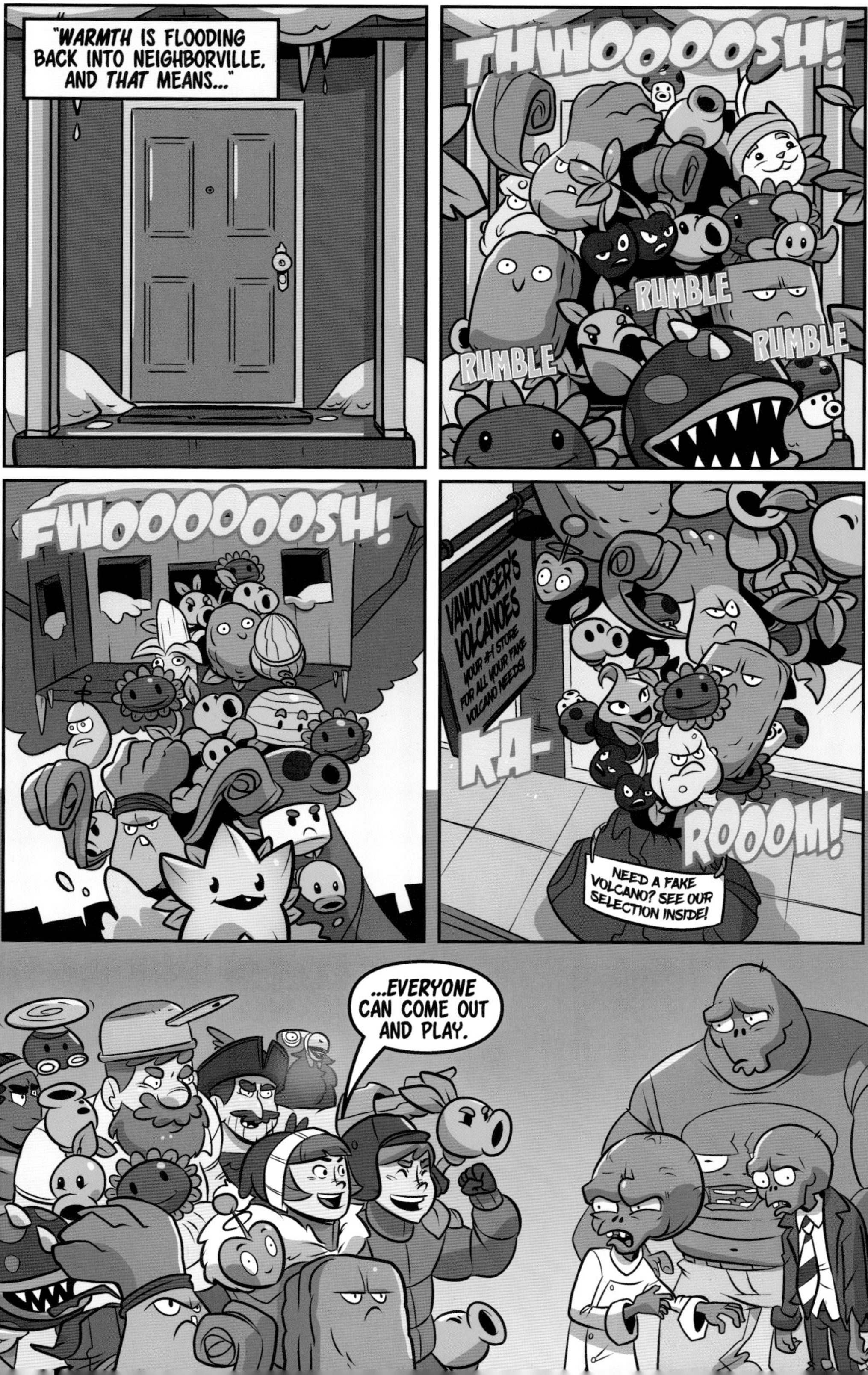

"WARMTH IS FLOODING BACK INTO NEIGHBORVILLE, AND THAT MEANS..."
THWOOOOOSH!
RUMBLE
RUMBLE
RUMBLE
FWOOOOOOSH!
VANHOOZER'S VOLCANOES
YOUR #1 STORE FOR ALL YOUR FAKE VOLCANO NEEDS!
KA-
ROOOM!
NEED A FAKE VOLCANO? SEE OUR SELECTION INSIDE!
...EVERYONE CAN COME OUT AND PLAY.

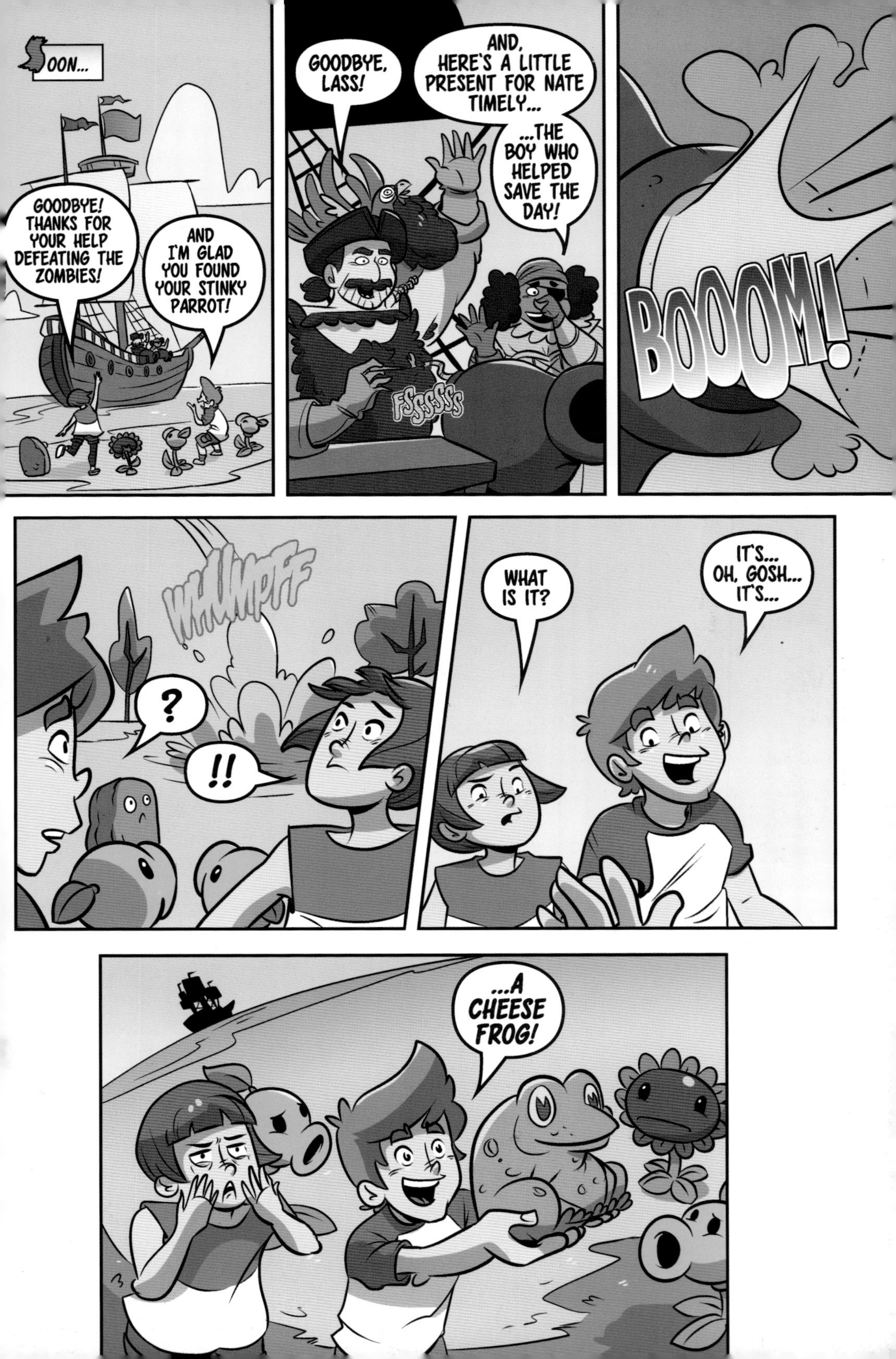
SOON...
GOODBYE! THANKS FOR YOUR HELP DEFEATING THE ZOMBIES!
AND I'M GLAD YOU FOUND YOUR STINKY PARROT!
GOODBYE, LASS!
AND, HERE'S A LITTLE PRESENT FOR NATE TIMELY...
...THE BOY WHO HELPED SAVE THE DAY!
FSSSSSS
BOOOM!
WHUMPFF
?
!!
WHAT IS IT?
IT'S... OH, GOSH... IT'S...
...A CHEESE FROG!

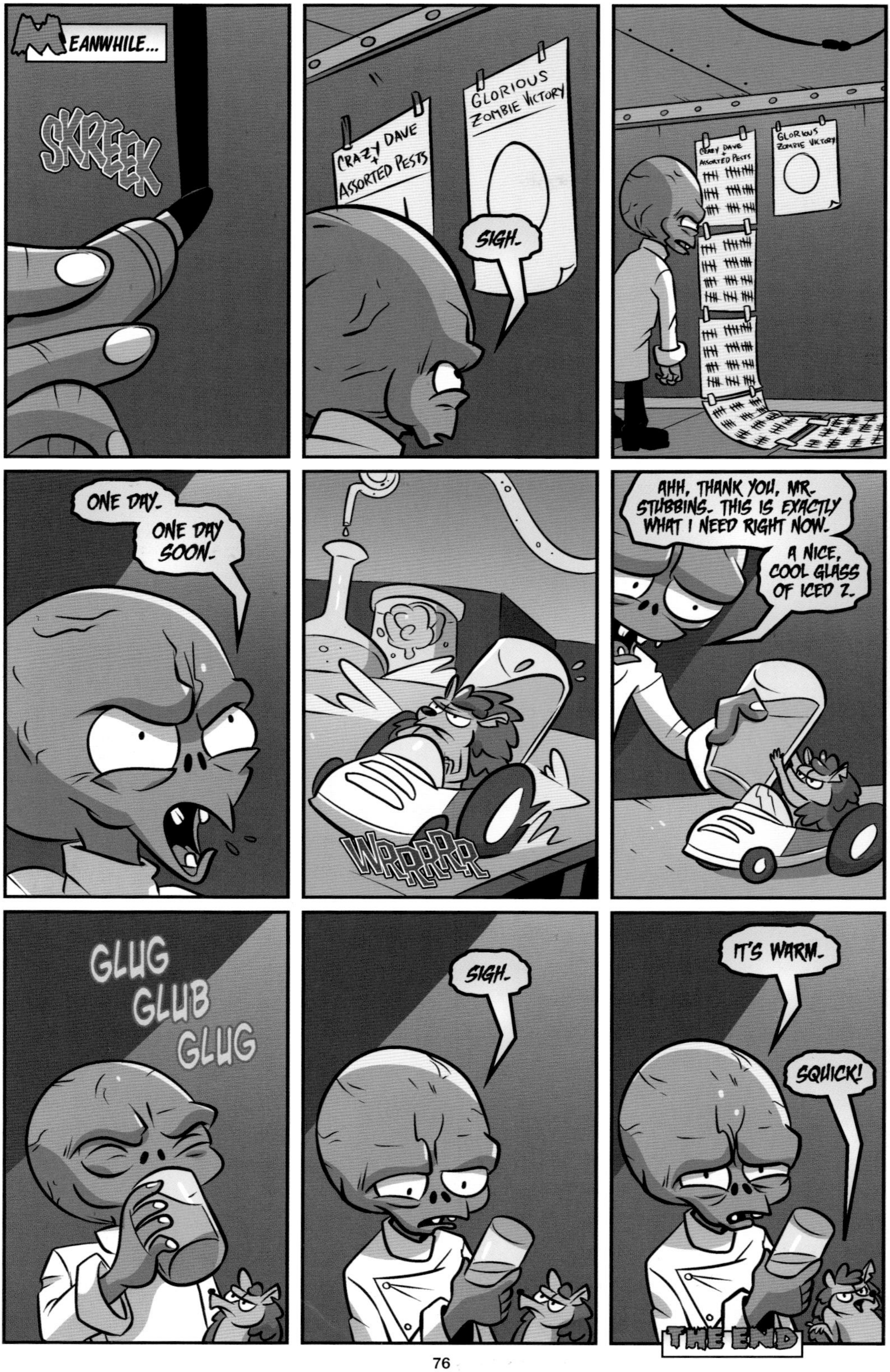

MEANWHILE...
SKREEEK
CRAZY DAVE + ASSORTED PESTS
GLORIOUS ZOMBIE VICTORY
SIGH.
CRAZY DAVE + ASSORTED PESTS
GLORIOUS ZOMBIE VICTORY
ONE DAY.
ONE DAY SOON.
WRRRRR
AHH, THANK YOU, MR. STUBBINS. THIS IS EXACTLY WHAT I NEED RIGHT NOW.
A NICE, COOL GLASS OF ICED Z.
GLUG
GLUB
GLUG
SIGH.
IT'S WARM.
SQUICK!
THE END

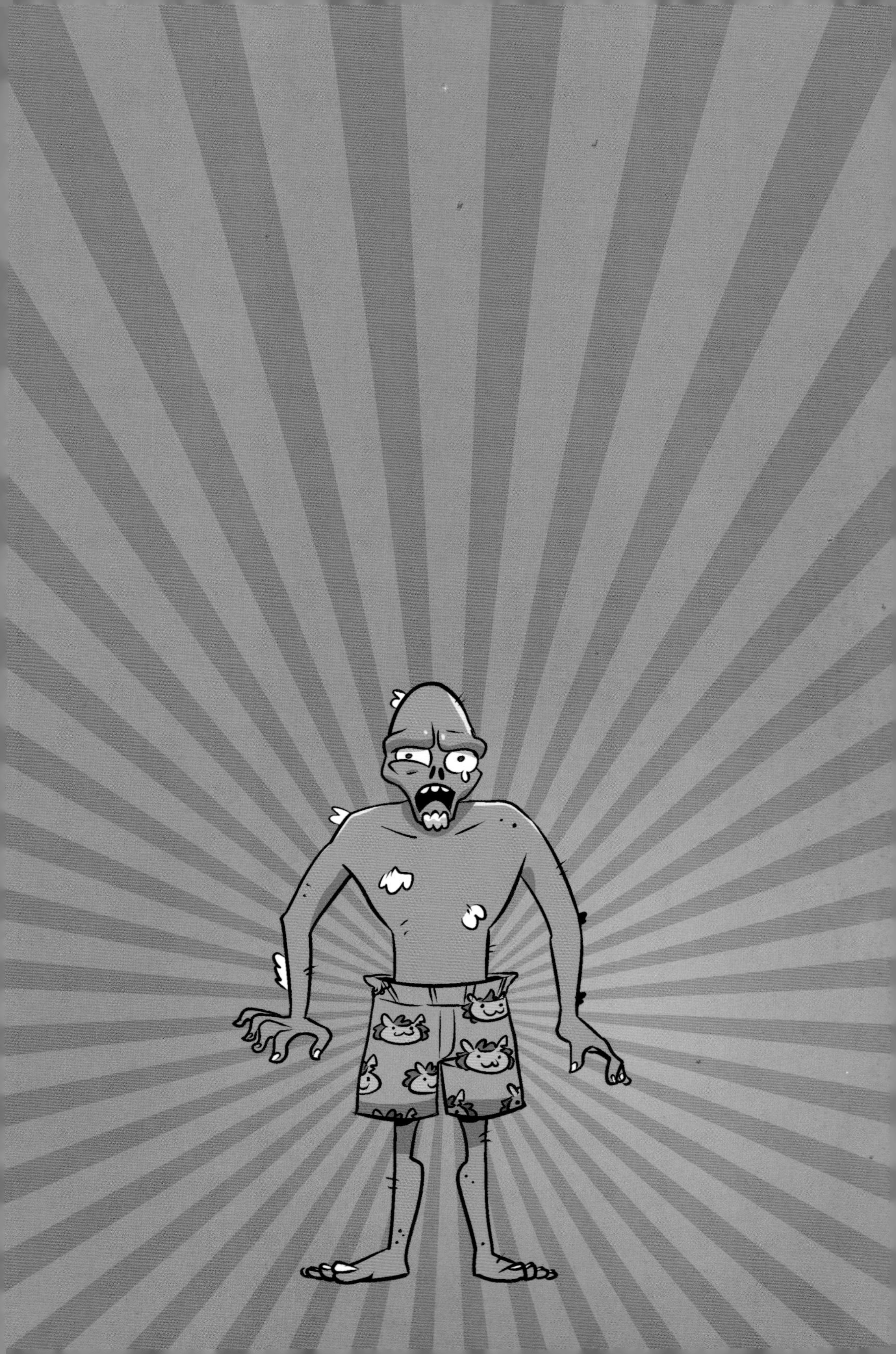

PLANTS VS. ZOMBIES: SNOW THANKS

cover pencils by CAT FARRIS

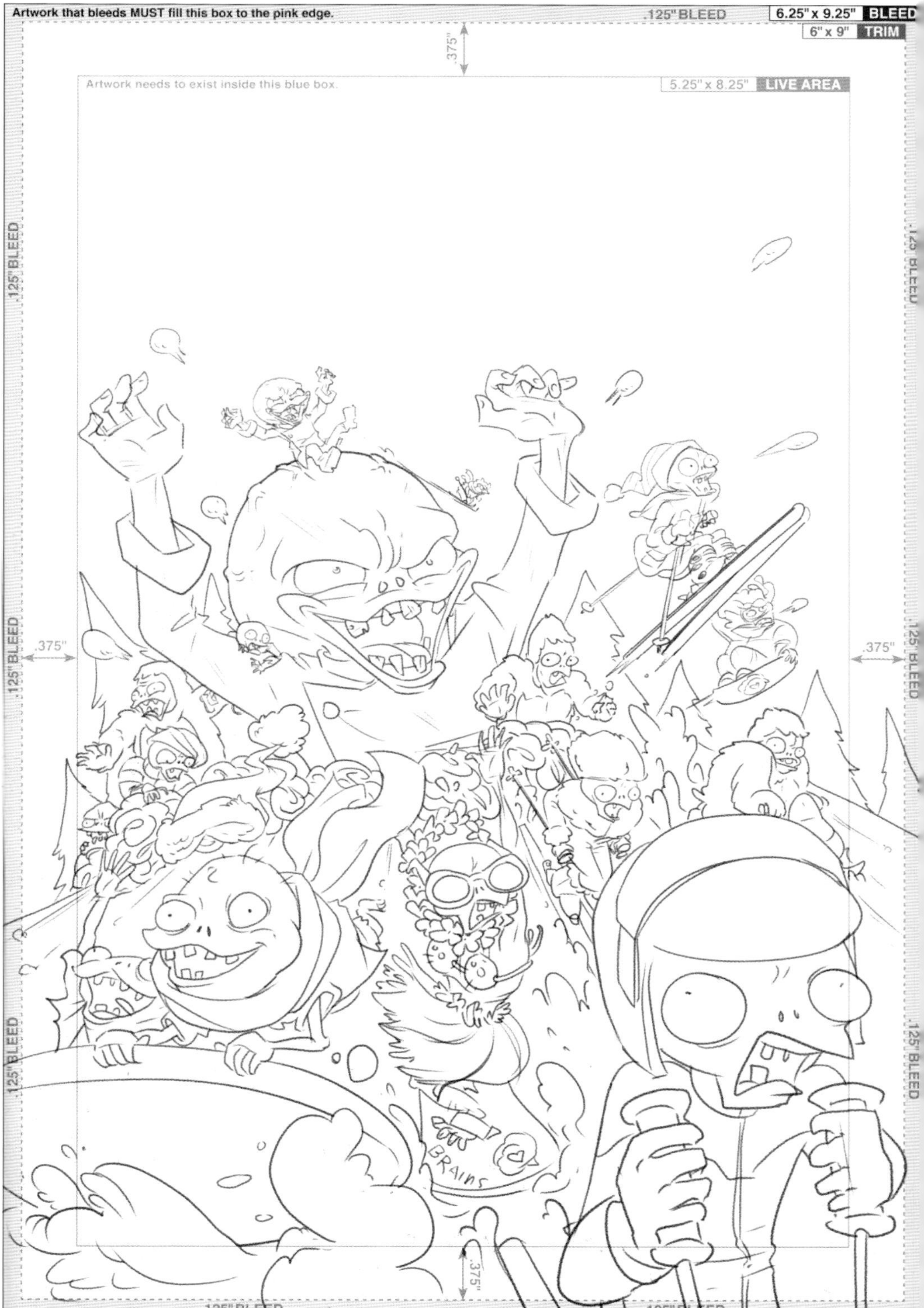
Artwork that bleeds MUST fill this box to the pink edge.
.125" BLEED
6.25" x 9.25" BLEED
6" x 9" TRIM
.375"
Artwork needs to exist inside this blue box.
5.25" x 8.25" LIVE AREA
BRAINS

PLANTS VS. ZOMBIES: SNOW THANKS
cover inks by CAT FARRIS

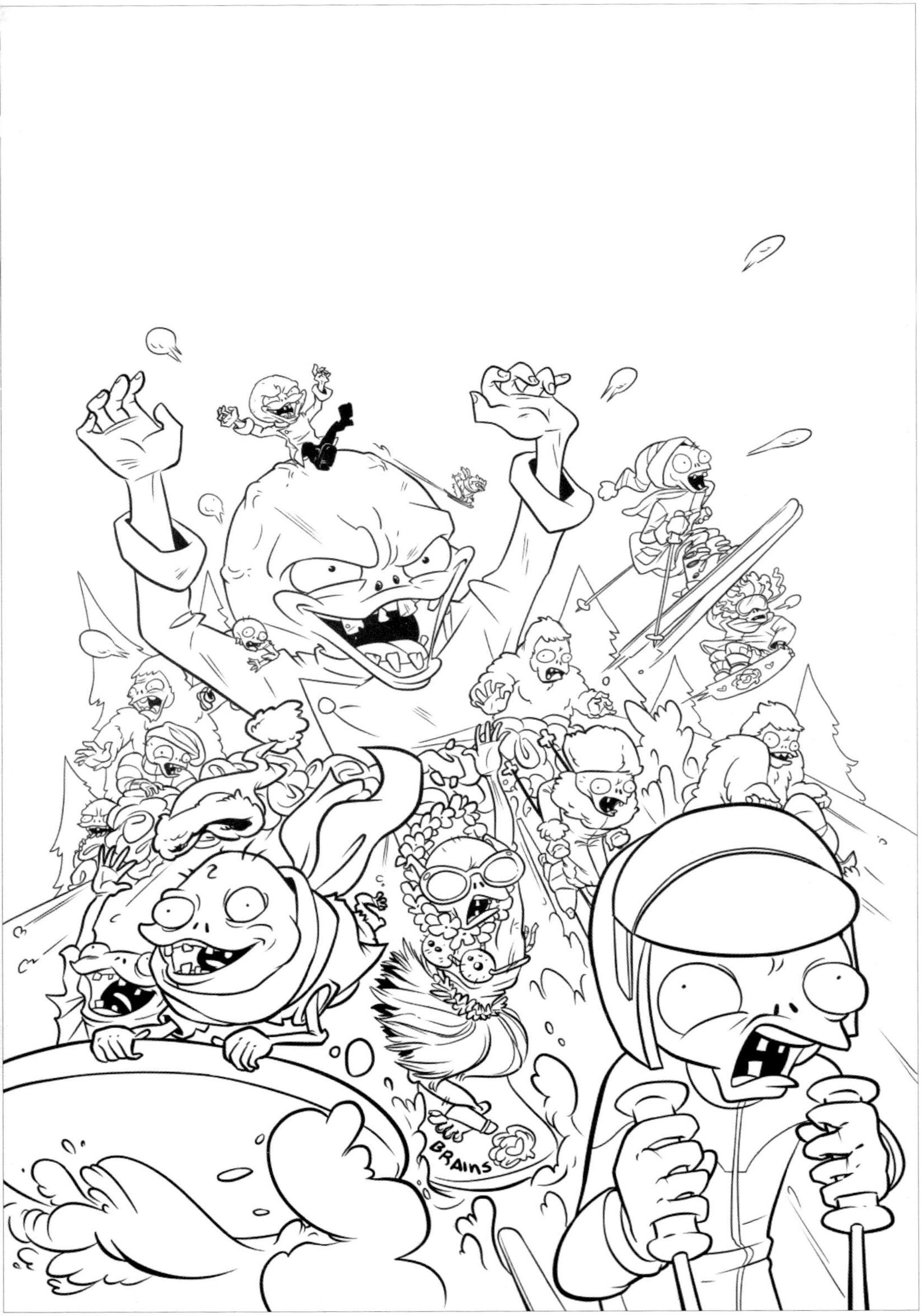
BRAINS

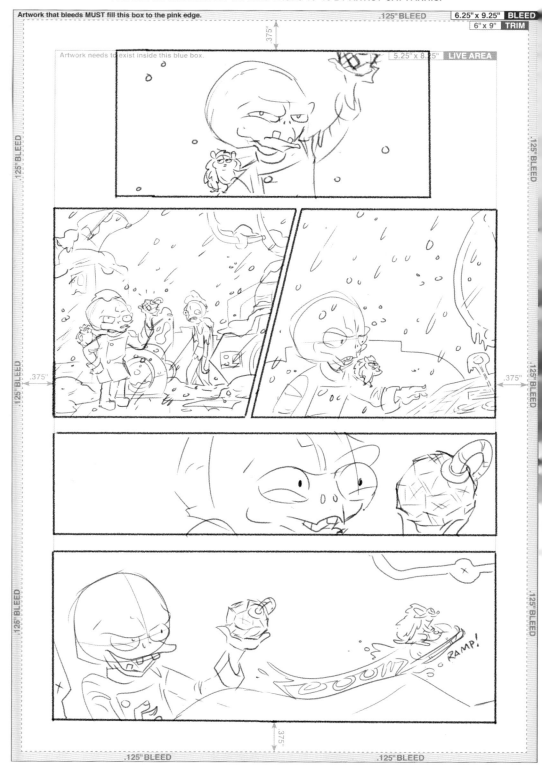

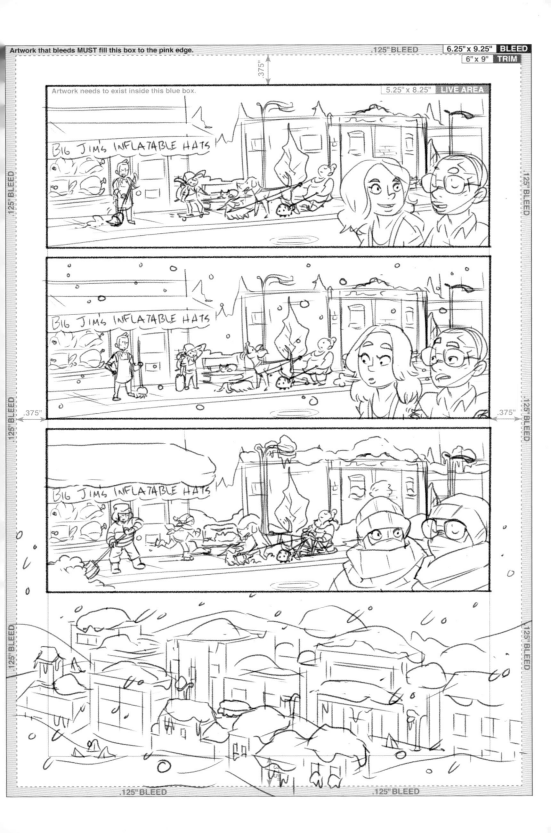

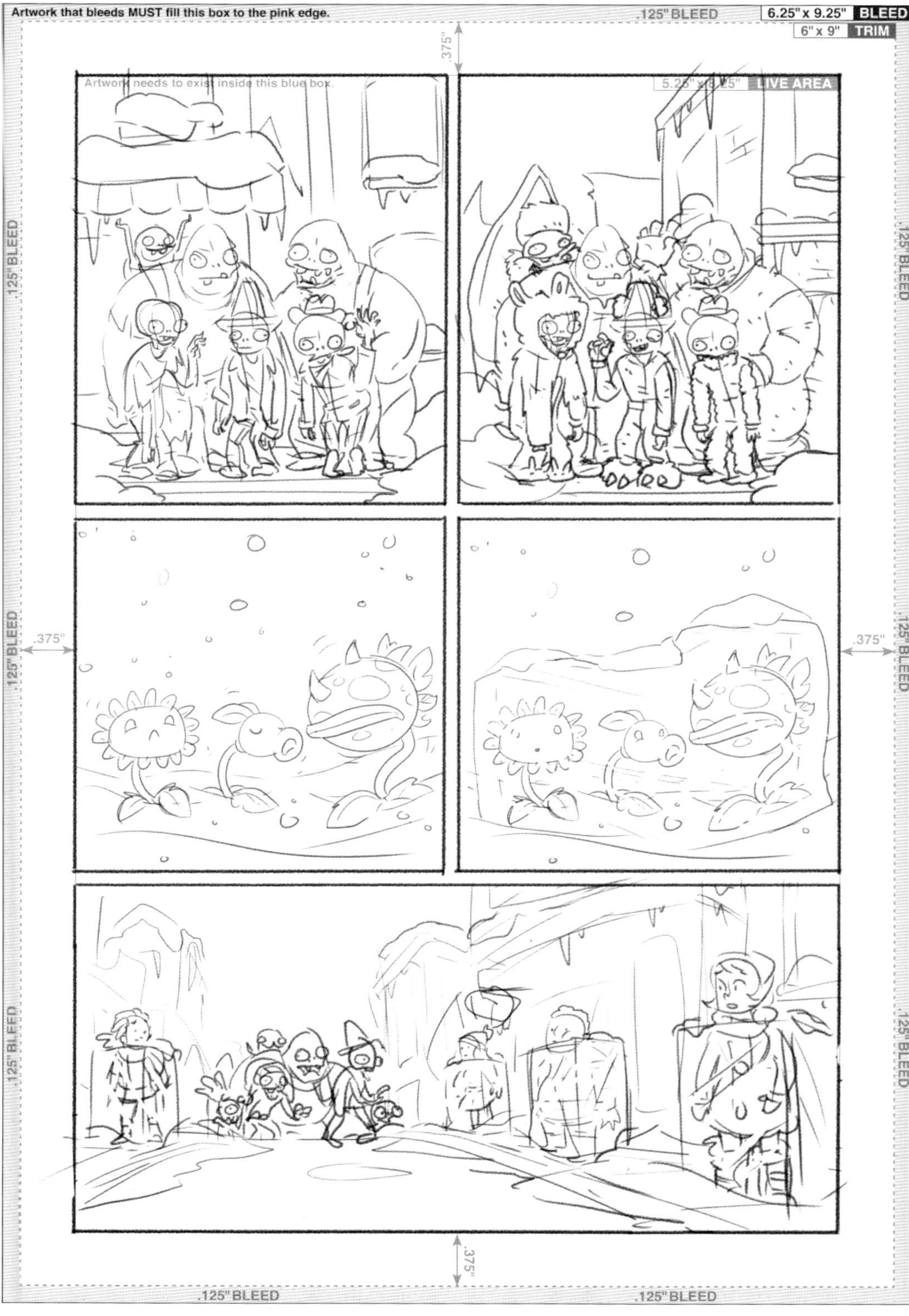

Artwork that bleeds MUST fill this box to the pink edge.
.125" BLEED
6.25" x 9.25" BLEED
6" x 9" TRIM
.375"
Artwork needs to exist inside this blue box.
5.25" x 8.25" LIVE AREA

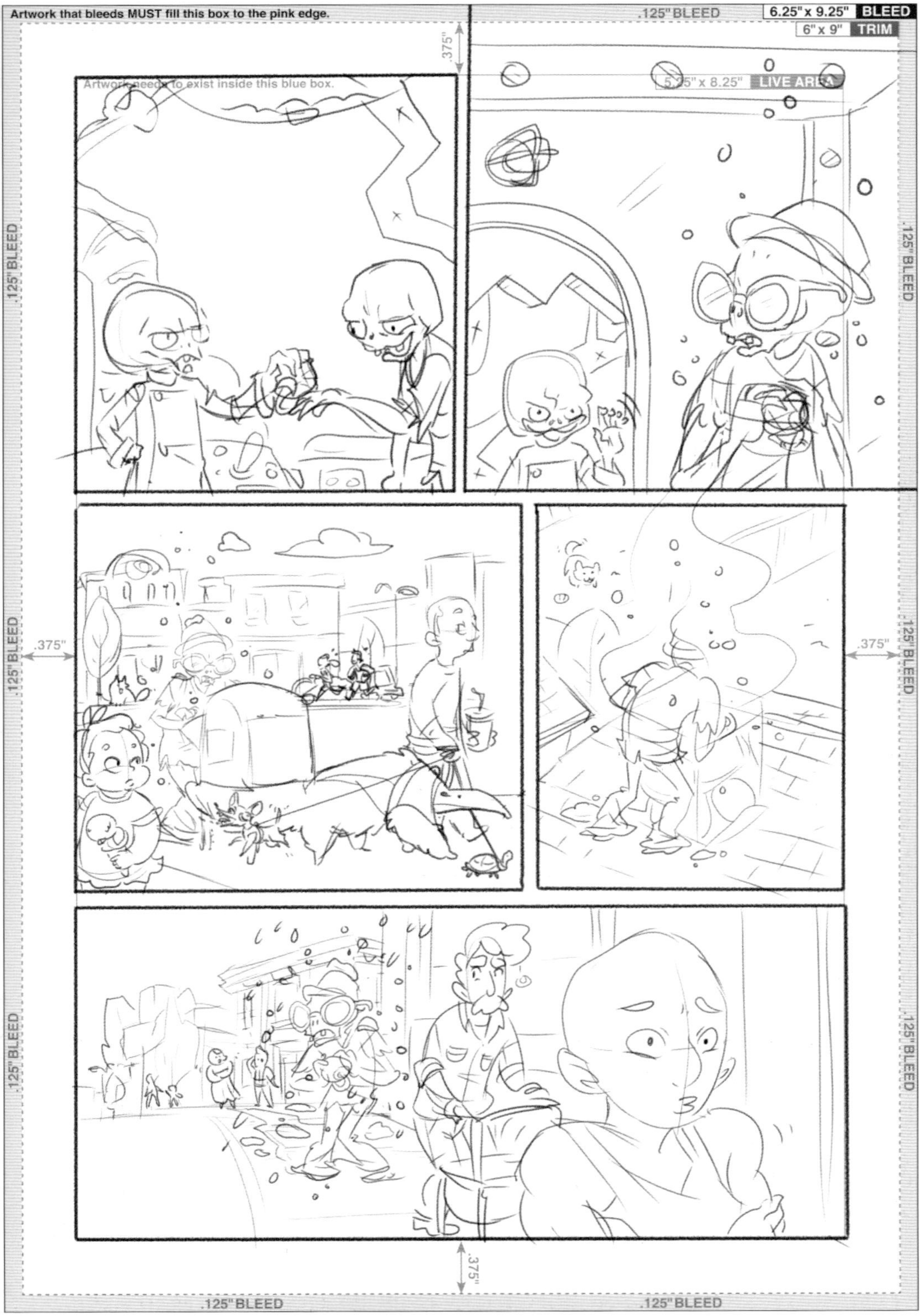
Artwork that bleeds MUST fill this box to the pink edge.
.125" BLEED
6.25" x 9.25" BLEED
6" x 9" TRIM
5.25" x 8.25" LIVE AREA
Artwork needs to exist inside this blue box.
.375"

CREATOR BIOS

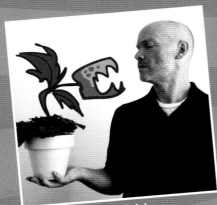

Paul Tobin

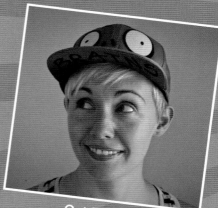

Cat Farris

PAUL TOBIN enjoys that his author photo makes him look insane, and he once accidentally cut his ear with a potato chip. He doesn't know how it happened, either. Life is so full of mystery. If you ask him about the Potato Chip Incident, he'll just make up a story. That's what he does. He's written hundreds of stories for Marvel, DC, Dark Horse, and many others, including such creator-owned titles as *Colder* and *Bandette*, as well as *Prepare to Die!*—his debut novel. His *Genius Factor* series of novels about a fifth-grade genius and his war against the Red Death Tea Society debuted in March 2016 with *How to Capture an Invisible Cat*, from Bloomsbury Publishing, and continued in early 2017 with *How to Outsmart a Billion Robot Bees*. Paul has won some Very Important Awards for his writing but so far none for his karaoke skills.

CAT FARRIS is a native Portlander, an artist, and pretty sure she's just making this up as she goes along. She is supported in this venture by the world's most beautiful husband, the laziest greyhound, and an all-star cast of Helioscope studiomates. She has done art for various comics, such as *Emily and the Strangers* (Dark Horse Comics), and *My Boyfriend is a Bear* (Oni Press). Her favorite plants are Wall-nuts and Tall-nuts.

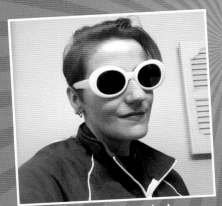

Heather Breckel

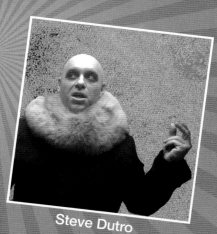

Steve Dutro

HEATHER BRECKEL went to the Columbus College of Art and Design for animation. She decided animation wasn't for her so she switched to comics. She's been working as a colorist for nearly ten years and has worked for nearly every major comics publisher out there. When she's not burning the midnight oil in a deadline crunch, she's either dying a bunch in videogames or telling her cats to stop running around at two in the morning.

STEVE DUTRO is an Eisner Award-nominated comic-book letterer from Redding, California, who can also drive a tractor. He graduated from the Kubert School and has been lettering comics since the days when foil-embossed covers were cool, working for Dark Horse (*The Fifth Beatle*, *I Am a Hero*, *Planet of the Apes*, *Star Wars*), Viz, Marvel, and DC. He has submitted a request to the Department of Homeland Security that in the event of a zombie apocalypse he be put in charge of all digital freeway signs so citizens can be alerted to avoid nearby brain-eatings and the like. He finds the *Plants vs. Zombies* game to be a real stress-fest, but highly recommends the *Plants vs. Zombies* table on *Pinball FX2* for game-room hipsters.

ALSO AVAILABLE FROM DARK HORSE!

THE HIT VIDEO GAME CONTINUES ITS COMIC BOOK INVASION!

PLANTS VS. ZOMBIES: LAWNMAGEDDON
Crazy Dave—the babbling-yet-brilliant inventor and top-notch neighborhood defender—helps young adventurer Nate fend off a zombie invasion that threatens to overrun the peaceful town of Neighborville in *Plants vs. Zombies: Lawnmageddon*! Their only hope is a brave army of chomping, squashing, and pea-shooting plants! A wacky adventure for zombie zappers young and old!
ISBN 978-1-61655-192-6 | $9.99

THE ART OF PLANTS VS. ZOMBIES
Part zombie memoir, part celebration of zombie triumphs, and part anti-plant screed, *The Art of Plants vs. Zombies* is a treasure trove of never-before-seen concept art, character sketches, and surprises from PopCap's popular *Plants vs. Zombies* games!
ISBN 978-1-61655-331-9 | $9.99

PLANTS VS. ZOMBIES: TIMEPOCALYPSE
Crazy Dave helps Patrice and Nate Timely fend off Zomboss' latest attack in *Plants vs. Zombies: Timepocalypse*! This new standalone tale will tickle your funny bones and thrill your brains through any timeline!
ISBN 978-1-61655-621-1 | $9.99

PLANTS VS. ZOMBIES: BULLY FOR YOU
Patrice and Nate are ready to investigate a strange college campus to keep the streets safe from zombies!
ISBN 978-1-61655-889-5 | $9.99

PLANTS VS. ZOMBIES: GARDEN WARFARE
Based on the hit video game, this comic tells the story leading up to the events in *Plants vs. Zombies: Garden Warfare 2*!
ISBN 978-1-61655-946-5 | $9.99

PLANTS VS. ZOMBIES: GROWN SWEET HOME
With newfound knowledge of humanity, Dr. Zomboss strikes at the heart of Neighborville . . . sparking a series of plant-versus-zombie brawls!
ISBN 978-1-61655-971-7 | $9.99

PLANTS VS. ZOMBIES: PETAL TO THE METAL
Crazy Dave takes on the tough *Don't Blink* video game—and challenges Dr. Zomboss to a race to determine the future of Neighborville!
ISBN 978-1-61655-999-1 | $9.99

PLANTS VS. ZOMBIES: BOOM BOOM MUSHROOM
The gang discover Zomboss' secret plan for swallowing the city of Neighborville whole! A rare mushroom must be found in order to save the humans aboveground!
ISBN 978-1-50670-037-3 | $9.99

PLANTS VS. ZOMBIES: BATTLE EXTRAVAGONZO
Zomboss is back, hoping to buy the same factory that Crazy Dave is eyeing! Will Crazy Dave and his intelligent plants beat Zomboss and his zombie army to the punch?
ISBN 978-1-50670-189-9 | $9.99

PLANTS VS. ZOMBIES: LAWN OF DOOM
With Zomboss filling everyone's yards with traps and special soldiers, will he and his zombie army turn Halloween into their zanier Lawn of Doom celebration?!
ISBN 978-1-50670-204-9 | $9.99

PLANTS VS. ZOMBIES: THE GREATEST SHOW UNEARTHED
Dr. Zomboss believes that all humans hold a secret desire to run away and join the circus, so he aims to use his "Big Z's Adequately Amazing Flytrap Circus" to lure Neighborville's citizens to their doom!
ISBN 978-1-50670-298-8 | $9.99

PLANTS VS. ZOMBIES: RUMBLE AT LAKE GUMBO
The battle for clean water begins! Nate, Patrice, and Crazy Dave spot trouble and grab all the Tangle Kelp and Party Crabs they can to quell another zombie attack!
ISBN 978-1-50670-497-5 | $9.99

PLANTS VS. ZOMBIES: WAR AND PEAS
When Dr. Zomboss and Crazy Dave find themselves members of the same book club, a literary war is inevitable! The position of leader of the book club opens up and Zomboss and Crazy Dave compete for the top spot in a scholarly scuffle for the ages!
ISBN 978-1-50670-677-1 | $9.99

PLANTS VS. ZOMBIES: DINO-MIGHT
Dr. Zomboss sets his sights on destroying the yards in town and rendering the plants homeless—and his plans include dogs, cats, rabbits, hammock sloths, and, somehow, dinosaurs . . . !
ISBN 978-1-50670-838-6 | $9.99

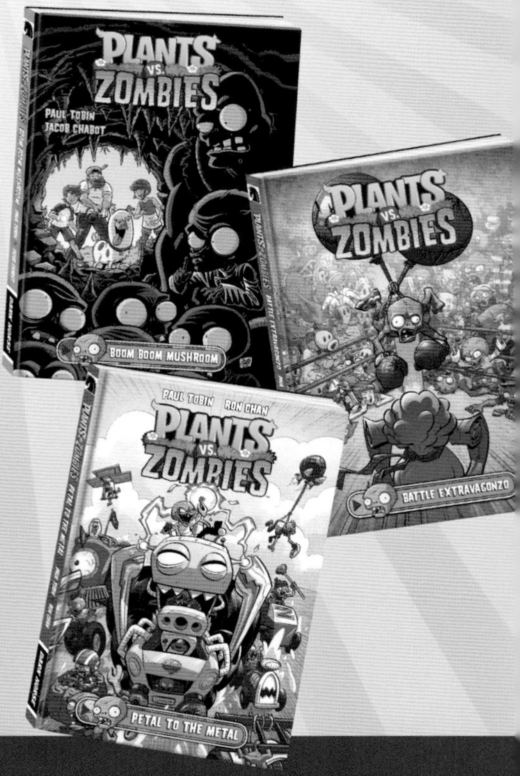
PLANTS VS. ZOMBIES
PAUL TOBIN
JACOB CHABOT
BOOM BOOM MUSHROOM
PLANTS VS. ZOMBIES
BATTLE EXTRAVAGONZO
PAUL TOBIN RON CHAN
PLANTS VS. ZOMBIES
PETAL TO THE METAL

AVAILABLE AT YOUR LOCAL COMICS SHOP OR BOOKSTORE To find a comics shop in your area, visit comicshoplocator.com. For more information or to order direct visit **DarkHorse.com** or call 1-800-862-0052

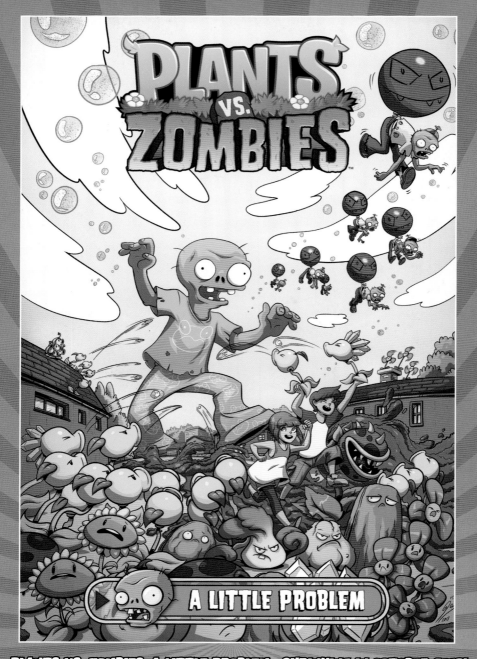

PLANTS VS. ZOMBIES: A LITTLE PROBLEM—SHRINKING IN OCTOBER 2019!

Dr. Zomboss creates an army of teeny zombies to try and sneak up on all the brains in Neighborville! To battle these miniscule menaces, the plants, Crazy Dave, Patrice, and Nate must shrink themselves to have any chance at defeating the zombies. But how will Neighborville's insects react to the invasion of their turf-of-the-tiny? And will this miniature zombie invasion mean the party for Crazy Dave's two-hundred-year-old pants gets cancelled? Don't miss the latest volume of the critically-acclaimed *Plants vs. Zombies* series that sees Eisner Award-winning writer Paul Tobin return to collaborate with artist Sara Ester Soler (*Red & Blue*) for this standalone graphic novel!

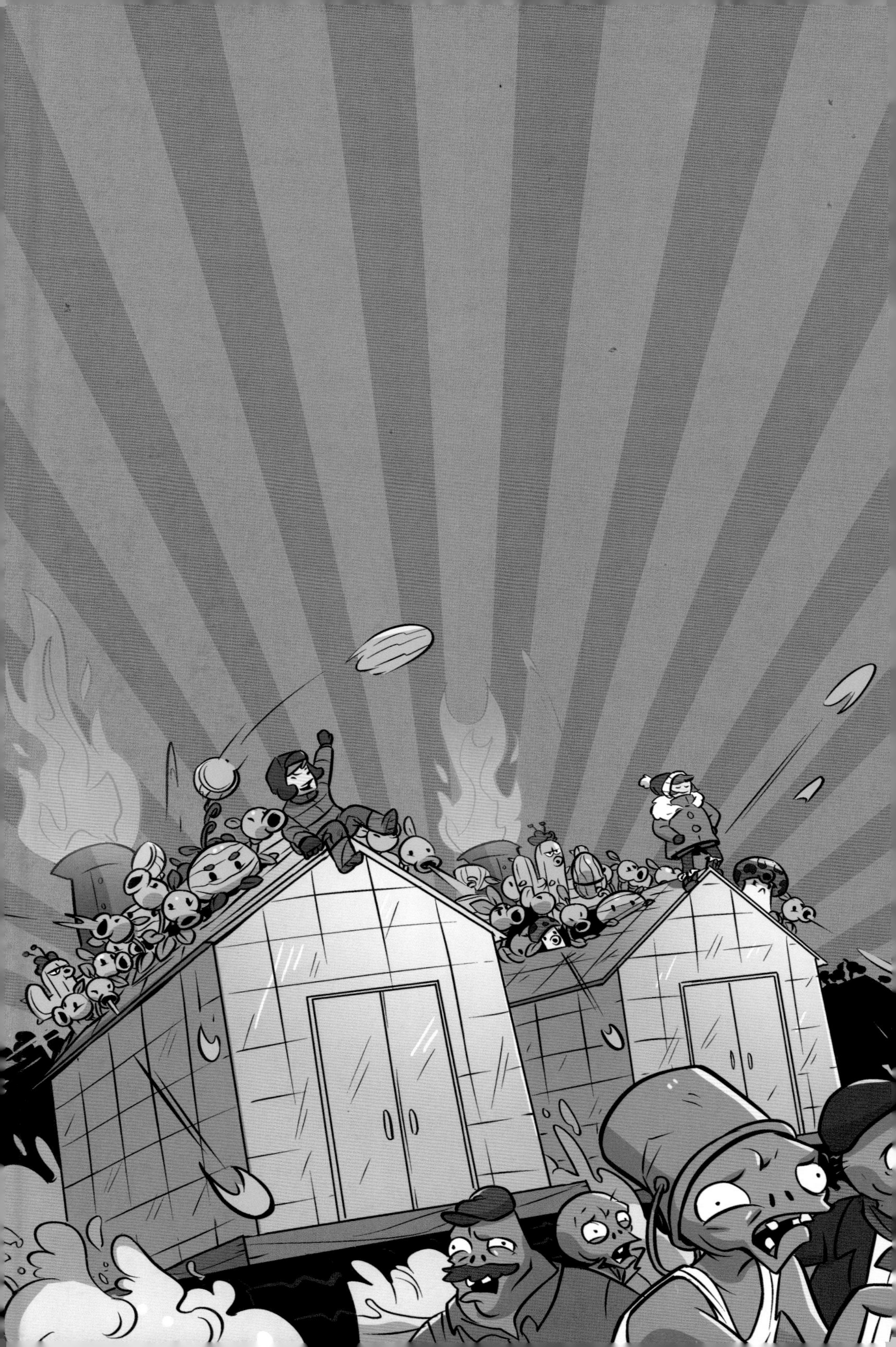

About the Author

"Sometimes I think I made a mistake," Robert Wolley says. "When I graduated from college I became the minister of a New England church which paid $3,600 per year. Out in California master masons were earning $30,000 a year. But I chose another way and augmented my income by writing. In graduate school I wrote magazine articles, D.J. scripts, even course papers; later I would write featured newspaper editorials and a weekly newspaper column. Eventually I did a lot of ghost writing. Perhaps laying words on words was a kind of masonry.

"There's no way to equate dollars with intangible rewards, but one reward of inestimable worth, whether in my ministries or through my counseling, working with adults and children and their families, has been to be let into someone's life and to have that person or family say, 'You made a difference.'"

Wolley had ministries in New York and Massachusetts and left the parish ministry to become the Director of Extension for the Universalist Church of America and later the Unitarian Universalist Association. His insights in the field of the sociology of religion led to interim lectureships at several universities here and in Europe, and eventually to counseling institutional and industrial leaders, often dealing with interpersonal relationships and thus with individual managers' personal concerns.

"I was prepared for the role of 'pastoral counseling,'" Wolley says. "And when I became a city's designated 'counselor-of-choice,' I was prepared for that. But later, when dealing with management leaders, I was not fully prepared for what often became a concern: an individual manager's personal situation. 'My husband/wife and I....'; 'I don't understand my son/daughter'; 'I can't communicate with...'—family issues, including marriage problems, that affected one's day-to-day job.

"Additionally, since I worked in the Deep South for two or three months each year, there were intense racial questions and

great anguish. It was hard to disguise my Boston accent in Georgia, the Carolinas, Florida, Alabama, and Mississippi, yet I had to deal with both blacks and whites. In the late 1950s and the 1960s it was difficult to establish trust. I was not always successful.

"The times were difficult for many people, although not more so than other times in history. There was a lot going on that impacted individuals and society and a great need for understanding counseling.

"The whole counseling bit began almost by accident. My first year in a Boston area college I worked a couple of afternoons and on Sundays as a youth leader in a large suburban church. A graduate student I knew worked in a Boston youth center. One night he was stabbed as he left the center. He quit his job. I applied for it and became the late weekday afternoon and evening activities director of a Boston youth center. I was a kind of counselor—without training or education, a perfect example of the 'blind leading the blind.'

"So when I changed schools, I took every psychology and sociology course I could manage to work into my schedule and was fortunate to obtain psychology internships that greatly broadened my insights and skills—and, of course, such skills as I had were put to work almost immediately. Such work eventually took me from a part-time parish and an internship in a New York state mental hospital to two full-time parishes and a counseling role and later to businesses, to the public schools, and a Massachusetts prison—and throughout into the lives of parishioners, troubled citizens, public school children, and their families.

"It is that background which allows me to write about a senior issue with which I dealt many times, as have other counselors and psychologists, but which has received little or no attention (in the hope, I guess, it will either go away or that by ignoring it, it will disappear): the concern for and about senior romance and love.

"In my senior years, by people who knew what I had done most of my life, I was asked often for assistance by other seniors contemplating a second chance at love. Then my own excursion.

There was little or no help in print. I hoped to fill that void, and thus was born this book."

Wolley lives on Cape Cod and works full time as a freelance writer, these days writing mostly poetry and fiction and an occasional essay.

Recent Books by Robert Wolley

The Pranks an' Enlightenment of Frank an' Me. 1997. An adventure story for young readers brings to life a colorful harbor town full of characters, including young Frank and his best friend.

Testament (with artist Gobin Stair.) Philosophy.

Between Sisyphus and Me: Story Poems. 1999. Poetry

The Jaguar People. 2004. Fiction

Green Hell. 2004. Fiction

Turn from the Jaguar. 2005. Fiction

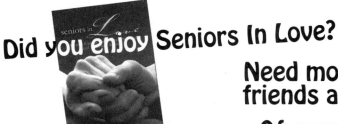

Did you enjoy Seniors In Love?

Need more copies for friends and relatives?

Of course you do!

Show the World that Love Knows No Age!

Order the Car Magnet

An Ideal Wedding & Anniversary Gift!

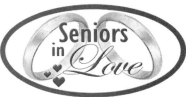

6¼ x 4½", red, white and gold

Order directly from the publisher at

www.geroproducts.com

or use the order form below (may be photocopied)

Name:			
Address:			
City/State/ZIP:			
Daytime Phone:		Evening Phone:	

QTY	ITEM	PRICE	TOTAL
	Seniors In Love Book	19.95	
	Seniors In Love Car Magnet	11.95	
		Subtotal	
Missouri residents only: at 5.25% sales tax			
SHIPPING & HANDLING: 1 item $4.95 Each additional item: $1.00 For larger orders (over $500) email for shipping price quotation: editor@geroproducts. com			
		TOTAL DUE:	

Send Check or Money Order
HATALA GEROPRODUCTS
P.O. BOX 42
GREENTOP, MO 63546

Written by PAUL TOBIN
Art by CAT FARRIS
Colors by HEATHER BRECKEL
Letters by STEVE DUTRO
Cover by CAT FARRIS

DARK HORSE BOOKS

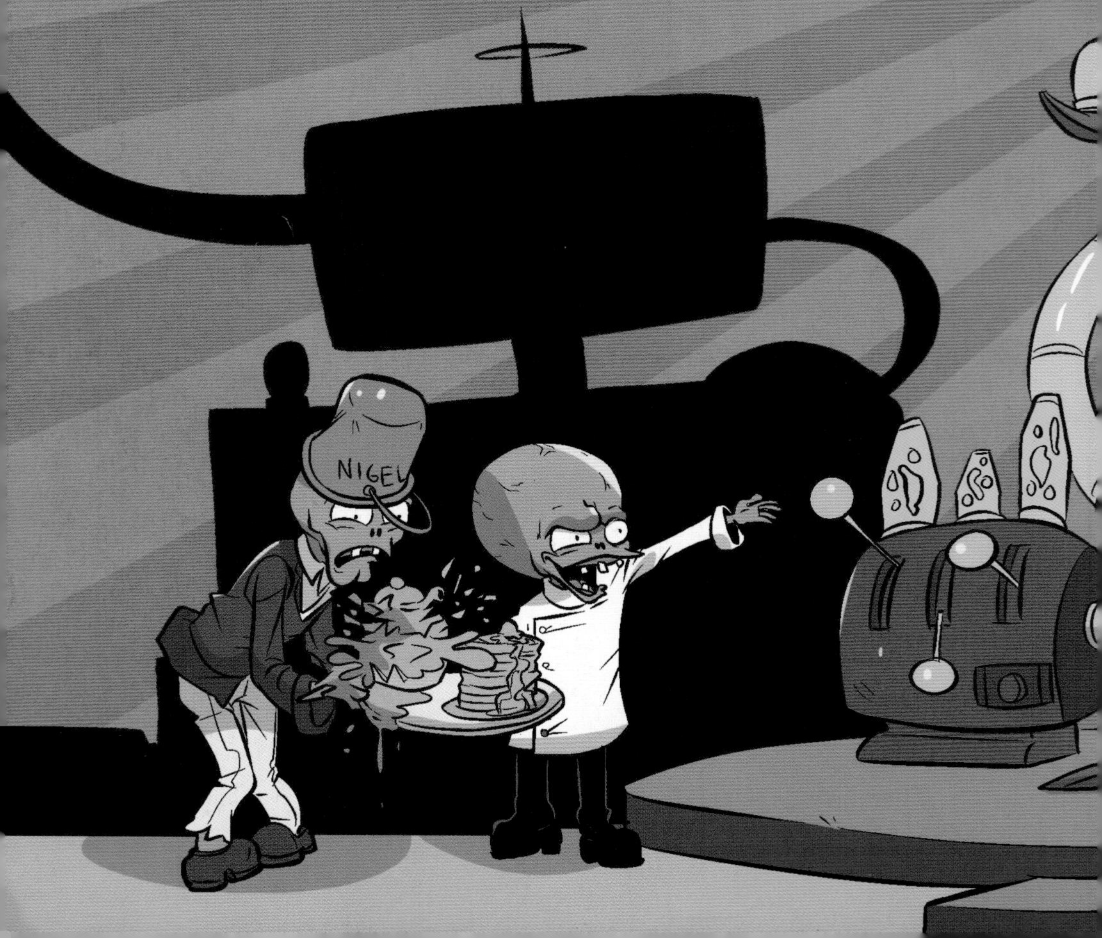
NIGEL

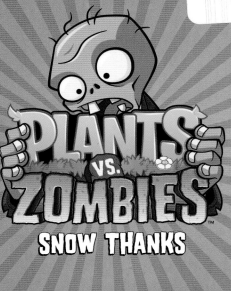

Plants vs. Zombies

SNOW THANKS